The one filling the truck's radiator had shaved off his beard, but the face was the same, and Ragnon knew he was the third picture on the wanted poster. His heartbeat nearly doubled as he moved closer to Sergeant Cruz and whispered tightly, "Goddam, man, it's them. All four of 'em! You got your pistol ready?"

"Ay, no, Tomás, it's in the jeep." Cruz's voice was husky and dry with his own tension.

"Jesus H. Christ," but it was more a prayer than a curse. "Then let's just ease on back across the road real careful like."

"I think it's too late," Cruz whispered. "I think the one with the water jug suspects we're cops—what do you think?"

"I think we're in for it, partner," Tom Ragnon said.

DEATH RAID

Richard Harper

A DELL BOOK

Published by
Dell Publishing Co., Inc.
1 Dag Hammarskjold Plaza
New York, New York 10017

Dell ® TM 681510, Dell Publishing Co., Inc.

ISBN: 0-440-11685-6

Printed in the United States of America

June 1986

10 9 8 7 6 5 4 3 2 1

WFH

"Pobre Mexico, tan lejos de Dios y tan cerca de los Estados Unidos."

Porfirio Diaz
Mexican general &
president
1830–1915

(Poor Mexico, so far from God and so near the United States.)

AUTHOR'S NOTE

Though based on fact, *Death Raid* is a work of fiction. There is no Mimbres County in Arizona. There are police and criminals, and criminal police, on both sides of the border. But any similarity to real criminals or police in this book is purely coincidental.

PROLOGUE

It was nearly seven P.M. and barely into the third month of the new year as thin wisps of cloud raced across the face of a pale, late winter moon that shed its cold light over the desert landscape like a shroud. A coyote yammered from a distant arroyo, and another answered from a hill above the isolated ranch house where windows looked out with warm yellow eyes on the telephone lines that were severed and dangling, swaying gently against the pole in the chill night breeze.

The dirt road that ran past the front gate was empty, the nearest neighbor four miles away, the nearest town twelve. And the same cold wind that moved the dangling wires stirred the greasewood and mesquite and palo verde, and rustled the dry wands of the ocotillo clear to the low range of barbed hills and barren mountains fourteen miles to the south that marked the Mexican border.

In the living room of the house a mesquite log burned low behind the glass of a heatilator fireplace, and sixteen-year old Sandra McNeal was arguing with her little brother Tad over what TV show they were going to watch.

Bob McNeal had already put in a long day, and his tolerance for his children's moods was on a short fuse. "Tad—you've got your own TV in your room—use it!"

"But Daddy, it's black and white—I want to see the Fonz in color!"

"Your room, Tad—now!" The tone of his voice told more than his words. Tad knew that any further argument would mean a licking, and with a meaningful glare of vengeance at his older sister, he raced up the stairs to his room.

"Thanks, Pop," Sandra said, tossing her long blond braids. "He's a pest!"

"He's got his rights too," McNeal grumbled at his daughter, then belched and reached for a roll of Tums. Once more he'd eaten too much for supper, and once more he swore he was going to cut down. He was out of shape, but he wondered why —surely he got enough exercise, what with running the ranch and helping out at the feed store in town; and for the second time he picked up the evening paper.

"Bob—come in here." His wife's voice from the kitchen made him groan and mutter under his breath as he set the paper down again and heaved himself out of his chair.

In the kitchen Helen McNeal had dished up a pot of leftover stew and was wrapping one of her fresh-baked loaves of bread in a tea towel. "Here." She laid a cube of butter on top. "Take this out to those new hands you started yesterday. They're probably tired of beans."

Bob McNeal thought of calling Tad downstairs again, then let it go and lifted his plaid jacket off the hook in back of the kitchen door. "Anything else?" he asked wearily, picking up the stew pot by the handle and slipping the bread and butter between it and the lid. "This is the last chore I'm gonna do tonight."

Ten minutes later Sandra came into the kitchen as her mother was putting the last of the supper dishes into the dishwasher and turning on the machine. "Mama, the telephone isn't working; I tried to call Julia; can I take the car over there to do my homework?"

"Homework?" Helen McNeal turned on her daughter. "You just argued your brother out of a TV show, and now you say you've got homework? Get upstairs and do it, young lady!"

"Oh, Mama, doing it alone is the pits; it goes so much faster when we do it together—please?"

"It's late—you'll have to ask your father."

"Where is he? Shouldn't he be back?"

Helen McNeal had just begun to wonder about that herself, but she had no time to answer, or even think. Because the kitchen door crashed open and the intruders were inside with a gust of cold night air even as the two women screamed in unison.

Two of the assailants were on the older woman in a couple of quick strides, stripping off her apron and dress and undergarments in a matter of seconds. As she went down in shocked horror on the cold linoleum floor, she had only a glimpse of her daughter, already naked and writhing beneath two more.

Her seven-year-old son, screaming "Daddy! Mommy!" and rushing down the stairs in a rage of terrorized panic, was quickly seized and stuffed into a half-empty freezer chest set along one wall, and the lid was slammed shut, cutting off his final cry.

For the next few minutes there was only the low, steady roar of the dishwasher working away at its chore; then, as it paused for a change in one of its cycles, the incessant ticking of the big kitchen clock overlay the long sobbing gasps and moans, and the rutting, grunting animal sounds.

Mercifully, the woman's daughter had fainted before they were halfway through. And afterward, both their throats were slashed and they were left in widening pools of their own blood, which began congealing quickly in the cold wind blowing in through the open kitchen door.

PART I
The Investigation

ONE

When Detective-Sergeant Tom Ragnon tried to draw a mug of coffee from the big aluminum urn in the detective squad bay on the second floor of the Mimbres County Sheriff's Department, and found it already dispensing only the dregs, he knew it was later than he thought, and that he was in for a bad day.

Charlie, the duty officer leered over his own steaming mug. "You ain't gonna have time for coffee this morning, Rags. Old Ironballs wants to see his numero uno homicide specialist right away—a multiple killing down on the border. Somebody wasted one of Pantana's leading families and he's been rattling his cage for an hour trying to find you. Big night?"

"Shit," Ragnon muttered, scowling and thinking instantly of the vacation time he planned to ask for, and feeling guilty for putting his own needs ahead of the tragedy of murder.

When he walked into the chief of homicide's office, he saw Sidney Poole's small hooded eyes flick automatically to the wall clock as its minute hand ticked to 8:21. Poole's drooping mustache, round cheeks, and double chin gave him the look of an anxious walrus as he asked tersely, "Where the fuck you been, Rags? I tried to call you at your trailer and got that damned recording machine. And your wife hadn't heard from you or seen you over at her place; you get lucky last night or what?" Chief Poole paused in his tirade to light up one of his foul little cigars.

"Overslept, Chief," Ragnon muttered. "Had a rough night." He slumped down on the vinyl couch by the wall without being asked, and put his head in his hands. "Charlie says there's trouble in Pantana." He seemed to always refer to homicide simply as *trouble*.

"Three bags full, Rags," Poole answered. He had set down his bronze horse desk lighter and was puffing tiny smoke rings toward the ceiling. Then he pushed his chair back and eased his bulk away from his desk as he eyed his homicide specialist critically over half-lensed glasses. "Too bad about the rough night, but you're not going to catch up on any sleep on this one.

Jesus, you look like shit warmed over—where *did* you spend last night?"

Tom Ragnon looked up from his hands. "To tell you the truth, Chief, I was going to ask for some time off—"

"Forget it." Sidney Clayton Poole waved his cigar like a magic wand. "This one's nasty, and important. See if the chopper's free to fly you down to Pantana, or check out a car."

"What happened?"

"A whole family savaged in cold blood. The lab boys are already there, and the Border Patrol. A sheriff's deputy has secured the scene; three bodies, lots of blood—"

"Who found 'em?" Ragnon got back on his feet, shrugging off the lethargy and wondering, as he had wondered so often in the past, why he thought homicide was such a great line of work.

"Telephone lineman, about two hours ago. He was tracing a downed line and found theirs cut and dangling from the pole. Lights on in the house and the kitchen door standing wide open. When he looked inside, he puked." Chief Poole refired his cigar with his big desk lighter and blew more smoke toward the ceiling. "Anyway, get down there and sort it out—check in with the town marshal"—he glanced at some notes on his desk —"name's Edwin Duff. He's probably at the scene, too, by now. Ranch is twelve miles southeast of town—and don't let him give you any lip about jurisdictional shit; this is your case—take control of it. Oh, one more thing, there were four in the family, but only three bodies. A kid is missing, a seven-year-old boy, so we may have the goddamned FBI in on this one, too, if it's a kidnapping."

"Terrific," Tom Ragnon said. "Might as well call in the Marines."

Ragnon decided to skip the chopper ride, and checked out an unmarked county car instead. Getting to the scene before it was too messed up was important, but from the sound of it, it would already look like Indianapolis on race day. Besides, it was only a forty-minute drive, and he needed time to think. A kidnapping? he mused, taking the elevator down to the garage. After they'd killed the most likely source of a ransom? Not likely. Maybe the poor kid witnessed it, and scared shitless, was still hiding somewhere.

As he drove out of the underground garage below the Sheriff's Department building, a few thick drops of rain splattered the windshield, reminding him of the uncertainty of the weather forecast the night before. A large storm system was tracking across the higher elevations of northern Arizona, with snow above 5000 feet and temperatures in the southern deserts dropping into the lower forties with rain. And since he didn't know when he'd be getting back, he stopped by his trailer to get his country working clothes.

Inside, he switched on the radio and tuned it to a news and weather station while he changed to old blue jeans and boots, and then dug out a long-sleeved flannel shirt and fleece-lined denim vest. Taking his crumpled, sweat-stained Stetson from the top of the closet, he tucked a fresh pouch of Redman Chewing Tobacco in his vest pocket and felt as ready as he'd ever be to face a fresh homicide.

He'd quit smoking two months ago, when his wife threw him out, and taken up this worse habit; but he found it calming in times of stress, and at least he didn't chew as much as he'd smoked before. He was clipping his holstered .38 Cobra snubnose to the back of his belt when the news gave a brief report of the bodies of a family found on their ranch near Pantana, with no names given until next of kin had been notified. Police investigators were at the scene, and an update was promised on the regular ten o'clock newscast.

Turning off the radio, he closed the trailer door behind him and locked it, wondering why he bothered. There was nothing there worth stealing. Even the TV was secondhand. Since his wife had kicked him out, it was a place to change clothes, shower and shave, and maybe grab a few hours sleep. But it sure as hell wasn't home.

The house on Old Father Road was home. It was on the outskirts of the city, on the way to Pantana; and today was the anniversary of their second month of separation. Impulsively, he decided to stop by. He hadn't realized it would hurt so much —the old heave-ho—but it had. The pain was almost physical. It was Angie's second marriage, and her kids. But for three years now, since they were babies, they had been like his own. And he had deliberately waited late himself to marry, postponing it, running from it, finally taking the plunge only when he knew this one was for real. He'd known it wouldn't be easy, and it wasn't. Goddammit, it sure as hell wasn't.

Widowed when her husband was killed in a construction accident, and ten years Ragnon's junior, Angie was a surgical nurse at one of the biggest hospitals in the city. Liberated and strongly career-minded, she also had ideas about his own career now; like how much better off he'd be as a lieutenant, off the street and seated safely on his hemorrhoids behind a desk, like Lieutenant Poole. Her occupation, like his, also required odd hours, and that had been another burr under their marriage saddle. But they should have been able to work it all out. They hadn't.

The threat of rain hadn't materialized, but the clouds remained as he pulled up the long, curving drive of the tri-level set among tall cottonwoods on a quarter acre. His six-year-old, Brian, was out in the yard with his lunch pail, arguing vehemently with his four-year-old sister, Melissa, threatening her with violent bodily harm if she didn't do something or other, or maybe if she did. Ragnon wasn't sure which, because when they saw him pull to a stop, they both ran over screaming, "Daddy! Daddy!"

Melissa started telling him what Brian had done, and the little boy started blaming her as they argued all over again. He wondered why he wanted so badly to get back to all this, and then he gave them each a bear hug and a kiss, and sent the boy off to school after digging a Monster Cookie out of his pocket for each of them and sweeping the little girl up in his arms.

Angie had come to the side door in her housecoat and waved him into the kitchen. With her shoulder-length black hair framing a long narrow face, she reminded him of Veronica Hamel on the TV show *Hill Street Blues.* "I just fixed breakfast, and there's plenty if you want some." Her smile was warm, and he wondered why she always seemed so friendly, yet so happy when they were apart. Or was she simply pleased he had stopped by? It had been a whole week.

"No time to eat," he said, letting Melissa down in the kitchen and handing her a half-finished glass of milk from the table to wash down her cookie. "Triple killing down near Pantana—and a kid missing. Just coffee and one of those sweet rolls will do."

"I heard it on the radio; it figures they'd assign you." Her voice had a familiar bitter edge, but he didn't take the bait.

Instead, he eyed her speculatively over the coffee. "It's been two months, Angie," he probed delicately, "two months today."

"Are you coming back for good, Daddy?" Melissa interrupted, as an Indian girl about nineteen came into the kitchen from the porch.

"Daddy and I have to talk now, Missy," Angie told the four-year-old, "and then he has to work. You run along with Rosa; you'll see Daddy again this weekend." Then she introduced her husband to Rosa Flores.

Tom Ragnon kissed Melissa, and as the two left the kitchen Angie answered his questioning look. "That's the sitter—I finally found a good one."

"You've got a sitter?"

"I had to have some help, Tom. Missy won't be in kindergarten for another year, and you're not here to watch them now."

"That's right, I'm not here, and who's fault is that?"

She sighed heavily. "What about the lieutenant's exam—you going to take it?"

"Angie, please, you know I don't want a desk job. I'm a field man."

"Then at least get out of homicide."

He shook his head. "We've been down this road before, it's what I am; it's my life."

"It'll be your death, Tom, can't you see that?" She sighed again. "We just don't need each other; we've proved that. We're both too independent."

"I need *you*," Tom Ragnon said.

She looked away. "I don't want to argue about it. Look, I'm off today—come by for dinner."

"I don't know, I may not be back—"

"Even if it's late. I'll make meat loaf and heat it in the microwave. We can talk then, okay?"

"About getting back together?"

"Just talk, no promises. We never did talk enough. Maybe that was part of our trouble."

Tom Ragnon nodded, staring through the open dining room door at the aquarium by the window. It needs cleaning, he thought absently. That had been his job.

As he drove away from the house on Old Father Road, he thought about his work in homicide. In a way she was right: to progress, you had to move up; it was part of the bureaucracy. Except that he liked what he did; he was good at it. He wasn't at all sure he'd be any good higher up. Why couldn't she understand that? Not understanding made for a difficult family life. But most of the men in his unit were single or divorced, and now it looked like he was headed that way, too, in spite of all his careful plans.

Tugging the pouch of Redman from his vest pocket, he tucked a hefty pinch in his cheek. His love for Angie and the kids, and his love for his profession, were tearing him in two. He didn't want to lose either of them. The thought of Brian skipping off to school reminded him of where he was headed now: a place where sudden, violent, senseless death had struck a family, ending it. And a boy was missing. A boy about Brian's age.

TWO

Monday, March 8, 9:40 A.M.

He covered the forty-mile drive to Pantana in as many minutes, through a desert that was changing slowly but inevitably. Ravaged by years of overgrazing, it was worn down now with the erosion that followed. And the tall, distant smokestacks of one of the mine smelters sent a constant trail of dirty haze adrift across the miles-wide valley, scouring the once blue sky.

He supposed that was progress, too, these days, in spite of anything the Sierra Club or Greenpeace or any of the other environmentalist groups could do about it. The entire earth was being ravaged; worn down, used up, wasted. But it was the waste of individual human life that was his own particular concern. Homicide and murder. And sometimes even that seemed hopeless.

Rolling down the car window, he rested his arm on the sill and sent a squirt of tobacco juice onto the roadway. Nearing forty, he'd been an Arizona lawman for fifteen years; a homicide detective for seven of that; and things never seemed to get better. He just got older and the violence got worse.

Most killings were among relatives, or at least the victim and his murderer knew each other; and every killer left traces of himself at the scene and took something of the scene with him. Sometimes it took long months of legwork and endless questions, and sometimes the killer simply sat down beside his victim with the weapon in his hand. Somehow most of them got solved, eventually; but the really vicious ones, or those seemingly without motive or purpose—those were the gut-busters. He wondered about this one as he slowed to enter the main street of Pantana, with its lone gas station and corner bank, its bar and general store.

The schoolhouse built on the edge of the town was the only modern building. Twelve miles beyond, he turned in through the open ranch gate, where he stopped and got out to examine the end of the phone line dangling from the pole. Spitting out the rest of his tobacco, he got back in the car and drove on down the dirt road to the house, past newly posted signs: CRIME SCENE—KEEP OUT BY ORDER OF MARSHAL DUFF.

A green Border Patrol jeep was just leaving, the two agents waving as they passed him; and Ragnon spotted the Pantana town marshal by his ten-gallon Texas hat and the holstered hog-leg pistol strapped to his thigh. He was talking to a uniformed deputy sheriff and they were standing beside the deputy's county car with its bar of rooflights still flashing.

A police lab van was parked in front of the house. Ragnon pulled in between it and the county coroner's station wagon. A photo-news team was being held off by two more deputies, and one of them called to him for a statement as he got out of his car. He brushed them off with a "no comment—I just got here" and referred them to Lt. Poole for all releases.

As one of the lab technicians walked out to their van with the deputy coroner, Ragnon showed them his shield and asked, "What's it look like?"

"A mess." The technician shook his head. "One adult male found in the doorway of a house trailer out back with his skull crushed. This looks like the weapon." He held up an old ironbound wooden singletree. Bagged and tagged for evidence, the dried blood and hairs caught in the cracks of the weathered wood were clearly visible through the plastic covering.

"Two more in the kitchen of the house," the deputy coroner said. "One adult female and one juvenile female, both stripped and apparently raped and their throats cut from ear to ear. No weapon found there—kitchen cutlery looks intact, but could be one missing."

"A single assailant?" Ragnon asked him.

"Possibly, but I doubt it—I'd say two at least, maybe more. A surprise attack for sure, about supper time last night, give or take an hour. We should have a report on everything in a couple of days."

"Thanks. You know if they got any prints?"

"Print men just left." He nodded toward a car that was pulling out the front gate. "Mostly smudges, I understand. They'll have to separate the victims' from any others, but there were a couple of possibles in blood: half a palm and a thumbprint on a freezer lid. Nothing took on this old singletree." He paused to light a cigarette. "Photographer's still inside taking pictures, but we're ready to bag the bodies whenever you're finished. Just let me know."

Ragnon nodded as the uniformed deputy walked over and officially turned the crime scene over to him. Then he turned and headed reluctantly for the open kitchen door as the Pantana town marshal fell in step beside him. "You Sergeant Ragnon? I'm Marshal Duff. They said you'd be taking over. I sure don't envy you none. Looks like a bitch, don't it?"

The detective shook hands without breaking stride. "They usually are," he said.

"No telling where the bastard's run to," Duff continued, "but probably over the border. McNeal's car is still in his garage, but his late model pickup's missing—a white GMC. I got an APB out for all the good it'll do, but everybody's looking for it and the missing boy—the Border Patrol, deputies, the state police—and I suppose the FBI will be in on it, too, if it's a kidnapping."

They had reached the kitchen door and Ragnon paused on the threshold. "Why would they take the kid and kill the parents?" he wondered aloud. "Who's going to pay the ransom—the grandparents?"

"Maybe they took him for a hostage—till they got away safe," Duff suggested as Ragnon admired the border of winter flowers planted neatly on either side of the door. A few feet away a lawn mower sat in the middle of the brown and dormant Bermuda lawn, and a rubber tire swing hung motionless from the largest limb of an old oak tree that shaded the long screened porch.

"What's missing besides the truck?" Ragnon asked as they stepped inside the kitchen, then forgot his question as he stared at the dried blood and naked bodies of the two female victims. One was sprawled on her back on the linoleum floor, and the other was belly down across the kitchen table. He forced himself to watch a moment as two lab technicians chalked around them. The older female's hair was done up in curlers and resting in a pool of congealed blood that had drained from the hideous gash across her throat.

Then the detective turned back to the door where the marshal was waiting, and pushed past him to stand outside again, taking a few deep breaths while his stomach calmed down. No matter how he tried to prepare himself, he could never get used to it—the aftermath of murder. But it did make him all the more determined in his work, and his cases had an unusually high percentage of positive results.

"They broke into a gun cabinet in the living room and emptied it," the marshal was saying, ignoring his distress, "and they rumaged around some upstairs, but can't tell what else is missing. Big console TV's still here, and the stereo in the girl's room. A relative's flying down from Phoenix to take a look—McNeal's older brother. He'll make the funeral arrangements too. . . ."

Keep talking, Ragnon thought miserably; keep talking so I can concentrate on not throwing up.

"It's a dirty goddamned shame," Marshal Duff rambled on obligingly. "Folks around here never used to have to even lock their doors. Nowadays a body needs an armed escort to go to a ball game. I tell you, Sergeant, the assholes of the world are taking over and nobody seems willing to stop 'em. Even the justice system is all fucked up—they turn most of 'em loose on technicalities, or their shyster lawyers plea bargain 'em down to misdemeanors just to clear the dockets and empty out the jails."

"Life is tough all over," Ragnon mumbled, recovered now as the photographer took a last flash picture before moving toward the door.

"That's it," he said. "I already shot everything in and around the trailer. Should be ready by tomorrow if you want to look."

Nodding, Ragnon stepped inside again and began to study

the shambles of the death scene where the lights were still on and a pot of stew had dried and burned on the back burner of the stove. Surprise was written over everything, from the stew on the stove to the freshly baked bread on a white cloth, the cloth folded back and the long serrated-edge knife lying cleanly innocent amid the crumbs. "Looks like they may have brought their own knives," the detective said.

"Looks to me like burglars caught in the act and turning it into a rape-murder," the marshal suggested.

"That's what you think?" Some of the drawers and cabinets had been turned out and the contents dumped on the kitchen floor, but it didn't look like a planned burglary by any stretch of the imagination.

"That's my guess," the marshal said. "And probably wetbacks. It's been getting worse all along this border the past few years. Used to be the wets came just to work. They were decent men; you could go off and leave the house open, nothing touched, ever. Now they come just to burgle an isolated place. They hit and run for the border. Hell, it's only fourteen miles away here. Ranchers are keeping their guns loaded now and not leaving their places alone for even a few hours."

Tom Ragnon wasn't ready to say yet what he thought had happened. It was too early in the investigation to try to make assumptions, but he had an uneasy feeling about this one, like it was going to be one of the gut-busters.

He led the way through the rest of the house, working carefully through each room and making notes and rough sketches as he went. The ransacking seemed to support the burglary, but it also seemed too random for professionals. A pro would have turned out all the drawers and closets and emptied them in piles on the floor. Some places were untouched, and there had been no attempt to even move the big color TV or some other easily disposable appliances. And upstairs only the McNeal's bedroom had been searched.

The big question persisted: Why a burglary with the family all at home? Burglars broke into empty houses, and they sometimes killed when surprised in the act; but here the burglars had done the surprising. And with no forced entry, it looked more like an armed robbery turned to murder.

"That the trailer out back?" Ragnon asked, looking out a bedroom window.

Marshal Duff nodded. Old, with its paint flaking, it was parked beside an empty horse corral and partially hidden by a huge pepper tree. "McNeal kept his wets out there; there, and sometimes over in that big Quonset he used for a barn when he took on extra hands in the fall."

"Where are they now—his workers?" Ragnon asked as they walked back downstairs.

"Don't know if he had any this early in the year. I'll have to ask around. Usually had two or three on the place all the time, though. You think maybe they did it?"

Ragnon didn't answer. Outside he told the deputy coroner it was okay to remove the women's bodies, then he followed Duff around back toward the trailer as the perplexed marshal shook his head and muttered, "Killed by his own wetbacks—that's hard to believe, Sergeant. Some I know treat their Mexicans rough, but not McNeal—he was a saint. And that missus of his has been postmistress at Pantana for at least four years, and president of the PTA. You know McNeal's old man was the late state senator?"

Ragnon noted that the horse corrall appeared unused, and remarked about it as they passed.

"McNeal's girl got throwed and hurt bad a couple years back, and he got rid of the horses. Understand the boy's been naggin' him to get another—not that it matters now. There's a cow and some chickens I'll have to get the neighbors to look after."

They had come around to the open trailer door where the body of Bob McNeal lay face down across the threshold. "A hell of a blow," Duff commented, staring down at the back of the head, which was dented in, the hair matted with dried blood.

Ragnon studied it a moment, then moved up on the first of two wooden steps and leaned across the body to the open doorway so he could see inside. Somebody had lived there, and recently. It was dirty, but not the dust and cobwebs of being vacant and abandoned. It smelled lived-in too, and as he stepped carefully over the body and inside, he noticed that a blanket crumpled on a bunk had a fairly fresh blob of beans spilled on it.

"Maybe they just ran off when the trouble came," Duff called from outside. "But wets or whatever, unless they're picked up in that white truck, we'll never find 'em. Mexico's too close. The Border Patrol and Customs is all there is down there, and you know how thin a line that is. They only catch a fraction of the dope and wets that come in all the time."

Ragnon was back kneeling in the doorway now, examining something that appeared to have been spilled recently and had soaked the wooden floor and dried. There were bits of freshly cooked meat and vegetables, an overturned pot nearby, and a loaf of what looked like fairly fresh bread lay in one corner. "Looks like the same bread and stew that was in the kitchen, Marshal. What was McNeal doing, bringing his hands their evening meal?"

"By God, it looks that way, don't it? And he was hit from behind with that old singletree."

Stepping back inside, the detective moved slowly through the cramped trailer, hoping the lab men got some prints here that might be compared to those found in the kitchen. It didn't take long to examine the two small rooms and tiny bath. Dirty dishes were stacked in the chipped enamel sink, and old Army blankets were piled loosely on the bare, stained mattresses of the bunk beds. Pictures of naked girls torn from girlie magazines adorned the walls and were crinkled and yellowed with age, but a freshly crumpled empty pack of Mexican cigarettes lay under one of the bunks.

Moving outside again, Ragnon waved the coroner's men over with their body bag as Edwin Duff asked him, "Well, Sergeant, what do you think?"

"I think we've got a ball-buster, but let's wait till we get the lab reports and autopsies and maybe find the missing boy and the truck before we start thinking anything. McNeal have any known enemies? That phone line out there was deliberately cut, which indicates intent. Maybe they just took enough to make it look like a burglary."

"I told you they were saints, the both of them. Everybody around here thought highly of them. McNeal was on the town council; the girl was the lead in the school drama class. The little boy was like any little boy—Christ, Sergeant, I wish we could get the bastards!"

"Yeah," Ragnon mused, his uneasiness growing, unexplained as he patted his vest pockets for his Redman and tucked a pinch comfortably in his cheek while he stared around at the empty ranch yard. Only hours ago it had been a home, a warm throbbing thriving place of human habitation, a shelter from the storms of life—until last night.

"Well, I'm going back to town," the marshal was saying, heading for his car. "If you need me for anything more, I'm usually at my office or at home—it's right next door. I've got a base radio for long range communications if you need it. Meanwhile I'll call around and see if anybody's found anything."

Ragnon watched as the marshal's car pulled away and the coroner's wagon followed him. Then, left alone at the scene except for a pair of deputies on guard at the front gate, he spat into the weeds at his feet and tried to puzzle out what had happened here and why. But none of the pieces quite fit.

He searched the big Quonset carefully, but it yielded nothing. Used for storage mostly, it contained an old '48 Ford blocked up off its wheels, an empty feed bin and loft, and some old salt licks for cattle. He even looked in an abandoned privy and the attic of a toolshed, calling out the missing boy's name, which the marshal had said was Tad, but got no answer.

Returning to the house, he walked slowly through the rooms again, this time turning off any lights that still burned. Sunlight streamed in through all the east windows, and upstairs he paused again to survey the girl's room, barely touched by the intruders; then the boy's, with its toys and posters and models all undisturbed.

In contrast the McNeal's bedroom had been turned inside out. Even the bed had been overturned, the dresser drawers dumped and the clothes from the closet strewn around the floor. A douche bag and a dildo lay beside the open bathroom door, and on the bathroom vanity a tube of Preparation-H lay beside a shower cap. Murder did that, he pondered, opening a window and spitting outside; it laid bare the personal lives of its victims, disrupted their existence in midstride, and left them exposed and vulnerable, even after they were dead. He wondered that it still got to him, but it did, even after years in homicide: the awful fragility of life and the sudden finality of death, and the incredible unfairness of it all.

Downstairs again he moved back through the house to the kitchen. He even poked around in the open knife drawer with his pen, but the set appeared complete with the serrated bread knife accounted for nearby. There was even a cleaver, untouched; but he decided to have the cutlery all tested anyway, in case something had been used and washed and put back. But they really hadn't been that careful, whoever they were. They had been sloppy and hurried, but deadly.

He opened a broom closet and peered inside. He even looked in the refrigerator and opened the oven door. Turning, he stared a moment at the big chest freezer set along one wall and at the bloody palm and thumbprint on the lid. And an eerie, gnawing suspicion needled the back of his mind as he forced himself to trip the latch and open it. He caught his breath at what he found inside.

THREE

Monday, March 8, 12:30 P.M.

"Chief? Ragnon. Send the coroner and lab people back out here, and the photographer—I found the missing boy."

"What—dead?"

"Yeah. They stuffed him in a half-empty freezer right there in the kitchen. No apparent marks or wounds on him, so he was probably alive at the time." Ragnon paused to open the phone-booth door and send a spew of tobacco juice into the street before resuming his conversation. "And Chief, can I have John Antone down here on this one? If I'm gonna get these guys, I need to sort out the tracks. There's so many now, it looks like they held a Shriner's Convention out there."

"Shit," Poole growled. "Where in hell are you?"

"Phone booth in the school yard at Pantana. I didn't want to put this out on the car radio. Can you get Antone?"

"I can try."

"Goddammit, do more than try—he was a seven-year-old kid!"

"Okay, okay, and I'll call off the FBI. At least it's narrowed down to a murdered family with everyone accounted for. Oh, the Border Patrol's found McNeal's truck, about an hour ago, abandoned with a busted oil pan."

"Where?"

"Lower end of Pájaro Canyon, two miles from the border. Engine was cold, so the perpetrators are probably deep in Mexico by now. The lab boys are down there now, but I'll route 'em back when they're through. I still don't know what good Antone's gonna do you, now we know where they went."

"Just get him, Chief. I at least want to sort out how many there were and anything else he can come up with, and we don't know for sure they actually crossed the border. They may have doubled back."

"All right, but it's damned obvious they were heading for Mexico and staying off the roads. They just didn't know the back country, or got lost and blundered into that canyon—it was a cloudy night."

"Or maybe they want us to think that. Anyway, I'll get back to the ranch and look around some more while I wait for Antone. Leave the truck where it is until I can get a look at it."

"Okay, Rags, but a look is all you get. Once you and Antone establish they actually crossed the border, it's over. Even if they could be found on the other side, you know what a hassle extradition is with those grease balls."

Ragnon didn't bother to say anything about the chief's slur; long ago he'd realized that the chief's attitudes wouldn't change. "Right, Chief; and tell Antone to bring his own camera and a close-up lens."

Tom Ragnon drove hard the twelve miles back to the ranch, returning to the kitchen to stare down again with a peculiarly acute anguish at the pitifully small, stiff corpse in the freezer. He had always prided himself in maintaining a professional coolness in his work. No emotions, just methodical, calculated police procedure. But some cases were hard to treat as a simple piece of work. Sometimes old people were bludgeoned to death for their few miserable pennies; or young people cut down in their prime; or like now, whole families, including children. It was hard not to become emotionally involved, not to seek revenge rather than justice. Because what was justice anyway? Justice for whom? Death was so irreversible for the victims. No matter what he did, the cold flesh couldn't be warmed, the smile couldn't be returned to the twisted features, nor the light to the eyes.

For Ragnon there was only the justice of finding the killer

and stopping him, before he killed again. And this kind would, he was sure of it, for whatever twisted motive. He sat down wearily at the kitchen table, and removing his .38 he flicked open the cylinder and checked the loads. His job was clear if not easy: find them, along with the evidence to convict. Only why did his good work always have to come after the fact? After the deadly deed was done? Snapping shut the cylinder he decided, as he always did at the start of an especially grisly case, that he had chosen a sometimes deeply depressing profession.

An hour later he had completed another tour of the house and grounds and found nothing new except an outline of something in dust on a dresser in the boy's room—a portable TV, by the size of it. But he'd come to no particular conclusion about the crime, except that the boy had probably been killed because he was a witness to the rest of it. And he still didn't know how many killers were involved. That's what Deputy John Antone's expertise would have to determine. As he rounded a corner of the house again, he saw the coroner's station wagon returning.

Directing them to the freezer inside, he reminded them not to touch the lid. "I want the print men to go over it again, especially the handle."

A few minutes later John Antone showed up in a county sheriff's jeep with a star on the hood and no doors. The young Indian deputy had worked with Ragnon on cases before, and by his own admission he was part Papago, part Apache, and part coyote. Whatever he was, he had earned the detective's keen respect for his competence as a cop. He wouldn't be rushed, couldn't be bullied, and never failed to show a wry, bemused smile when reminded of the white man's concept of law and order.

Dismounting from the jeep and pushing back a stiff-brim hat, the uniformed deputy held out a firm brown hand. "Morning, Sergeant. It's been a while." His words were low but distinct, and softly accented.

"About six or eight months—how you been, John? Still walking tall and chasing bad guys?"

"Sometimes I think it's all a losing battle, Sergeant." He smiled, then glanced around the ranch. "I heard what happened. You found the missing boy in a freezer?"

Ragnon nodded. "I can't even tell how many assailants there were, but more than one."

The Indian was looking around at the ground. "I don't know either, man. Looks like somebody held a Sunday school picnic —I never saw so many tracks on top of tracks."

"Sorry about that. See what you can do."

John Antone looked at him. "You really expect me to sort all this out?" he asked half seriously. "It would take a Gypsy fortune teller."

"Just take your time and do your thing, John," the detective told him, "so I can do mine."

Antone shrugged, smiling. "I already started. The phone man must have parked out by the pole on the road. His hobnailed boots lead right up to the kitchen door walking, and back to his truck on the run, so I can eliminate him."

"Did you bring your camera?"

"In the jeep. I've got to decide what to shoot first. What's the estimated time of death?"

"Supper time, between five thirty and seven thirty, give or take."

"Well, there was a heavy dew here last night after midnight, which will help separate the tracks made before then from those added this morning. That will leave just separating the victims' and the killers'. Luckily it hasn't rained here yet; it's pouring in the city. I'll yell when I've got something."

Tom Ragnon watched the Indian start on the far perimeter of the grounds surrounding the house and trailer and begin working his way in a slowly diminishing circle. Then he returned to the house just as they were carrying the small body out in a bag. "I wish you could get the scum who did this," the deputy coroner said, slamming the station-wagon door. "But it beats me how the fuck you'll do it."

"Good autopsies and lab work will help," Ragnon answered. But he knew the main thing now was where the killers had gone. If they were already in Mexico, which was likely, and had the sense not to return . . .

Forty minutes later he was still nursing a lot of negative thoughts about the whole case when Antone called to him from the trailer out back. "Hey, Sergeant—would you bring my camera? I think I've got things sorted out!"

Ragnon found the camera cushioned on a blanket between the seats of the jeep with the tripod behind it, and carried them around back to the trailer. A hobby photographer with his own color lab in his den, the Indian had an excellent reputation for taking his own crime photos.

Setting up the equipment, Antone adjusted the focus above a clear set of footprints just to one side of the trailer steps as Ragnon knelt beside him. "The light's good this time of day for shadows," the deputy said, "so we'll start here—with Two-Shoes."

"Two-Shoes?" Ragnon looked up. "What's a Two-Shoes?"

"There were four of them, Sergeant," Antone explained, changing his lens and adding a filter. "Nobody came on the place from outside the perimeter last night, so they were already here. Their tracks, mingled with those of the victims, were all made after that rainstorm three days ago, but before the heavy dew this morning. The other tracks are new—yours, the coroner's people, the lab and print men, with a lot of them overlapping. Luckily there are still several clean ones, like these of Two-Shoes by the steps. He killed McNeal."

"Jesus," Ragnon breathed, staring down at the tracks, "but why Two—" And then he saw it: the left print didn't match the right; they were different patterns—two different shoes. He looked up at Antone, was was smiling at his puzzled expression.

"Two shoes," the Indian said. "The guy was wearing a different shoe on each foot—both sneakers, right and left, but each sole has a different pattern: circles on one, diamonds on the other. And he killed McNeal. He knelt beside the detective. "See where the toes make a deeper impression—he raised up on the balls of his feet to deliver a blow with something heavy."

"An old singletree," Ragnon said. "They found blood and hair that will probably match McNeal's."

"And he was hit on the back of the head, right?"

Ragnon nodded. "And the blood was at the top end of the singletree."

"So McNeal was short, but standing on the steps," Antone continued, "and Two-Shoes, who is tall for a Mexican, still had to raise up to get force behind the blow, and got him on the back of the head instead of the top."

"How the hell do you know he was Mexican?"

John Antone smiled. "They were all four Mexican, Sergeant. I'd bet my best pair of moccasins on it. They were on this place, living in this trailer."

"And you think they were in it together?"

"Look here." He pointed to the confusing maze of tracks, evidently reading the sign like a map. "The three of them came out of the trailer and joined Two-Shoes." Kneeling again, he pointed out each track individually, some of them overrun and only partial, but a few clear prints of a left or right shoe. He worked with his camera and tripod while he talked now, taking close-ups of each one. "Here's Cowboy-Boots-with-Worn-Down-Heels; and here, this guy's wearing street shoes with a faint Cat's Paw design still visible in the right heel; and this one's wearing those tire-tread huarache sandals. And all four lead over to the kitchen door."

"And here's Cowboy. Boots heading over toward the garage all by himself," Ragnon pointed, amazed that he hadn't noticed it before.

"You got it, Sergeant. The McNeals' truck was parked there. Cowboy Boots must have driven it over here—see, it's got over-size rear tires worn on the outer edges from being out of balance. The front tires are new."

Tom Ragnon was shaking his head and making notes. He didn't see, not the way Antone did, but the explanation made sense.

Antone looked amused. "You did send for me to sort out these tracks, didn't you, Sergeant?"

"Jesus, John, *you* ought to be the fucking detective. They must have loaded the guns and whatever other loot they stole and left."

"That's the way I read it."

"But one thing puzzles me—if no strangers had come on the place for three days—"

"They were here already, Sergeant, waiting for the chance." He stared at Ragnon. "His hired help?"

Ragnon nodded thoughtfully and spat. "We'll have to check it out. The marshal didn't think he had any hands on the place. Get on your radio and see if you can raise him. Have him find out if anybody in town knew if McNeal had any hired help. And tell him to broadcast a description of these tracks to the Border Patrol and Customs."

"Okay, Sergeant. And I'll get these pix developed and blown up as soon as I can. But you think all of it will do any good, considering the truck's been found so close to the border?"

"Shit, I don't know, John." He spat again. "Maybe if the lab reports and autopsies just give us something, we can get a grip on this thing."

"But if they're in Mexico. . . ?" Antone persisted.

Ragnon stared hard at the deputy. "I'm not gonna worry yet about them being in Mexico, John, so don't start talking like the chief. And before you go back to the city and work on those photos, let's go have ourselves a look at McNeal's truck."

FOUR

Monday, March 8th, 3 P.M.

That Pájaro Canyon still existed in its natural state was due solely to its isolated location ten miles from any kind of road, and to the fact it had been purchased from the state and protected as a wilderness bird sanctuary by a private philanthropist.

Fed by a deep artesian spring, the seasonally dry arroyo that led into the canyon quickly became a flowing stream, its wide shallow banks thick with grasses and weeds and a forest of tall trees: cottonwoods and willows, walnut and ash and mulberry, the foliage already budding out to form its green summer canopy, while the canyon walls added to the shade and formed an oasis alive with a variety of birds. The shallow stream itself lapped gently over rocks for more than a mile, the rippling water edged and nearly overgrown in places with thick green watercress.

The stolen truck had broken through the barbed wire fence surrounding the preserve, and Ragnon and Antone followed the familiar tire tracks along the muddy bank, tracks overlaid now by the fresher tracks of the van used by the lab men. And as they jolted over the rocky, brushy terrain and rounded a turn, Ragnon was first to spot their quarry.

The white truck was hung up on a rock a dozen yards ahead, with the county's van parked beside it under a shaggy cottonwood and the two lab men still working with their brushes and bags and other sampling gear.

"Morning, Sergeant," the taller of the lab men greeted them

after they parked the jeep and got out. "We're finding you a few goodies, but most of the prints are smeared, and I'm afraid your birds have flown."

"They picked a strange escape route," Ragnon said, tucking a fresh pinch of Redman in his cheek as he peered in through the open door on the driver's side.

"Probably got lost and wandered in here in the dark trying to find Mexico. Border Patrol plane spotted it against the green foliage on its first flyover. Take a look in back."

In the truck bed a heavy metal toolbox stood open, full of assorted tools. A portable Sony TV, its glass screen broken, lay on its side beside an electric typewriter and a microwave oven. "All busted or too heavy to carry away on foot," the lab man said. "And look at this." He opened a redwood chest with a red velvet lining, to expose a set of sterling silver.

"What was in the glove compartment?" Antone asked, noticing it was open.

"Just the usual stuff—registration slip, some sales receipts, a flashlight and screwdriver and a box of tissues. McNeal's wallet was on the seat, emptied of cash." He held it up in a plastic bag. "No legible prints, but there was this *under* the seat." He held out another baggie containing a large silver coin. "An old U.S. Peace dollar—1928. Looks uncirculated, like it came from a collection. And it sure hasn't been under that seat long—no dirt or grease on it, or scratches. What do you think?"

"We'll have to find out if McNeal had a coin collection," Ragnon said, spitting. He watched the other lab man start to vacuum the truck with his portable equipment. Then he saw Antone moving on downstream, beginning to track through the thick undergrowth and stretches of damp sand along the bank, and he started after him.

A few yards farther on the Indian knelt again and then set up his tripod and camera. "All four are still together," he said, motioning the detective to the site and pointing at the tracks made where they had squatted down beside the stream. "See these marks—they're still carrying the weapons, rifles or shotguns, and laid them down while they drank."

Several fresh cigarette butts also lay discarded nearby, and when Antone had taken his pictures, Ragnon stabbed one of them with his pen and sniffed it. "Mexican brand," he nodded at the deputy, and then called one of the lab men down to bag them for saliva tests while he made a note of where and when they were found.

"This canyon only extends another half mile or so before the stream disappears underground," Antone said, folding his tripod. "The vegetation dries out and leaves only the hardpan desert again, almost impossible to track on. But if they held to this course, even on foot they must have crossed the border by midnight last night."

"A good fifteen hours ago," Ragnon said, glancing at his watch. "It's almost three thirty." He looked around at the cool green silence. Except for the singing of the birds and the babbling stream, it was eerily quiet. "Unless they just stayed here in the canyon somewhere."

John Antone shook his head. "Not from the looks of these tracks, Sergeant. They're hours old. Trash has already blown into them, and they're headed south in a hurry. I'd say it's ten to one they're drinking cold Dos Equis beers in some Mexican cantina right now."

"Well, my orders are to establish if they actually crossed the border, and we haven't done that yet." He spat again, more violently, and looked at the deputy. "But I could use a beer, too, how about you?" When Antone nodded, grinning, Ragnon added, "Good, let's go find someplace where we can look at your state highway map and give this all some serious thought."

In the back booth of a combination hamburger joint and gas station on the highway, they spread out the map on the table between them. Antone had checked in on the radio, but there had been no reports of either the fugitives or their tracks.

"Here's Pájaro Canyon," Ragnon pointed, "with its lower end two miles north of the border. And over here to the southeast the nearest Customs and Immigration port at Piedras Blancas, and a quarter mile on the other side, the Mexican town of San Ignacio."

"Nothing else for miles in any direction except the Sonoran Desert and some mountain ranges," Antone noted, "none of it very hospitable, even in winter."

"No, but notice that from San Ignacio the road continues southwest and eventually splits, one fork joining the highway south to Hermosillo while the other heads west to the California Gulf."

"You think they kept running?" the Indian asked. "On foot?"

"Not likely, not this bunch. They'd catch a ride or steal one."

"So what are we even speculating about, Sergeant? If they're in Mexico, even if you established who they are, the red tape of trying to extradite—"

"Goddammit, John, we don't have proof yet that they actually entered Mexico!" Ragnon was refolding the map. "And I want proof. They could have headed east or west along this side of the border after coming out of Pájaro, or even doubled back."

"But it's not likely." Antone leaned back as the waitress brought their burgers and beers and an extra order of fries. Glancing at the deputy's uniform and Ragnon's rawboned raunchy appearance, she asked, "You two huntin' them killers from the McNeal place?"

Ragnon smiled. "News travels fast. You got any leads?"

"No, but I just hope you catch 'em." She ripped their bill off her pad and laid it between them. "Murderin' Mexicans'll be coming back to kill again."

As she turned away, Ragnon asked the deputy, "Is she right? Are we sure they're Mexicans? Or maybe just four Anglos on the run and living like Mexicans?"

"They were Mexican," Antone insisted, and then hedged just a little. "At least they were *from* Mexico."

They wolfed down the meal mostly in silence, and as Ragnon picked up the check, he said, "Well, Mexicans or no, I'll spring for lunch, John, and dinner, too, if you find me exactly where those four crossed the line."

By late afternoon they had worked the desert for three miles east of the isolated U.S. Customs house at Piedras Blancas, cutting only the fresh sign of a party of six coming *into* the U.S. None of the tracks were made by the footgear they were looking for, either; two had been wearing the rubber-tired huaraches, but of the wrong tread design.

It was after five o'clock when they turned the jeep around, started tracking west of the Customs house, and met a U.S. Border Patrol jeep coming the other way with two uniformed agents doing the same thing. Dragging two heavy truck tires from a chain behind their vehicle, they had smoothed a wide stretch of sand to patrol for fresh signs of a crossing during their shift.

The two jeeps braked alongside each other and waited for the dust to settle, then the Border Patrol agent behind the wheel leaned out and peered at them through reflective sunglasses. "You guys looking for the McNeal killers?"

"That's right," Ragnon answered. "You get the broadcast description of their tracks?"

"Naw, but our radio's been acting up. What are you looking for? How many and what signs?"

"Four," the detective said, and he described the mismatched sneakers of Two-Shoes and the other tracks.

The border agent glanced at his partner, who had a cigar clenched in his jaws as he nodded. "That's them. We dragged across a set of tracks like that about two miles west of here, headed straight into mañana land, so I guess you're too late. You sure they're the ones?"

"Same tracks at the scene and at McNeal's truck, abandoned in Pájaro Canyon sometime last night," Ragnon answered.

"That's them then; too bad. They're probably in Hermosillo by now. Those tracks were hours old." The driver offered them a cigarette, and when they both shook their heads, he took one for himself and shielded the match while he lit it.

"We cut some fresh sign about a half mile out the other way," Antone told the agents, "six of 'em coming in, about an hour old."

"Thanks." The agent in sunglasses put his jeep in gear and revved the engine. "We'll check it out, and good luck—to all of us."

Checking their odometer, they drove beside the Border Patrol's smoothed tire trace for 1.8 miles, and there they were: four sets of tracks erased by the drag but still plainly visible on either side, though slightly filled now with windblown debris and the edges no longer sharply defined. Two-Shoes, Cowboy Heels, Cat's Paw, and Tire Tread. And all four were pointed south at a dead run.

Getting out of the jeep, Ragnon picked the binoculars from their rack, and while Antone set up his tripod to photograph the tracks, the detective walked over to the imaginary line; Imaginary because the International Boundary fence extended only about a mile out on either side of the Customs house, and on both sides here the land was the same: sandy, empty desert scrub, with only an occasional tall cement column to mark the border between two countries so close in geographical distance but so far apart in cultures.

Bringing the glasses to his eyes and adjusting the focus, Ragnon scanned the low barbed hills that hid the town of San Ignacio a short distance away. He knew that these same hills formed a narrow valley where the once full flowing stream that now surfaced only briefly in Pájaro Canyon also surfaced again on the Mexican side; shallow wells and irrigation ditches still supplied the water that supported the pastures and fields of cotton, corn, and beans on the little farms around the town.

He could see the tops of trees that marked the course of the river beyond the hills, and the tips of the twin bell towers of a Mexican church. But nothing else. And from San Ignacio the bastards could have headed anywhere, even east along the new road that led clear to Chihuahua. Or on unmapped roads into various mining towns in the mountains. Hell, they could soon be in Guaymas, or even Ciudad Obregón.

He let the binoculars hang loose against his chest by their strap and spat hard into the sandy soil at his feet as Antone came up to stand beside him. The reality of the killers' escape stirred a sick revulsion deep inside him as he thought of what they'd left behind at the McNeal ranch.

"Looks like you owe me a dinner, Sergeant," the Indian deputy said softly. "We've established they crossed into Mexico— hours ago, with no signs of their doubling back." Ragnon said nothing, and for a long moment Antone studied the expression on the detective's face. "But you're not going to let it go at that, are you, Sergeant?"

Tom Ragnon tucked a fresh pinch of tobacco in his jaw and worked it thoughtfully as he glanced at the deputy. Eventually he sent a spurt of juice onto the ground and handed the binoculars to the Indian. "Looks to me like their tracks continue on down that arroyo and between those hills. They probably crossed the stream right into the town, wouldn't you say?"

"So?" Antone asked meaningfully, raising the glasses and adjusting them to his own eyes.

Ragnon looked at his watch, then spat again. "So that Customs house doesn't close their gate till eight, and I'm wondering how much political dust we'd raise if we just drove back there and crossed the border."

FIVE

Monday, March 8th, 5:45 P.M.

Over the two-room weathered frame building that squatted forlornly beside the open chain-link gate and the dirt road, an American flag fluttered feebly against its staff. The uniformed Customs officer who strode out on the porch to greet them must have been close to retirement.

Burly, grizzled, and gray, he gripped Antone's hand and then Ragnon's with his own beefy paw as they introduced themselves. "I'm Randy Cain," he said, nodding sympathetically, as a fellow officer. "And I can feel for you and your partner, Sergeant. We're open twelve hours a day here, and it's like a graveyard most of the time, but after dark when the gate closes"—he shook his bristled graying head—"a river of aliens and dope flows north, while stolen vehicles and guns head south. Ford Broncos are a favorite now—but you must be after the ones that killed that rancher's family." He looked at Antone. "You track 'em back here to the border?"

The deputy nodded. "Looks like they crossed about midnight last night. Border Patrol put us onto their tracks some two miles west of here."

"Well, you can kiss them good-bye then—unless they're stupid enough to come back and try it again, or they pull something in Mexico. I been on this border for eighteen years and I shit you not, gentlemen, it's a tougher, meaner, raunchier breed that's coming north. No more just simple campesinos looking for work. The hard-liners are mixed in now, and this border's wide open. Where there's fencing they just cut through it, but most of it's open country. No way of stopping 'em without putting the whole U.S. Army across here, which in my opinion they ought to do. Goddamned Congress is worried about the Ruskies, and we got a fucking silent invasion of Mexicans,

Guatemalans, Salvadorans, and God knows what else coming across here every day of the year. Way it is, Customs and the Border Patrol, too, is a joke, a token force. Why, most of the dope—"

"We want to cross over," Tom Ragnon said, interrupting his harangue and spitting into the dust of the road, "see how far the tracks go and where, just for the hell of it."

"What?" Cain frowned in puzzlement, then shrugged. It was unusual, but not illegal. "Sure, why not? You want to come inside for some coffee first?"

"No—thanks, anyway. It's getting late."

"Okay, but you'd better at least leave your sidearms here till you get back or you'll be making an armed invasion of Mexico, and they're kind of touchy about that over there." He nodded toward the other small frame building with a covered drive-through. It was fifty yards beyond the gate along the road to the south, where a Mexican tricolor drooped against the flagpole. Ragnon had expected him to smile or wink, but he did neither. "You'll be conspicuous enough in that marked jeep, and the deputy in uniform," Cain added soberly.

"Are you sure this is a good idea, Sergeant?" John Antone asked cautiously.

Ragnon spat again as he unclipped his holstered snubnose and handed it over to Cain. "None of my ideas are good, John, unless they succeed. But you don't have to go. Wait here if you like, have some of the man's coffee. I'm just curious to see where those tracks go."

John Antone's sudden grin was mischievous. "Just testing you, Sergeant." He removed his service revolver and handed it to the Customs officer. "I wouldn't miss this for all the tortillas in Mexico. But you drive."

They changed places and Ragnon drove on through the gate, braking under the shaded drive-through of the Mexican custom house where the word ADUANO over the door had nearly faded out. Ragnon's Tex-Mex wasn't all that good, but when the middle-aged uniformed guard emerged, he used it to introduce himself and Antone, and showed his shield without either of them getting out of the jeep. He laid it out slowly and watched the Mexican official's frown deepen at his explanation of how they had tracked four murder suspects across the border less than two miles away.

The official's frown faded to puzzlement and then indifference as Ragnon told him they wanted to see if the tracks led into the town and then talk to the local *jefe* of police about the killings. The guard studied Antone's uniform with its empty holster, and the insignia on their jeep, then hesitated as he saw the camera nested on the blanket between them, and the binoculars in their rack. "Not jur camera," he said in thickly accented English, shaking his head firmly. "Or jur field glasses. Es contrabando."

Over Antone's protest, Ragnon leaned across and handed both the camera and glasses to the Mexican official. "You hold them for us—we'll pick them up on the way back, *'sta 'ueno?*"

The guard's face cracked in a huge smile as he took the equipment and stepped back muttering, *"Pasen, pasen gente, por favor."*

"Sergeant—"

"Relax," Ragnon told his companion, putting the jeep in gear and letting out the clutch. "You'll get your stuff back. He was just doing his duty—no contraband."

"But you didn't even get a receipt!"

"Trust." Ragnon spat into the road as they moved out of the shaded drive-through. "You've got to have a little trust."

"Okay, but if I don't get them back, you'll owe me more than a dinner." Then the deputy braced himself on the seat as Ragnon suddenly shifted into the granny gears and swung the jeep off the road, headed down toward the arroyo.

Picking up the same four sets of footprints, they followed the faint impressions down the wash and between the low hills where the stream surfaced again. There the tracks emerged on the far bank among the shallows and reeds and muck right in front of the jeep, and continued onto the roadway, where they vanished.

Stopping the jeep, they got out and searched in both directions along the road and across it, but even Antone was soon shaking his head. "Too much traffic—vehicles, footprints, even those." He pointed to a man on the high seat of a cart being pulled into town by a plodding burro.

"Could they have been picked up right here?" Ragnon wondered, returning to the edge of the road where the tracks had merged with everything else.

"Not likely. But they sure weren't waiting around. They were walking slowly but unswervingly, right to the road."

"And into town."

"Probably. It must have been a long day for them."

Climbing back into the jeep, they drove on down the dusty main street of the town. The wind was kicking up now, and a swirling dust devil danced across the weed-grown plaza where the church with its twin bell towers dominated the square. "We've lost them," Antone finally admitted. "They probably kept right on going toward Hermosillo."

"But not on foot," Ragnon insisted, downshifting as they reached the southern outskirts of the town, where the Indian deputy again failed to find any trace of their prints. "They either caught a ride or stole one," the detective said.

"Or they're still here, holed up somewhere," Antone suggested as Ragnon wheeled the jeep around and headed back toward the plaza.

Low clouds were gathering now and the temperature was dropping as he drove slowly, past tiny shops and residences that ranged from cramped adobe hovels to colorful brick homes with flowering gardens and patio walls or fences of ornamental iron. There weren't half a dozen people on the street to gaze curiously as they stopped at the one main intersection and waited for a dilapidated truck loaded with produce to pass.

Ragnon turned down several of the side streets off the plaza before he found what he was looking for—a two-story balconied old building with large patches of its stucco peeling off the adobe walls. It had once been painted a light blue, but that was obviously a long time ago, and the faded letters above the heavy wooden double doors were barely legible: COMANDANCIA DE POLICÍA.

Parking the jeep on the street in front, Ragnon stared past Antone up the broken concrete steps and through the open double doors that exposed a long shadowed hallway. "You really going in?" the deputy asked him. "Remember, we don't have much formal communication with our Mexican counterparts, Sergeant. No established procedures. We send them routine reports and wanted posters, but we seldom get anything back. We seldom even hear anything. We don't even know who the police chief *is* here in San Ignacio, do we?"

"Maybe it's time we found out," Tom Ragnon growled, stepping out of the jeep on his side. "Maybe this is our big chance to establish international police relations." He cleared his throat, spat out the last of his tobacco, then looked at the deputy and grinned. "You coming, or you chicken?"

"What's that the English say—'In for a penny . . .'" and he, too, dismounted.

Climbing the steps, they entered the long drafty hallway that opened into several empty offices as Ragnon called, *"Oye—hay ninguno aquí?"*

As if by magic a uniformed policeman appeared at the far end of the hall. He carried a Mauser rifle slung on one shoulder and he stared at the Anglo and the uniformed Indian curiously, but without hostility, as Ragnon asked him where they could find the *jefe*—the chief of police.

Motioning them forward, the policeman pointed into a large room lighted only by long narrow windows that reached almost from the worn wooden floor to the high-beamed ceiling. Without curtains or drapes the windows let long rectangles of fading sunlight angle across the floor toward a heavy wooden desk that had been set up on a six-inch dais. A Mexican flag hung on a pole beside the desk, and behind it a large wall map of Sonora framed the uniformed man who sat at it.

Another Mexican in civilian clothes was perched on a corner of the desk, and both had glanced up at the interruption, their playing cards still in their hands. Then the *jefe* stood up ponderously and set his cards carefully aside. His too tight uniform was sharply creased, and he wore a holstered Colt .45 belted around his heavy bulk. Ragnon judged him to be in his fifties, his balding black hair slicked back and his pudgy slightly pock-marked complexion clean shaven except for graying muttonchop whiskers. His dark glance which quickly took in both of his visitors was neither friendly nor warm as Ragnon introduced himself and Antone and showed him his shield and ID.

The *jefe* studied the ID a moment, then handed it back with a thin, slightly bemused smile. "Welcome, Thomas R. Ragnon, Sergeant, Mimbres County Sheriff's Department," he said in careful high-school English. "What brings you to San Ignacio?"

"Police business," Ragnon said, putting away his shield and card. "Can we talk?"

"But of course. I am Comandante Maximiliano Hernández de Garza, the *jefe* here—and this is Sargento Jacinto Cruz

Ochoa, the State Judicial Police agent for this area." He introduced the other man, who was standing now and holding out
his hand. Almost as tall as Ragnon, and wearing worn blue
jeans and a black leather jacket weathered with tiny cracks,
Jacinto Cruz had a thick black mustache and the dark lean look
and predator eyes of a hawk. But the eyes were curiously
friendly, and his grip was strong, not sweaty and weak like the
jefe's.

"Nice to meet you, Sergeant," Cruz said easily, with only a
trace of accent, and then shook hands with Antone. Pulling up
a couple of straight-back chairs, he invited them to sit down.

"I would offer you coffee," the comandante said, "but the fire
has gone out and the pot is cold." He nodded toward an iron-
bellied wood stove in one corner, on which a battered coffee pot
rested.

Outside, the rising wind rattled the windows and kicked up
the dust in the street as Jacinto Cruz cupped a light to a slim
brown cigarillo. Shaking out the match and tossing it in an
ashtray on the desk, beside a Spanish edition of Spiderman
comics and a lurid sex and violence Spanish weekly, he offered
them each a smoke and then rested one cheek on the desk again
as he inquired softly, "Now, Señores, what kind of police business would bring you here?"

Sitting between two old wooden filing cabinets and facing the
comandante on his raised dais with the map of Sonora behind
him, it took Ragnon about ten minutes to explain.

Comandante Hernández was sympathetic. They had, of
course, already heard of the killings, but he thought the Americans must be mistaken about the tracks. No such strangers were
known to be around here, or to have come through; it would
have been reported. And no vehicles had been stolen.

"You say you tracked them across the border and into this
town?" Sergeant Cruz asked.

"Yes." Ragnon nodded toward the deputy. "Antone lost
them when they mingled with the other traffic on the road, but
they must have come through here last night, sometime around
midnight."

The comandante shrugged. "If so, then they are gone by now,
anyway—to Chihuahua City or Hermosillo. I am sorry, but if
you can send us a written report we will of course do what we
can. You have their descriptions?"

"Not yet—only their tracks, the unusual patterns I described."

"Yes—Two-Shoes and Cowboy Boots, interesting." The comandante smiled skeptically. "That isn't much to go on, Sergeant."

"It's all we have right now," Ragnon responded tightly, feeling oddly like a fish out of water. "We hope to get more."

"Good." Comandante Hernández paused to light his own cigarette and insert it in a plastic holder. "Send us a full report. We will cooperate as best we can." He paused, letting the rank smoke trail out through his nostrils. "You, of course, think they are Americans."

"No." Ragnon replied almost too quickly. "We're sure they're Mexican illegals." He glanced at Antone, beginning to feel even more foolish to have come across with so little to go on. But he had really only intended to look at the tracks. Hunting up the Mexican *jefe* had been an afterthought.

The comandante's expression had hardened. "Of course— *mojados*. Well, Sergeant, we don't like murderers in Mexico either—whatever their race. Sure I can't offer you coffee before you go? We can build up the fire."

"No thanks." The detective and the deputy stood up almost together. "It's getting late, and we have to get back before the gate closes. We appreciate your cooperation." They shook hands all around again, and the two Americans left the building.

Outside in the blowing wind and dust, they sat a moment in the jeep and watched the gathering dusk. "Face it, Sergeant," the deputy said, "you're beating a dead horse. They got away clean."

"Maybe. That Comandante Max isn't going to lift a finger. Damn!" He started the jeep and was about to pull away when Jacinto Cruz came out of the building and waved them down. Descending the concrete steps and walking around to the driver's side, he leaned down and spoke to Ragnon. "I would like to help you, Sergeant," he said, his voice rising against the wind. "I know what you think we'll do about the report, and you're right. It will go into the file, how you say—thirteen?"

"You mean he'll throw it away."

"No, no, but in an unused file."

"A dead file."

"Sí, cases filed but not worked."

"Then how can you help, Sargento? And why?"

"One thing the comandante said was true—we don't like murderers in Mexico either. I will ask around—see if maybe somebody saw anyone suspicious. You're sure they weren't gringos?"

"Almost certain," Ragnon said.

"Then maybe if I could call you . . . collect?"

Tom Ragnon gave him his card. "Thanks, Sargento."

"De nada, Señor." Jacinto Cruz tucked the card in an inside pocket of his black leather jacket, and Ragnon glimpsed the butt of his .45 automatic in an underarm holster as the Mexican stepped back away from the jeep.

"You think he'll call?" Antone asked as they pulled out of the side street and swung around the plaza, back toward the Customs house, just as the first drops of rain began to fall.

"I'd make book on it, John." Thomas R. Ragnon was smiling contentedly now. "There's something about that Jacinto guy that appeals to my investigative nature."

"Well, before we make any more bets, you better hope my camera and binoculars are still in hock at the border. But for my money, that Comandante Max is just another two-bit hustling bureaucrat, and he's the one with the power."

"You think so?" Ragnon dug his Redman out of his vest pocket and scooped out a hefty pinch. "John, that Jacinto Cruz is a hunter, a real predator—couldn't you sense it?"

"Yeah," Antone admitted finally, thoughtfully, "you're right about that. At least if I were a Mexican desperado, I sure as hell wouldn't want him after me."

SIX

Monday, March 8th, 8:15 P.M.

"I said 'case closed,' goddammit, Rags!" Chief of Homicide Sidney Clayton Poole was out from behind his desk and pacing, his cigar glowing and belching blue smoke, his little walrus eyes glaring angrily at the detective-sergeant over his half-glasses.

"You know the odds against solving a homicide where the perpetrators aren't known by or related to the victims. When we get the autopsies and lab work-ups and Antone's pix, send the goddamned Mexicans the full report and let them wipe their asses with it if they want to. We can't waste any more time on a dead-end case."

"Unless they come back and kill again," Tom Ragnon said, pausing to send a squirt of tobacco juice twanging into the chief's plastic-lined metal wastebasket.

Poole stopped his pacing and stared at the detective. "Jesus, that's disgusting, Ragnon."

"It calms my nerves, Chief, and like I said, they could come back."

"Why the hell should they?"

"I don't know. I don't know enough about them yet— whether it was a random thing, or a planned burglary that escalated to rape and murder, or what. But they could come back. And there's this Mexican cop who's offered—"

"Don't give me any more shit about some gut-eating cop from across the line. He told you what they'd do with the goddamned report—that's the kind of help we get from the greasers, especially if it's one of their own. Their police system is as big a farce as the rest of their half-baked government."

"He took the trouble to follow us out, and offered to look for a lead." Ragnon started to spit again but decided against it and simply shifted the wad to his other cheek. "I told him he could call me collect if he got one."

"And you believed him? Jesus H. Christ, Rags—how much did he want for his 'lead'?"

"He didn't ask for anything."

"He will—whether he finds one or fakes one." Poole shook his head bewilderedly. "That's another world across the border, Rags, you know that. They don't think like us or act like us— they're Mexicans."

"They don't like killers on the loose any more than we do, Chief."

"Gringo killers maybe, but these are their own kind. And the murder site was here, and the victims gringos and not even turistas that might affect their pocketbooks. Look, it's as quiet as it's gonna get around here. You wanted some time off—take it. Go fly to Vegas or someplace, get laid by one of those hundred dollar hookers, live a little. Then get your life in order, make up with your wife or forget her. In the meantime"—he glanced at a note on his spindle and ripped it off—"here." He handed it to the detective. "I just got a call from that Marshal Duff. McNeal's brother is coming down to the ranch tomorrow to arrange for the funerals. He wants to talk to the detective in charge, so interview him as a formality. But lay it out for him: We're dead-ended with the perpetrators in Mexico, and we don't even know who they are—Two-Shoes and Cat's Paw, for Christ's sake? Just write it up and put in for that vacation."

Tom Ragnon smiled wryly and then spat viciously into Poole's wastebasket again. Watching Poole wince gave him a kind of perverse satisfaction. "Thanks, Chief," he said. "I sure appreciate the advice."

Leaving Poole's office about eight thirty, Ragnon stopped at his trailer for a quick shower and shave and then drove over to the house on Old Father Road, where he found Angie true to her promise. With the kids tucked in, she warmed up the meat loaf and tossed a fresh salad, and while they ate he told her about the case—a case to be closed almost before it opened.

"And that's it?" Angie bristled indignantly, her fork poised. "A whole family slaughtered in their own house—one a seven-year-old—and the killers are safe by stepping across the border? What about murder cases never being closed?"

"Technically it's not closed, it's just inactive—not worked."

"But what about extradition? And this Mexican detective, Cruz?"

"Extradition is a complicated process, even when we know who we're after, and we don't. I'm hoping Cruz will come up with something, since Antone tracked them right into his town, but it's a slim lead at best."

"I think four killers as vicious as these guys are going to leave more than tracks wherever they go," Angie said somberly.

For dessert she'd baked his favorite pie—a lemon meringue—and by midnight they were in bed, naked and warm and close. "This is crazy, you know," she whispered, nibbling at his ear. "I'm still divorcing you."

"I know," he sighed.

"I'm sorry, but a separation just isn't working. Look at us—you keep stepping on my life."

"You don't enjoy it?" he whispered back, the momentum building.

"I'm not just talking about sex, you bastard—the sex is great. I love you . . . miss you—"

"Then why a divorce? Why even a separation?"

"I need my space, Tom. I told you, and you still don't understand." He could feel her draw away emotionally in the darkness. The satin smooth warmth of her was still close against his lean muscular frame, the long dark strands of her hair still on his face along with her musky perfumed scent, but emotionally she had drawn away again, and that hurt.

"The chief says I can take some time off," he said, rolling away from her. "Suggests I go to Vegas or someplace if I can't make up with my wife."

"So maybe—"

They were interrupted by the jangling of the bedside princess phone, and Ragnon picked it up without thinking. "Yeah?"

"Sergeant? This is Antone."

Tom Ragnon sat up in bed, glaring at the digital glow of the clock-radio which had just turned to 12:22.

"Sorry to call so late," the deputy was saying, "but I couldn't get you at your trailer and Chief Poole said to try this number, since it's important."

"What's important?" Ragnon growled irritably.

"Customs agents just turned in a report to the Narcs, and they passed it on to us. It's a lead on Two-Shoes."

SEVEN

Tuesday, March 9, 1:10 A.M.

"Couldn't this have waited until morning?" Ragnon grumbled unconvincingly, taking the report Antone handed him and pouring the deputy a cup of coffee before he sat down at his tiny kitchen table and put on his reading glasses.

"It *is* morning, Sergeant," Antone said, smiling and glancing at the wall clock. "One-ten A.M. And that report is a direct tie-in with two of our murder suspects—Two-Shoes and Tire

Tread. The other two tracks couldn't be definitely identified—they were too messed up. But there were four of them at the scene."

The tail end of the storm system covering northern Arizona had finally reached the city, and hail rattling on the aluminum roof of the trailer was deafening as the wind buffeted its sides while Ragnon sipped at his own hot brew and skimmed briefly through the report. He had asked Antone to meet him here at his trailer, and the "scene" the deputy had referred to was a plane crash just short of an old abandoned World War II airfield in the desert, six miles north of the border and eight miles southwest of Pantana.

The pilot had been found dead in the partially burned wreckage, which included the cargo of baled marijuana. But the crash was only a few days old, and tire tracks also found near the scene, along with the footprints, were traced back to the outskirts of Pantana where two camper trucks were found abandoned in an arroyo. The campers had been reported stolen just four days ago, and a print in one of them matched the bloody thumbprint on the freezer at the McNeals'.

Ragnon looked up. "Then our Mexicans weren't farm workers, they were dopers and the deal went sour; so they wind up at the McNeal place *posing* as farm workers."

"Until Sunday night, when they decide to kill and rape and pillage as a little sideline before heading home."

"Jesus," Ragnon mused. "That wasn't very smart."

"It was crazy," Antone said, pouring himself more coffee and stirring in a spoonful of sugar while the storm raged outside. "But they almost got away with it—no dope money, but loot from a burglary for their efforts, so their trip north wouldn't be a total loss."

"Looks that way." The detective got up and rinsed his mug in the sink. "No other ID on them except what's in that report?" he asked.

"That's it, according to both the Narcs and Customs. No complete set of prints anywhere on the campers, and the tracks weren't familiar to them from any previous cases. The pilot's body was burned, but they're trying to ID that from dental records."

"So we're really not any better off than we were," Ragnon said. "No names, no descriptions, no real motive or witnesses.

Just a thumbprint and footprints and an empty pack of Mexican cigarettes found at the scene. Hell, John, they still could have been gringos!"

"But you don't think so either, Sergeant."

"No." Ragnon shook his head. "I agree with you, and thanks for bringing this over. I'll put it in the report to Comandante Max." He walked the deputy to the door. "Old Ironballs got another call from Marshal Duff earlier this evening. Says McNeal's brother is coming down to the ranch tomorrow—" He glanced at the clock. "Today. This afternoon. Maybe he'll be able to tell us what else is missing, or even get us a list from the insurance company."

"Want me to meet you there?"

"No, nothing he says is likely to lead to anything new. I'm afraid it's up to that Sargento Cruz now." The rattle of hail had eased off to a steady downpour of rain, but the wind continued battering the trailer with heavy gusts and Ragnon had to hold onto the door as he opened it.

"Should be the last winter storm!" Antone remarked as he put on his stiff-brim hat and ducked out into it.

"We'll wish we had more of it," Ragnon called after him, "once the summer heat hits! And leave us not lose all hope on this one, John. Instead we should be grateful! If this weather had hit twenty-four hours ago, we wouldn't even have those tracks!"

Charlie McNeal was ten years older than his late brother and forty pounds heavier. There wasn't even much of a family resemblance, but he was obviously grieving. A mechanical engineer in Phoenix, he'd flown down to Tucson and rented a car for the drive to the ranch near Pantana.

Outside, the afternoon temperature stood at fifty-two degrees under a cloudy sky, but there was a deeper chill here in the unheated house, a clammy empty shadow of wasted lives as McNeal sat on the living room couch, his elbows on his knees and his face in his hands, sobbing heavily as the reality of his loss was reinforced amid the still bloodied shambles of the home.

He had walked into the kitchen first, where the chalk marks of the bodies were still on the table and floor, the blood dried now to dirty brown stains. And the shock still hung like a silent scream in the air around them.

"I'm really sorry about this, Mr. McNeal," Ragnon offered woodenly. It was such a trite, empty phrase, and yet he meant it. He glanced over at Marshal Duff while they waited for the brother to regain his composure.

The marshal shook a fresh cigarette loose from a pack and offered it to the detective, who shook his head, then put it between his own lips and cupped a light.

"And you've no idea who—" McNeal looked up at Ragnon. "Who did this? Who *could* have done this?"

"Mexicans," Duff answered, shaking out his match. "Illegals. They're hitting a lot of places along the border these days. Fortunately they don't usually kill, but these did."

"We don't know who they were, Mr. McNeal," Ragnon said. "They were living in the trailer out back, but only for a day or two, and we tracked them across the border."

McNeal shook his head despondently. "So what chance is there of ever catching them now?"

"Well, I told you about the tools and silverware and things we found in the truck," Ragnon said. "It might help if you could identify anything else that's missing—like the guns that must have been in that locked cabinet over there. Were you here often?"

"No, not often. But we were close. Holidays, special occasions. Just last Christmas—" He was staring at the broken door on the empty gun cabinet as his thoughts wandered off. "Bob liked to hunt," he started again. "He was teaching Tad—" His voice caught in a sob. "I'm sorry, but this just hit me sudden . . . what's really happened—they're gone."

"Take your time, Mr. McNeal," Tom Ragnon said, taking out his notebook. "About the guns. . . ?"

"He had half a dozen," McNeal continued. "I don't know—a .357 Magnum revolver was his favorite, but he had a .22 Luger for target practice. And a rifle, bolt action—thirty-ought-six, I think it was—and a couple of shotguns. I don't know what size. I don't own a gun myself—I don't hunt." He stared hard at Ragnon. "A lot of good they did him—all those guns."

"If we could maybe get a list from the insurance company. . . ?" the detective asked.

McNeal nodded.

"You've looked through the house, Mr. McNeal," Ragnon said. "Can you tell if anything else is missing—small things maybe, valuables. They didn't seem to be after any really big stuff."

"I . . . no, no, I can't tell—"

"What about cash? Did your brother keep a lot of cash in the house? Or maybe a coin collection?"

McNeal got up and walked over to the hutch that stood against one wall. The knickknacks behind the glass were untouched, but the lower drawers had been yanked out and dumped upside down on the floor, their contents scattered. McNeal knelt down. "Not much cash," he said. "A hundred at most—but he had a set of old silver dollars, twenty of them in a clear plastic case with individual pockets. He kept it taped to the bottom of one of these drawers." He looked up. "It's gone."

"Silver Peace dollars—say 1928?"

McNeal looked puzzled. "Yes, all of them that same year, uncirculated. How—"

"They found one on the floor of the pickup, under the front seat," Ragnon said.

"Oh . . ." McNeal turned over one of the drawers. "There was something else, too, that's missing—a bag of dimes. Nothing special or old, just dimes. He kept them in this hutch, too, in a velvet bag."

"A velvet bag?"

"Purple velvet—one of those kind that fancy booze comes in —I forget the brand. A purple velvet bag with a yellow drawstring—full of dimes."

"Seagram's Crown Royal," Ragnon said, adding the information to his notebook. "What about jewelry, Mr. McNeal? Could you tell if any jewelry was missing—say from the bedroom?"

McNeal shook his head. "Helen didn't go in much for jewelry; a little costume stuff, nothing expensive except her wedding ring—a plain gold band." He looked at Ragnon. "Was it. . . ?"

"Gone," the detective said. "No rings on any of the victims." He made another notation in his book. "Any inscription on the ring?"

McNeal shook his head. "No, I don't think so." His anguished stare fixed on Ragnon again. "There's no real chance of catching them, is there, Sergeant? Realistically—"

"There's always a chance, Mr. McNeal. The more details we can uncover, the better the odds."

"But if they're in Mexico—"

"Even in Mexico," Ragnon insisted, "I'm already in touch with the Mexican police."

"And they'll help? They'll—"

"They'll try." He was tiptoeing along the edge of a lie, and he knew it. "We'll all try, Mr. McNeal, but so far we haven't got much. No names, not even a description. And if they have to be hunted in Mexico, there'll be some bribes to pay—it's the custom. Here." He handed him his card. "If you think of anything else, call me."

"I want to set up some kind of reward anyway," McNeal said, tucking the card in his wallet, "a fund—" he looked at Marshal Duff. "I'll talk to the bank in Pantana, get the sergeant some cash to work with."

Edwin Duff nodded sympathetically. "The town council will help too. We all want to help." He looked at Ragnon. "And we do have a description of sorts, Sergeant," he said. "I meant to tell you earlier. I talked to a farmer who remembers picking up four Mexicans on the outskirts of Pantana four days ago. They rode in the back of his truck with his fourteen-year-old son and he dropped them off about a half mile from this ranch. They said they were looking for farm work, but now he's had time to think about it, he says they didn't really strike him as farm workers—too arrogant and mean looking. He was sorry he'd picked them up and glad to be rid of them."

Tom Ragnon was staring at the marshal, almost holding his breath. "For Christ's sake, man, what did they look like? What's the description?"

Duff shrugged. "Just ordinary Mexicans—dark skins, black hair and eyes. But his kid did notice one funny thing about the biggest one—his shoes."

EIGHT

Tuesday, March 9th, 10 P.M.

By evening the storm had passed on eastward into New Mexico and Ragnon had talked to both the farmer and his son. Back at his desk in the detective squad room of the Sheriff's Building downtown, he was typing up the first Homicide Report on Case #PAN-82-0307.

It still wasn't much, and leaning back in the armless swivel chair, he stretched cramped muscles and wondered how a secretary stood this kind of work all day. The hands on the big wall clock above the map of Mimbres County were at 10:08, and it was quiet. Other than the sounds of the duty officer at the switchboard, who was popping his gum, and the faint hum of the janitor's buffer in the hall downstairs, it was like a tomb, and he guessed there was no one else in the building.

He knew he should have left by now, too, but this report wasn't just the brief summary Chief Poole had wanted. It was going to be read by Jacinto Cruz in San Ignacio, and he was putting into it all the details he could, including the matching print and tracks at the site of the plane crash and the missing items described by McNeal's brother; everything the Mexican lawman might need, assuming he was going to continue the search.

Reaching for the bottle of whiteout, Ragnon blotted out his last error and then began typing slowly again. The back window on the farmer's truck had been out, so he could talk to them as he drove and make his observations about their not seeming like farm workers. Between his half-assed Spanish and their butchered English, it evidently hadn't been much of a conversation, but enough to get by.

Although they were just ordinary Mexicans—and he said they all looked alike to him—he did remember the biggest of them had a two-inch scar under his left eye, a thick straight mustache, and wore a red rag for a headband to tie back his shaggy black hair. And he seemed to have the best command of

English. The youngest had a long, narrow face with a hook nose, and was clean shaven, with slightly buck teeth; while the oldest had acne scars on his cheeks, a drooping mustache and goatee. The fourth wore a full beard and had a chipped front tooth.

And the farmer's kid, riding in the back with them, had noticed the odd shoes that Red Band was wearing: both black sneakers, but the right one had diagonal white stripes while the left had straight orange ones. It had struck the kid as funny, but he hadn't laughed. Something about those four had discouraged his making any jokes about the one with two shoes.

Ripping the report out of the typewriter, Ragnon read it over one more time, then made triplicate copies on the Xerox. He would still have to have it all translated into Spanish, and even amended, if the autopsy and lab reports showed anything unexpected, but for now it was all he could do. He knew it wasn't enough. But a police artist had been working with the farmer and his son when he left, doing composite drawings that he could include with the report. And that was a start.

Except that once old Ironballs got his copy, that would end it. Comandante Max would get his on the other side, and that would end it there, too, unless—he kept seeing the Mexican detective's dark hawk eyes and quietly deceptive manner, and wondered why in hell he hadn't called. Why had he bothered to come out after them and offer his help if he wasn't sincere? He hadn't even asked for anything—yet.

Shifting his pinch of Redman to his other cheek, he sent a shot ringing into the nearby wastebasket, then chalked himself off duty on the board and turned out the lights in the squad bay as he left.

He hadn't meant to drive by the house on Old Father Road this late. And she'd warned him not to drive by at night at all unless he called first. Not because she was seeing anyone else, she insisted, but just on principle. Angie was big on principle.

But as long as he was here. . . . A light still burned in the living room, and her car was parked on the carport as he pulled up behind it. Slamming his own car door, he stepped up on the porch, rang the bell, and waited. He could hear stirrings inside, but it was taking her a long time to move from the living room through the hall to the front door, and he began to get an uncomfortable feeling in the pit of his stomach.

He glanced around. There were no other cars on the street. Then her voice came through the door and he knew she was at the peephole. "Tom—what are you doing here?"

The lock mechanism rattled, the door opened as far as the safety chain would allow, and she peeked out. The tone of her voice had made his stomach tighten a notch further as his brain busily denied what his instincts were insisting. "I told you never to do this, Tom," she said, closing the door to free the chain and then opening it again just as a car engine roared to life in the alley out back and squealed its tires getting away.

When he spoke, he didn't recognize the sound of his own voice through the sudden ringing of the anger in his ears. "An alley rat, Angie? You're dating alley rats?"

"It wasn't a date, Tom—it was just a friend stopping by, someone I met at work last week." She was fully clothed. That's all he seemed able to think about at the moment—she still had her clothes on and her hair didn't seem disheveled. "We were just watching TV," she was saying, "a movie—that old one we like: *Same Time Next Year*, with Alan Alda."

"Very appropriate," he mumbled angrily, realizing they had moved into the living room with this strange conversation, and she had turned on the rest of the lights. "And your friend—does he always park in alleys and leave by the back door when someone knocks?"

She smiled, trying to ease the tension. "That's my fault. He knows I'm still married, and I told him you were a cop and that we're still friendly."

"Are we?"

"I told you I need my space, Tom."

"You sure do."

"So why did you come by? To spy on me?" She had fumbled a cigarette from a pack on the coffee table, and he knew she was nervous now. She had all but given up smoking. And the brand was new to him, some kind of menthol lights. Ragnon wondered if they belonged to her late departed friend as she steadied the table lighter in her hand.

"Actually I just wanted to share this case with you," he said. "It's beginning to break a little, a few small cracks around the edges—at least on this side of the border."

"And I want to hear about it, Tom, but it can't be like before, can't you understand that? I don't want to hurt you, but I can't breathe—you're pushing me too close. Maybe we can get back together, I don't know—I'm all mixed up now. You should have called."

"Yes—I will next time." He was aware that his fists were clenched and his breathing constricted. "If there is a next time." He knew he was going to have to face the fact that his marriage was really ending. Maybe he would take that vacation in Vegas. "Good night, Angie," he said softly. "I'm sorry."

"Tom—" She put a hand on his arm. "As long as you're here, sit down. Tell me about the case." She mashed out the partially smoked butt in an ashtray. "I'm really interested."

"Not now, Angie—maybe later. Nothing important yet anyway—just small things, and a gut feeling about this one."

"You've always said it's the small things that are put together to make the big picture, and your gut instincts have been right before. What about this time?"

He was tempted. Tempted to sit, to take her hand and try to wipe out the last few ugly moments of agonizing reality about his marriage and his life. To make a final desperate grasp at saving it, but he resisted. That's what he had been doing for the past two months, and obviously it hadn't worked. They were getting further apart. And now someone else was moving in. If not this one, some other. He had reached the door and turned. "Good night, Angie—I'll call you." She seemed so small and helpless, sitting there on the couch; yet somehow strong and capable at the same time; independent, efficient, and sure. "Good night," he repeated needlessly, and stepped back out into the night.

NINE

Wednesday, March 10, 8:05 A.M.

Two messages were spiked on Tom Ragnon's desk when he entered the squad bay next morning after a restless night in his trailer. The first was from John Antone. The autopsy and lab reports were ready, and the deputy had gone over to the morgue to pick them up. The second message was off the switchboard: an hour earlier a collect call had been accepted for him from one Sargento Jacinto Cruz of the State Judicial Police in Sonora, Mexico. Ragnon was to call back and arrange a meeting. Cruz had a lead on Two-Shoes.

"Bingo," he muttered. He poured himself a brimming mug of coffee and sipped it thoughtfully while he contained his excitement and tried to decide what to do. He called Antone first, told him about Cruz and to cool his heels at the morgue until he got there. But when he put a return call to Cruz through the switchboard, the Mexican police agent was out, whereabouts and time of return unknown.

"Shit," he grumbled, finishing his coffee and glancing at the clock. It was 8:22, and he was thinking: They don't take siestas down there in the morning, do they?

Two doors down the hall he walked into Sidney Poole's office without knocking, his mind made up. "I'm ready to take that vacation, Chief," he said.

Old Ironballs had his mouth full of Danish, and it took him a moment to clear it with a swallow of his own morning brew. But at least he was smiling. "Finally," he beamed, "a sensible decision from you, Rags." And the smile became lecherous. "What's it gonna be—Las Vegas and one of those statuesque showgirls with the tassled tits?"

"No—Mexico and Sergeant Jacinto Cruz. He just called."

"Oh fuck, Rags, you're sitting on your goddamned brains again. I just got through talking to Antone over at the morgue. Autopsy and lab reports are zilch too. Nothing significant. Two clear prints—count 'em." He held up two stubby fingers. "An index finger off the TV found with the truck, and a thumbprint with half a palm in blood off the freezer. Everything else that was legible belonged to the victims. Now what's this shit about a vacation in Mexico?"

"You said I needed a vacation, Chief; I agree. The homicide case load *is* lighter than usual, probably as light as it'll get this year. So I'll take some time off. How I spend it is my business."

Poole shook his head in disgust and lighted one of his foul cigars. "You so much as put your foot in a cow pie down there, Rags, you'll wind up so deep in one of their spic slammers they'll have to shoot your beans to you with a peashooter, don't you know that?"

"Cruz has a lead on Two-Shoes, Chief—that was the message he just left. He wants a meet."

"Bullshit. How could he have a lead so quick? All you gave him was tracks—footprints, for God's sake."

"I'm going to call him, talk to him, meet with him. I'll hand carry a copy of my report on the case, and I'll pick up copies of the composites a police artist is making up from the farmer and his son who saw them. I've got the scent on this one now, Chief, and I can't let it go."

"You've got your head up your ass," Poole snorted, "that's what you've got. He'll want money, your greaser cop—*la mordida*—they always do."

"McNeal's brother is already starting a reward fund—five thousand dollars. And Marshal Duff says the Pantana town council is going to meet on it and probably match it. The town is in an uproar, Chief. The McNeals were well liked and the family is influential. His father was the late state senator, so they're going to want more than a paper tiger on this case."

"I know who his goddamned father was, Rags—the brother's already had the attorney general's office on my case. But I also know what it'll cost to chase this thing all over mañana land and what it'll result in—zip. Four Mexicans in their own country, among their own friends, aren't exactly gonna stand out like four turds in a toilet bowl."

"Look at it this way, Chief," Ragnon said, smiling, "I'll be on my own. Me and Cruz. And with the reward money, it won't cost your budget so much as a rusty centavo."

Sidney Poole was studying the detective closely now over his half-lenses. "You're really a little crazy, you know that, Ragnon? You know the problems they're having down there, with their peso devaluations and another one of their half-assed elections coming up. Think about it—you'll be over there with no jurisdiction, no official status, no gun—if you weren't my A-fucking-one homicide specialist, I'd have you committed." He was squinting one eye and tilting his head away from his own cloud of cigar smoke. "I don't really want to lose you, Rags, and a stunt like this could get your ass shot off. They're not all that crazy about gringos anyway, unless they're rich turistas. In a lot of ways, they're still primitive as hell. But I'm not getting through to you, am I, Rags?"

"No, Chief, you're not getting through. I'm as dense as ever."

"And stubborn. Okay, I tried. Sign a leave slip and get the fuck lost—but keep in touch. Even if you should get lucky and find 'em, we'll still have all that extradition shit."

Tom Ragnon smiled again. "Thanks for the speech, Chief—see you."

Sidney Clayton Poole stared after him at the closed door, shaking his head and thinking, Well, what could he expect of a man whose favorite tune was something called "Classical Gas."

In a vacant conference room at the county morgue, Ragnon met with Deputy John Antone and they went over the autopsies on each of the victims, along with the lab reports. The grisly full-color photos of the bodies were spread out on the table between them, and they still made Ragnon a little queasy.

"The little boy was asphyxiated in the freezer," Antone said, glancing back at the report. "Both female victims died of severed jugulars, the weapon being the same: a smooth, sharp instrument, probably a knife."

"What about the bread knife and those in the kitchen drawer?"

"All tested out clean. If one of them was used, it was thoroughly washed. Not a trace."

"And there would have been—at least a trace."

"According to these autopsies, both women were raped, and the one facedown on the table—the daughter—was sodomized."

"A real bunch of sweethearts, these four." Ragnon tucked a fresh pinch of Redman in his cheek.

"Blood groups of the victims were A and O Positive," Antone continued reading, "but tests on traces of semen and sweat and saliva stains are grouped O and AB. Also found some pubic hairs, not the women's."

"What about McNeal himself?" Ragnon asked, chewing thoughtfully.

"Death due to a fractured skull. The singletree tested out—human blood and scalp hairs in the cracks of the wood matched his blood group and his hair." Antone looked up. "But that's all we've got from the lab. No full set of prints on anybody but the victims. A right index on a broken shard of the TV screen found in the truck, and the left thumbprint on the freezer, both at least twelve points. I can try cross-checking with Immigration files, and the FBI's single print processor—it's all computerized now."

Tom Ragnon nodded. "Looks like our best lead will be the composites. When will they be ready?"

"You can pick them up this afternoon."

"Good. I want to take the whole package with me to show Jacinto Cruz."

John Antone smiled. "Somehow I'm not surprised he called. And I guess I'm not surprised you're going either—but on your own time and expense? I'd think the chief could work out some kind of financing."

"Not old Ironballs. He's always got a hard-on over his tight budget. Even with a multiple murder only two things move him to spend time and money—an open and shut case or political heat."

"There may be some political heat on this one," Antone said, "if McNeal was as well connected as they say."

"There already is, only I can't wait for it to build. The trail gets colder every hour, and we've got to strike while Jacinto's iron is hot, if I can just get hold of him and set up the meet. I put the call through again from downstairs, but no luck."

"I wish I could go with you, Sergeant. I'd even sign a leave slip, too, but I just got back off vacation."

"Poole wouldn't okay two of us anyway." Ragnon closed his notebook and began putting the photos back in their envelopes. "I get the idea he thinks I might be dead meat nosing around for killers in Mexico."

"He could be right. At least you're going to have good company. I see in the papers the new president-elect is touring northern Sonora next week, making speeches about all the great things he's going to do. But watch yourself. You've got my number at home if you need anything—officially or otherwise. And stay in touch anyway, in case I get something more here, though I'll be working unofficially too. It's open but off the active list now that the report's going to Mexico along with the suspects."

"I don't plan to be away long," Ragnon told the deputy as

they mounted the stairs to the first floor of the building. "I'll be taking my own car and just playing everything by ear."

Back at the sheriff's building they put away the original copies of the report and pictures, and Ragnon arranged for Spanish translations to follow. "I want this one, John," he said somberly as they shook hands. "I want this one bad."

"Just don't get caught with your ass hanging out in a cold wind down there, Sergeant. I like working with you."

At one P.M. Ragnon tried again with a call to San Ignacio without success. At three he picked up the completed police artist's drawings of the four suspects as described by the farmer and his son. He was sitting at his desk, studying them intently, when Jacinto Cruz called again.

When Ragnon had described the evidence he had accumulated, the Mexican detective said, "Fine, can you meet me about seven here in San Ignacio?"

"Okay. At the police station?"

"No. The Cantina Linda, on Calle Cajón, four blocks south of the police station. You will be alone or your partner will come too?"

For just an instant Ragnon hesitated, a touch of anxiety nibbling at the back of his mind. Then he answered, "Alone. I will be alone."

"Hasta la vista, Sargento," Jacinto Cruz said, and hung up.

TEN

Wednesday, March 10, 6:30 P.M.

Driving through the International gate in his old four-door Ford Falcon an hour and a half before closing time, Tom Ragnon was waved on by the Mexican Customs agent and entered San Ignacio just as long blue shadows were stretching down the dusty streets and alleyways and a chilling evening breeze brought a few spatters of rain out of the west.

The Cantina Linda was right where Cruz had said it would be: four blocks south of the police station, a stuccoed adobe painted bright blue with pink-trimmed doors and windows. A uniformed policeman stood on the corner, and an ornamental iron gate opened into a courtyard where a pulsing red globe flash-lighted the deeper shadows of the parking area.

Inside, the smoke was thick enough to walk on, and kerosene lamps disclosed a scattering of patrons along the bar and seated at small round tables in front of an empty bandstand. At the moment there were more girls than customers, and when Ragnon entered with his worn leather briefcase tucked under one arm, several of them gave him inviting glances which he ignored.

In the moments it took his eyes to accustom themselves to the dim interior, one of the men at the bar picked up his beer and walked casually over to a table in the center of the room, and Ragnon recognized Jacinto Cruz by his crinkled leather jacket. As the Mexican started to sit, Ragnon shook his head and motioned him over to a table by the window, where they sat down on opposite sides.

Ragnon laid the briefcase on his left and put his Stetson down on his right as a bartender came for their order. Cruz was drinking Carta Blanca and ordered another. Ragnon shook his head. "Maybe later." And while Cruz lit a fresh cigarillo off the butt of an old one, the American moved over to the window and opened it about six inches.

The cold air made the candle on the table between them gutter as they studied each other in silence while Ragnon patted the pockets of his sheepskin vest for his pouch of Redman. "I'm nervous," the detective said. "And I chew when I'm nervous. And since they don't seem to put spittoons in saloons any more, I need an open window, or an empty can."

"You don't look nervous," Cruz observed, smiling. His white teeth were bright as Pepsodent in his dark hawkish face and his eyes glinted yellow as a cat's in the candlelight. "Didn't you bring your gun?"

Now it was Ragnon who smiled. "No. It's against the law."

The American noticed the slight bulge of the shoulder holster under the Mexican's leather jacket as Cruz nodded at the briefcase. "What *did* you bring, Sargento?"

"Evidence. Everything we've gathered so far." He leaned back as the bartender brought Cruz another sweating bottle and

placed it on the table between them. "You said you had something for me," Ragnon said, "so I brought something for you."

"No money?" Cruz asked, still smiling. "I thought maybe it
was money." He blew several perfect smoke rings that drifted
over their heads to mix with the already blue haze hanging just
under the ceiling.

Ragnon chewed thoughtfully for a moment; so that was the
way it was going to be. Well, Old Ironballs had warned him. He
spat out the six-inch opening of the window and leaned closer
to the Mexican. "I thought maybe we should talk first," he said
carefully.

Jacinto Cruz shrugged expressively. "Por seguro, why not?
You talk, I'll listen." He took a long swallow of his Carta
Blanca.

Unzipping the briefcase, Ragnon spat once more out the window, then lowered it to ease the sputtering of the candle while
he laid out what he had on the table between them, including
the full-color shots of the victims. Watching the Mexican study
the evidence, Ragnon told him of the farmer and his son who
had picked up four men just two days before the murders and
how the boy had remembered the one with two shoes. He had
saved the composites for last, and he laid them now in front of
Cruz. "These were drawn by a police artist from the descriptions. Do you recognize any of them?"

Cruz, smoking, studied the four faces for long moments in
silence, then looked up and shook his head. "Sorry, no." He
swept his hand over the rest of the evidence, the autopsy and
lab reports, the working notes of an ongoing investigation, and
he looked up in amazement. "All this—so fast?"

"Just lucky," Ragnon answered, stuffing the pictures of the
victims back in their large envelope. "Lucky there was dew over
the tracks that night and no rain; lucky all four were seen; lucky
one wore two different shoes. Just lucky."

Jacinto Cruz nodded. "We have a saying in Mexico: *Toda la
vida es suerte.*"

"All of life is luck," Ragnon translated. "Well, maybe not all.
Not in this business anyway. Sometimes we have to make our
own luck. You know how it is—most murder cases take weeks,
others maybe months or years. But the longer they take, the less
likely they are to be solved. We've got a dozen cases that are
several years old, but we never close a murder investigation. It

may not be worked if there are no more leads, but it's never closed."

"So what about the money?" Cruz asked, ignoring the speech. "You mentioned a reward—five thousand dollars."

"Did I?" Ragnon asked, surprised. "I sure didn't mention the amount."

"But that's what it is—so far. The victims' relatives have put up five, and the town of Pantana may match it." He smiled sardonically, lighting another cigarillo. "We have our sources, too, Sargento."

Tom Ragnon's respect for the Mexican lawman's ability had suddenly broadened, while the trust had diminished. "For apprehension and indictment—of all four," he challenged.

Jacinto Cruz was still smiling. "It doesn't work that way, Sargento; not here."

"I know—*la mordida*—the bite."

The Mexican grew serious. "Bribery is not unheard of in your country, *verdad?* And cops have—how you say—on the take?"

"Some cops," Ragnon said evenly. "Not this cop."

"Of course. I respect that. But you respect this, gringo, the exchange of money is the way of business in this world and has become traditional here; everybody gets his share." He leaned back, tilting his bottle of Carta Blanca, then laughed infectiously. "Why are you gringos always so shocked, so angry? I tell you it is the way business is done all over the world. Besides, you think I can support my family on my salary as a policeman?"

"So how much do you want?" Ragnon raised the window, spat out the last of his tobacco, and lowered it.

Opening the envelopes again, Jacinto Cruz thumbed idly through the composites and color photos, then looked up. "These are evil men you seek, Sargento." His insinuation was plain.

"So, how much?"

Cruz took a last long pull of his beer and wiped his mouth on his sleeve. "If the reward is ten thousand? Only half—twenty-five hundred now, and the rest when they are caught, if they are caught. That leaves you five thousand, you and your partner, the Indio."

"We don't share in the reward money. Catching them is our job—what we're paid for, year in and year out."

"But not much," Cruz implied.

"No," Ragnon admitted, "not much; but a living. And before I give you anything, I'll have to see evidence of your results. I'll have to move with you on the investigation, and you with me—a cooperative effort. Your resources and mine. Agreed?"

"Such an arrangement is possible," Cruz commented, mashing out his cigarillo in a jar lid. "It might even prove interesting."

"So these are yours," Ragnon said, and before the Mexican could change his mind, he pushed the pile of envelopes and reports across the table and zipped shut his empty briefcase. "Now what do you have on Two-Shoes?"

"One of the girls here is an informant," Cruz said. "She serviced four such men three nights ago, in the early hours of Monday morning. One of them wore two different shoes."

"Can we talk to her—show her the drawings?"

"Not here. Follow me." He gathered up the envelopes and tucked them under his arm.

Outside in the dusk the fading daylight had turned the air a pale yellow as the wind kicked up little swirls of dust along the street and the two policemen walked around the building and then crossed over to an alley, where a green four-door Plymouth, almost as battered and old as Ragnon's Falcon, was parked close against a high adobe wall.

Cruz opened the door and they both got into the front seat. "This is Anita," the Mexican said, pointing to the skinny painted girl huddled in the back. Ragnon, chewing again, pushed back his Stetson and stared. She looked scared but determined, her mascara-thickened lashes blinking. "Show her the drawings while there's still enough light," Cruz said.

When she had had a chance to look at all four, she began nodding her head, handing them back and chattering rapidly in Spanish, which Ragnon couldn't quite follow. "What did she say?" he asked. "Does she know who they are?"

"No. They are the four she serviced, but she doesn't know them. They were strangers to San Ignacio. They told her they worked at the mines in Cananea, but they did not seem like the usual miners she is used to. And they were not farm workers. She says they were more like animals; very dangerous men.

They made her afraid, and she was glad when they were gone. And I already asked her if they indicated where they might be going; they didn't." He smiled. "But one more thing agrees with your report, Sargento. They paid for her services in American dimes—from a big purple bag."

Ragnon picked up the four drawings and handed them back to her. *"Enseñeme Dos Zapatos,"* he told her. Show me Two-Shoes.

Without hesitation she pointed out the one with the scar and the headband, and then she voluntarily described the shoes with accuracy. "And this one had a chipped tooth," she added, pointing to the one with the full beard.

When she could tell them no more, Ragnon asked Cruz if he had paid her, and he nodded. "She is taken care of."

"Well, here's a little more," Ragnon said, handing the girl a thousand note.

She smiled, exposing crooked and missing teeth which spoiled the effect of her rouge and mascara, and she spoke rapidly again in Spanish.

Jacinto Cruz grinned. "Did you get that?"

"I think so—she wanted to know if I want a piece of tail."

Cruz nodded. "She'll give you a special price since we are friends. I can take a walk if you want to use the car?"

"Maybe some other time." Ragnon smiled at the girl. *"Otra vez, Señorita."*

Anita shrugged indifferently, then spoke rapidly again to Cruz, something about toros, and he laughed. "She says she prefers gringos as customers because she can make more money," he translated. "She says Mexican men are like bulls and can punch her for twenty minutes, while gringos she can get off in five."

"Terrific," Ragnon said, and spat out the car window.

"Wait here till I see if it's clear for her to go," Cruz told him, and started walking toward the end of the alley where the sky was dark now, with only a faint pinkish glow in the west.

Anita leaned forward, resting her arms on the back of the front seat, and smiled again. "Jur married, yes?" she asked, trying out her English.

"Separated," Ragnon answered, wondering if she really thought she had to make conversation while Cruz was gone.

"Jur wife, she geeve ju French?"

"What—oh, French? Yeah, sometimes she did."

"Ju like French now? I geeve good French. No charge. Ju friend of Jacinto, he friend of mine."

Ragnon shook his head, smiling. "Next time, Anita. Maybe next time."

The girl shrugged. "Sure. Meantime ju catch these guys, yes?"

Before he could answer, Cruz was signaling from the end of the alley and she left the car, running to join the Mexican agent and then disappearing around the corner, back toward the bar.

When Cruz returned he sat behind the wheel in silence, smoking in the darkness. "Now what?" Tom Ragnon asked.

"I am thinking," the Mexican answered.

"About the evidence?"

"About the money."

"We'll have to work that out," Ragnon said, still hedging. "I'll be staying at the hotel tonight."

"Then I'll see you tomorrow—say around noon. Maybe I'll have something more."

Cruz started the car and drove back to the cantina, where he let the American out beside his own car. "I think maybe we can work together, gringo," he said, and his expression seemed genuinely friendly. "I'll keep these." He put a hand on the accumulated reports and pictures. "Maybe they will help. And I'll see you tomorrow, eh?"

"I'll look forward to it."

"Meanwhile, you think some more about the money. And Sargento . . . ?"

"Yes?"

"That Anita—she's a reliable, what you call—snitch?" He smiled. "She is also a good piece of ass. You should have tried her."

ELEVEN

Thursday, March 11, 10 A.M.

Tom Ragnon did not ordinarily sleep well in strange beds. But the night he had just passed had been an exception, even though the Hotel Corona was not exactly a San Ignacio Hilton; it was just the only hotel in town.

A drafty old masonry building built sometime during World War II for God knew what, it had been converted in the late sixties when the border towns had begun to boom and an electronics factory had been established in San Ignacio as part of the twin-plant *machiladora* system to provide U.S. companies with cheap, docile labor and avoidance of American safety laws.

Skipping dinner in sudden remembrance of a New Year's pledge to eat less and exercise more, Ragnon had limited his intake to a couple of beers in the hotel lounge, where he had struck up an acquaintance with the shapely brown girl lying naked beside him now; her friendly persuasion had been more than he could resist.

She was not Anita, but she was a lot like Anita. He had even forgotten her name, but he remembered that she spoke much better English than Anita and seemed suspiciously curious as to what he was doing in San Ignacio; especially what he was doing hanging out with a policeman like Sargento Cruz who, she noted, was one very tough hombre.

He lay there, staring a moment at the ceiling, where the original dark blue paint was showing through the peeling layers of more recent additions, and realizing it was the first night in a long time that he hadn't even thought of Angie.

Rising stiffly and wincing at the squeaking bed springs, he went to the window naked and drew aside the heavy drape. Shivering, he stared out at the rain-drenched plaza. Another storm had passed on through during the night, and a pale sun was shouldering aside the thinning overcast and had formed a rainbow behind the church. He hoped it was a good omen.

Behind him the springs squeaked again and he turned, but the girl was only stretching sleepily and burrowing deeper under the blanket. "Jesus," he muttered, "it must be ten o'clock." Confirming the time by his watch, he patted the pockets of his vest which was hanging over a chair, found his pouch of Redman, and tucked a pinch in his cheek. Still shivering, he stepped in a patch of sunlight coming through the glass while he pulled on his shorts and pants, and assured himself that his wallet and shield were still intact. Though the hotel was unheated, the colorful wool blanket had provided plenty of warmth for sleeping, but getting up was a bit of a challenge.

Remembering Jacinto Cruz, he thought that the more he got to know the man, the better he liked him—*mordida* and all. Not that he trusted him yet, but he was working on it, all his instincts fighting to overcome his stubborn professional cynicism. He was almost convinced the guy was what was once called in the old west "a man to ride the river with." As he stepped down the hall to the communal bathroom, he was even beginning to think that catching the killers of the McNeal family might just be possible.

After a quick spit-bath and cold water shave, he brushed his teeth and returned to the room, where he slipped on his flannel shirt and sheepskin vest and combed his hair in the cracked mirror. The girl was still sleeping. Leaving a handful of peso notes on the scarred dresser, he put on his Stetson, picked up his empty briefcase, and decided he'd better at least get a hot meal under his belt before he faced Jacinto Cruz and the inevitable bargaining that was to come.

He passed up the hotel café and walked the two blocks to the old railroad tracks, where he found what the Mexican detective had recommended—an old adobe residence with a corrugated iron roof, the front of which had been converted into a restaurant complete with red-checkered oilcloths and fresh flowers on the tables. The only occupant of the place was a wrinkled old woman who was bending over a black iron stove where a pot of beans was simmering. She said nothing, but gave him a toothless smile of welcome and a thick white mug of café con leche, and in minutes followed it with a heaping plate of huevos rancheros and soft flour tortillas with a side dish of green chile salsa.

Ragnon had just finished off a second helping and was gulping his third mug of coffee when the door opened and the rope-lean figure of Jacinto Cruz ducked inside. "Ah." He smiled ingenuously. "I see you found it." Turning to the old woman he cried out, *"Madrecita! Qué tal?"* and gave her a fierce hug.

Dragging up a chair, he straddled it backward and rested his chin on his crossed arms. "You slept well, Sargento?" he asked, with just a suggestion of irony.

"Like a babe in arms. And you?"

"Ah, I have been busy—no time for sleep." He cupped his hands and lit one of his slim brown cigarillos, nodding grate-fully to the old lady as she set a steaming mug of black coffee before him. "You like my madrecita's cooking?"

"I'm just finishing seconds and thinking about thirds." He glanced toward the woman at the stove. "She's not really your mother . . . ?"

"She's everybody's mother. Used to have a lot of business here when the railroad ran, she and her papacito. Railroad quit running about a year ago, when trucks took over, just about when the old man died, so it's all she can handle alone anyway. She cooks up a pot of beans every day and makes fresh tortillas. I just see to it she never runs out of anything."

The woman brought Ragnon more coffee, and as he stirred in a spoonful of sugar, he eyed the Mexican detective closely. "You've found something more haven't you, Sergeant? I know the look."

"Maybe." Cruz's half smile was wicked as he tapped the ash from his cigarillo into a battered tin ashtray. "Maybe several things. I have a cousin working on the new highway that goes east to Janos in Chihuahua. There is a difficult detour around a bridge site; he guards the construction equipment at night and was on duty from midnight to eight the night of your killings. I checked with him and he said there was very little traffic, and none such as the four we seek. Not that night nor in the two nights after. So if he didn't fall asleep or turn his back too long to piss, we can eliminate their escape in that direction."

"Unless they went in the daytime," Ragnon suggested, sip-ping his coffee.

"That is not likely. These are night people, and they were too late for the eleven P.M. bus to Hermosillo."

"How many buses a day out of here?"

"Just the one, and no one answering their descriptions was

seen the next night, or the night after that. Also there is something else that reinforces all this. An incident was reported at a bar and gas station twenty miles southwest of here, at the junction where the road joins the highway going south to Hermosillo and another road going west to the California Gulf. It happened four nights ago—about two in the morning on Monday— a fight and a minor knifing by four men."

Ragnon leaned forward with interest; the murders had been on Sunday evening. "Our four?"

"Not enough of a description," Cruz said, "not even the shoes. The bar was dark and it happened just as they entered. So your drawings couldn't be identified either. But just as the fight started, one of them was heard to brag about having just killed some gringos up north."

"Jesus," Ragnon breathed. "Okay, let's check it out. Where are they being held?"

"They're not."

"You mean they were turned loose?"

Sergeant Cruz smiled indulgently. "Of course. It was only a minor stabbing, a fight. They paid a small, unofficial fine to the local police and departed."

"Terrific. And of course it was too dark for the local police to have a description?"

Jacinto Cruz shrugged, as if that said it all. Then he pulled a notepad from the pocket of his black leather jacket and consulted it. "They left in an old blue van with the right door missing—Sonora plates—but nobody got a number. And no one noticed if they took the highway to Hermosillo or the road to the coast."

Tom Ragnon pushed his coffee mug away with a sigh. Then he fished in his vest pocket for his Redman and sat there turning the pouch over in his hands, thinking.

"You're getting nervous again," Cruz said, smiling.

"Yeah." He opened the pouch and tucked a pinch of tobacco in his cheek. The calming effect was comforting, and he made his decision. "All right, let's go. You take Hermosillo and I'll head for the coast."

"No," Cruz answered, shaking his head and mashing out his smoke in the ashtray. "I've already advised the Hermosillo police—I have a cousin on the detective force there, a lieutenant."

Now Ragnon smiled skeptically. "Another cousin? And an honest cop?"

"No. He is—how you say—as crooked as the back leg of the dog. But he owes me a favor. I will send him the posters after I make more copies. I will go myself to the coast. There is a shrimp port and several small fishing villages."

"I see. And what will I do, Sergeant?"

The Mexican's smile was broad now. "You will return to your own jurisdiction and arrange for the reward money."

Ragnon stared at him. "I've really got to trust you, don't I?"

"Not really. When you come back with some cash we can work together, side by side, wherever the outlaw trail leads—unless, of course, they are already apprehended."

"Okay. So how much to start the investigation? Twenty-five hundred is too high. Let's say a thousand."

"But it's already started, Sargento. I will need at least two thousand."

"You alone?"

"No, there is the comandante, and my cousin in Hermosillo."

"The lieutenant owes you a favor already, remember?"

"He can do more now. And my own expenses—our expenses —will be high." He was watching Ragnon closely. "How much did they give you, Sargento?"

Tom Ragnon smiled. "I got a cashier's check for fifteen hundred, to start. It's in the Pantana bank."

"The exact amount I had in mind," Cruz said, and he, too, smiled. "Bring it with you when you return."

But Ragnon was not quite through. "How much does Comandante Max get?"

"Three hundred."

"And your cousin?"

"Two hundred."

"Which leaves you a thousand. Not bad."

"We," Cruz said, leaning forward, "you and me, gringo. We get five hundred each."

"I told you, Sergeant, I'm already getting paid. It's my job."

Jacinto Cruz gestured expressively with his hands. "A thousand for me, then," and his sly grin warmed the little restaurant, "and I'll buy the gas for your car."

"Done. I'll call you when I'm ready to bring it across. Or leave word with Comandante Max if you're not here."

Cruz frowned and his dark eyes grew darker. "No, my friend, you will not talk to the comandante—only to me. I'll contact you as soon as I return from the coast and I have news from my cousin. Our dealings with the comandante must be very limited in this matter, with regards to both the financing and the information. We will share with him as little as possible of both. I do not trust him."

Ragnon shook his head, tucking a fresh pinch of Redman in his cheek as they got up to go. "But you trust your crooked cousin in Hermosillo."

"I do not trust him either," Cruz said as he opened the door and waved good-bye to Madrecita, "but we must deal with someone, no?" He looked at the American. "I'm not sure I even trust you yet, Sargento, but I am trying."

"I am trying too," Tom Ragnon answered, smiling. Outside, at Ragnon's car, they shook hands firmly.

TWELVE

Thursday, March 11, 1:15 P.M.

"Trust? You're talking about trusting a goddamned gut-eater, Rags?"

"I better trust him, Chief—and he better trust me. It's the only way it's gonna work." The detective emphasized his words by sending a spurt of tobacco juice ringing into Poole's metal wastebasket.

Poole in turn puffed up his best angry walrus look and mashed out his cigar in his ornate brass ashtray in a fit of self-righteous disgust and loathing. "Jesus, Ragnon, I swear sometimes you're a bigger asshole than you look."

Tom Ragnon glanced over at John Antone with a slow, tolerant smile and continued chewing calmly. "And this is one of the chief's good days," he explained sarcastically. He had called the Indian deputy as soon as he got back to the city and briefed him on what Jacinto Cruz had turned up in Sonora, explaining that now it was a matter of the reward money.

"How much money?" Antone had asked him.

"Fifteen hundred up front."

"Dollars?" Deputy John Antone had whistled.

"Charlie McNeal is putting up five thousand," Ragnon was explaining now to the chief. "He's already given me fifteen hundred in working capital. If the Pantana town council comes up with another five thousand, we just might get something going down there. It might even cost less. This Jacinto Cruz seems reasonable enough."

"Shit, it's still bribery! Extortion!" Poole was lighting another cigar with his big horse lighter.

"Mordida, Chief," Ragnon explained patiently. "It's the custom. There's the comandante, and Cruz, and a cousin in Hermosillo—"

"And God knows how many other cousins, or who else— probably the fucking governor of Sonora before it's over!" Poole, puffing on his cigar like a steam engine, was flicking sharp glances at Antone, who was taking it all in with irritating stoicism. "The Mexican president-elect is campaigning across Sonora next week," the chief said, looking back at Ragnon. "You think they're gonna want you running around down there looking for killers?"

"Antone warned me about that, too, Chief. I won't get in their way if they don't get in mine."

But Poole was still fuming. "And what's our guarantee— trust! You want us to *trust* the fucking greasers!"

"It's paid out only as we gather evidence, Chief," Ragnon reminded him.

"Instead of after arrest and indictment, never mind extradition. He'll lead you around by your dick, Ragnon."

"Well, that way I'll at least be with him every step of the way, Chief." He spat again. "And when the evidence gathering stops, the money stops. He understands that."

"More bullshit," Poole grumbled. "And with only you in Mexico to see we're getting our money's worth."

"I'm all you've got, Chief. And it's McNeal's money, and the Pantana town council's. With me on vacation there's not a tin peso coming out of your budget."

"If the town council will go along," Antone reminded them. "Nobody's talked to them yet."

"I'm talking to them this afternoon," Ragnon said.

Sidney Clayton Poole had slumped down behind his desk.

He'd run out of arguments. "Okay, Rags, if the town council agrees to this bullshit, who am I to say no. But Antone's got his own job—he's not on loan to us anymore."

"I'm working with the sergeant on my off hours, Chief."

"No shit." Poole shook his head in disbelief of the whole business. "It's crazy—it can't work. When a case goes to Mexico, it's dead." He looked back at Ragnon. "There's something else—a fresh stiff was found in the desert this morning, probably an O.D., so if the autopsy confirms it, the Narcs will handle it. If not, I'm pulling you off vacation and you can forget about Mexico."

"I'll call in sick, Chief," Ragnon said softly.

"You would, too, you bastard." Poole stared hard at his homicide specialist. "Oh, fuck, I may as well tell you, I heard from the attorney general's office again this morning. They're still walking around with a hard-on for this McNeal thing too, said to give you—what's that French shit? Carte Blanche? But you're still on your own. You can't operate officially in Mexico. And if you get in any real trouble, you got nothing but that frito bandito Cruz for a back-up, which means you got zip."

In the hallway outside the chief's office Ragnon asked Antone if he wanted to come to the Pantana council meeting, but the Indian shook his head. "Can't. Got the duty; but keep me posted. Meanwhile I'll keep my ear to the ground up here. And Sergeant, take care, okay? Old Ironballs may be a racist sonofabitch, but he's got a point."

Tom Ragnon nodded, and as Antone walked away down the hall, the detective thought that surely with the Indian deputy on this side of the border and Jacinto Cruz on the other, something ought to work out right. But as he dug his Redman out of his pocket and tucked a pinch in his cheek, he wondered if he was biting off more than he could chew.

Going to the nearest pay phone for privacy, he called the house on Old Father Road. It rang four times, and he was angry with himself at the relief he felt when a man didn't answer. "Hello, Angie," he said.

"Tom—I was in the shower—glad you called. You coming over?"

"No, just calling. Everything okay? How're the kids?"

"Fine. Everything's fine. Did you go to Mexico again? What happened?"

He touched briefly on the new developments in the case and on the fact that he was taking an unofficial working vacation south of the border.

An uncomfortable silence resounded in his ear. "Angie. . . ?"

"I'm here. I thought when you mentioned a vacation, you meant a real vacation—time to get away and think, about us."

"I am thinking about us."

"Sure. Here we go again. You just can't cross your *t*'s and dot your *i*'s like everybody else, can you? You always have to do something totally different. If there's a more dangerous, more unorthodox way, you'll find it."

"That's not fair, Angie."

"And isn't this the month they're giving the administrative exam? You'll miss it—again. Or is that planned too?"

Slipping back to that old barb again, he thought. "I'm a street cop, Angie. I work homicide cases; it's what I'm good at, not that administrative shit. We've gone through all this before, can we get off it?"

"Sure." The word came like a sliver of ice through the receiver and into his ear.

"I'm probably going to haul my trailer down to Pantana and base out of there," he said, "since I'll be going back and forth a lot. I've got to meet with the town council this afternoon about the reward money."

Silence.

"You said it's what we need, a real separation." He felt like shit, using that as a kind of excuse. He thought about her alley man; he thought about the kids. The silence on her end gave him time for a lot of painful thoughts.

"Are you taking your gun, Tom?" she asked suddenly.

"My gun? No. I'm not even down there officially. I can't take my gun."

"Be careful, Tom," she whispered.

"Jesus, Angie, you sound like you mean it."

"I do."

THIRTEEN

Thursday, March 11, 4 P.M.

The five-member council of Pantana met quarterly in the school cafeteria, with an always uncertain attendance and the usual agenda including things like what to do about off-road vehicles from the city driving on ranch property, and leaving gates open or cutting fences. But a special meeting had been called to consider the proposed reward fund for the McNeal killings, and all five members were present.

Tom Ragnon, had just presented the cumulative evidence, along with a report of the proposed unofficial investigation in Mexico, his initial meeting with the Mexican police, and how it would be financed. He returned to his seat at a separate table, where Marshal Edwin Duff and Charlie McNeal also waited, while the members conferred around their coffee cups.

As a trial jury, the detective had a feeling the entire council would be challenged by attorneys for one prejudice or another; tucking a fresh pinch of Redman into his cheek, he wondered how they ever managed to function as a group. They seemed to agree only that the McNeal family had been liked by everybody. The tragedy had hit the town hard. They were scared and they wanted the killers caught.

The actual pay out of the reward money seemed to be the biggest stickler, and Ross Windom, a banker who looked the part with his head of thick gray hair and distinguished bearing, glanced over at Regnon. "A few questions, Sergeant. . . ?"

"Go ahead," Ragnon answered, spitting into a coffee can he had brought along for the purpose.

"You mention paying fifteen hundred up front and more as the case progresses, with the final payment upon arrest, not on indictment, like here in the states. So with the process of extradition and a formal trial to follow, we have no actual guarantees, do we?"

"None at all," Ragnon said. "It's just the best chance we've got of catching these guys under the circumstances."

"Sergeant Ragnon." Del Roberts, an ex–Air Force colonel spoke up. His hair too was gray, but receding in a close-cropped crew cut that expressed a lifetime of bristling authority. "Assuming we agree to this somewhat unorthodox proposal, just who is to judge how the case is progressing—the Mexicans?"

"Me. I'll be the one in Mexico, working the case unofficially with Sergeant Cruz."

"Why can't we hold the money in a sort of escrow account, and pay on apprehension and indictment?" Myrium Tyler asked. The only woman on the council, she was a rancher, too, a crusty old spinster with a face wrinkled by a lifetime under the Arizona sun.

"Because it's a foreign country, Miss Tyler," Ragnon explained patiently. "Different procedures, different customs and traditions."

"Like bribery—*la mordida*—the bite," Bert Dawes grumbled sardonically. A rancher-attorney, he was relighting his big briar pipe, and a thin film of sweat glistened on his bald head.

Ragnon smiled indulgently. "It's an acceptable way of doing business in a lot of countries, Mr. Dawes. And under-the-table deals aren't exactly unknown in this one."

"In other words, Sergeant, we're being asked to trust you, and you're trusting this Sergeant Cruz," Myrium Tyler said.

"We all have to trust somebody," Ragnon answered, spitting into his can.

"And what's in this for you, Sergeant?" Benjamin Torres, Mexican-American owner of the Pantana Mercantile Store, spoke up for the first time. His slight smile was skeptical and not at all friendly. "I understand you'll be on your own time, at your own expense; a paid vacation true—but why a working vacation?"

"Let's just say I'm dedicated to my profession, Mr. Torres, and let it go at that."

"Or maybe you hate Mexicans."

For a long moment there was total silence in the cafeteria. Then Colonel Roberts let out a long sigh. "Ah, shit." He glanced apologetically at Myrium Tyler. "Here we go again with that Affirmative Action crap. C'mon, Ben, this is a murder investigation, for Christ's sake, we're not putting him up for the school board."

"The job is in Mexico, Colonel," Torres persisted stubbornly, "hunting Mexicans. Wouldn't a Spanish-speaking detective have more rapport, more insight into—"

"No!" Charlie McNeal was suddenly standing. "Five thousand of the reward money is mine, and I appreciate you people putting up more, but Sergeant Ragnon is a specialist, and he already has a contact in Mexico, a contact who speaks both English and Spanish."

Even Marshal Duff was on his feet now. "Could I say something on Sergeant Ragnon's behalf?" he asked.

The other council members nodded their assent, Colonel Roberts waving down Ben Torres's attempted rebuke.

"Mr. McNeal is right," Duff said. "The sergeant was put on the case because of his record for closing murder investigations with positive results. I know, I checked. Even the governor's office is backing him. So why bring in somebody new, of any race?"

As a murmur of assent went around the table, Torres shook his head in resentful resignation.

"Look," Ragnon was standing now, "this is getting embarrassing. I've laid it out for you—what I've got, how I propose to work, and what it's likely to cost. I want these guys bad, and you want them too. But it's up to you about the money and who goes after them. I'll just step outside in the hall while you decide."

Upwards of twenty townspeople were milling around in the lobby and hallway outside, including a photographer who tried to take his picture and two newshounds who began belaboring him for a story. "Can you give us any details on the reward being offered, Sergeant?"

"You'll have to wait for the official news conference." Ragnon began pushing through the crowd.

"Have you got any firm leads yet—any names?"

"The Mexican police have it now. They're following several leads."

"Does that mean you'll have to extradite if and when they're caught?" one reporter persisted, until Ragnon pushed passed him, referring any further questions to the sheriff's public relations office after a terse "No comment."

Fortunately it was McNeal they were really after for a background story on the victims, Ragnon thought as he moved around the corner of the hallway, pausing to bend over a drinking fountain outside the swinging side doors of the cafeteria. As he rinsed out the last of his tobacco and moistened his throat, he could hear the buzz of heated conversation through the locked doors, but he wasn't worried. Benjamin Torres would be arguing a little, but mostly for show. The others would overrule him. He wondered momentarily who in the governor's office had put in a word on his behalf. Usually he was up to his ass in crocodiles with any brass and always got the dirty end of any political stick.

As he straightened up, wiping his mouth, he found he was still not alone in the hallway. An attractive young woman was standing a few feet away, watching him with a bemused smile. "You must be the detective—Sergeant Ragnon?" Wearing fashionable slacks and an expensive fringed buckskin jacket, she didn't strike Ragnon as being a townie as she extended a slender hand. He shook it firmly. "I'm Wanda Henderson," she explained. "My father is Colonel Roberts—inside." She nodded toward the glass windows in the swinging doors. "How's it going?"

"I don't know; they're deciding now." Large dark eyes, ash-blond hair worn in a ponytail, a narrow nose, and thin lips—and not at all bad in the chest department, he mused.

"I'm sure you got my father's vote," she said. "He likes a man with a devil in his eye. He never liked my Henry—my ex—even if he *was* Air Force." She had taken an embossed cigarette case from her bag. Opening it, she offered him one, smiling again as he shook his head. "I noticed your coffee can through the window. Didn't you forget it?"

"No, I just stepped outside for some air. They might take all night."

She had selected a cigarette for herself as if they were candies and was tapping it on the closed case before putting one end to moist red lips. "No light either, I suppose?"

"Sorry." He watched her take a slim pencil lighter from her bag and snap a slender flame to the tip of the cigarette.

"You don't talk much," she observed candidly, exhaling the first jets of smoke from her nostrils. "You're not shy are you, Sergeant? I assure you I'm not a reporter."

"Not especially shy, no. I just learn a lot more by listening.

How about you?" He smiled. "Are you always so unsure of yourself?"

Her own smile radiated confidence. She'd make a good ad for just about anything feminine, he thought. "I—" she started, but the doors swung open suddenly and Charlie McNeal looked out.

"Okay, Sergeant," he said, "they're ready."

"Excuse me, Mrs. Henderson," Ragnon said.

"Go right ahead. From the look on that man's face, I think you've won whatever you asked for. And nice to have met you, Sergeant. Would you tell my father I've got the car out front?"

Inside, Ragnon had his hand shaken all around. Even Ben Torres expressed his apologies and confidence, however reluctantly; and Windom, the banker, promised him an amount to match McNeal's, the account to be at the mutual disposal of McNeal and the council.

Myrium Tyler's tanned and leathery face was beaming, and Colonel Roberts told him, "I know you'll get them, Sergeant. You've got the look of an eagle."

"I'll try, Colonel," Ragnon said. "Your daughter's here. She said to tell you she's got the car out front."

McNeal and Duff were the last to leave, and Ragnon asked the marshal about bringing his trailer down for a base.

"I'm sure we can find a foundation and hookups that aren't in use, Sergeant," Duff said. "There's even one down by the volunteer firehouse that's a possibility."

"I'll probably bring it down tomorrow then, and take the first fifteen hundred over to Cruz."

"You'll be crossing right away, then?" McNeal asked.

"As soon as Cruz calls with anything new, or before, if I haven't heard from him in a couple of days."

"Thank you again, Sergeant—for everything."

"It's my job."

"No," McNeal said, "I think you're a man who does more than his job. I think you go the whole nine yards and then some."

"Thanks. And there's a reporter or two waiting for you in that crowd out there; you might watch what you say."

Outside again, Ragnon was heading for his car when he saw Wanda Henderson standing beside a shiny red Porsche and he stopped. "You didn't see your father, Mrs. Henderson?"

"He went with Mr. Dawes—something about an unfinished chess game. Can I give you a lift, Sergeant?"

"Thanks, but I have my car." He wondered why he was no longer moving toward it.

"Then may I buy you a drink, to celebrate? I take it you did win your cause, and I'll hear all about it from Daddy, but I'd rather hear it from you. The Hangman's Lounge is just down the road, and it's not only the best bar in town, it's the only one. Unless you don't drink either?" Her eyes held a real challenge.

"I've still got a few bad habits," Tom Ragnon said. "Your car or mine?"

They drove the Porsche to the watering hole, which was half restaurant and half bar and an accumulation of relics from the past. Rusty spurs and branding irons hung from the walls between paintings of fat cattle in high grass. Bits and pieces of ancient firearms were nailed to the beamed ceiling between wagon-wheel lamps, and the floor was actually covered with sawdust.

Alone except for two guys playing a Pac-Man game in a corner, they settled into a booth on the bar side where Wanda Henderson ordered a vodka-7 with lime and Ragnon settled for a beer.

"Still not talking?" She eyed him over her straw.

"I'd rather hear about you."

"I'm sure your murder case is far more interesting; a horrible thing to happen, but it's already slipped to an inside page of the paper. It said you'd tracked them into Mexico and lost them."

"Is that what it said—we lost 'em?"

"What's really happening? You may as well tell me what went on in there, my father will anyway."

"Not much to it. They got up a reward to match McNeal's— ten thousand total. That will be released to the papers. But since the killers are in Mexico, the reward will probably be paid out there, and I'm elected to do the negotiating and paying."

"What you're really saying is you're going into Mexico after them."

"Unofficially. I'm taking a little vacation."

"But isn't that dangerous?"

Ragnon shrugged.

"So when are you leaving?"

"I'll bring my trailer down here tomorrow and park it, probably next to the fire station. I'll base out of here until it's done. Now what about you? Somehow your clothes, your sophisticated ways, don't add up to a nowhere place like Pantana. What are *you* doing here?"

She shrugged elegantly over her vodka. Ragnon couldn't help flashing a comparison with Angie and mentally kicked himself for it. But then Angie had her alley rat, he consoled himself instantly.

"I just came home to the ranch to recuperate from my divorce," she said. "It got rather nasty, the money being on my side of the family. But it's finally over, and I think I won. At least there were no children to drag through it. You married, Sergeant?"

"Separated. My fault. Two kids. We're trying to patch it up; not very successfully." He realized he didn't want to talk about Angie. "You were raised around here, then?" he asked her.

"Hell, no. Phoenix mostly. And California and New Mexico. I'm an Air Force brat. But Daddy's always had money and an itch to retire on a ranch. So he did, eight years ago; here in Pantana, three years before I was married. But I was off at college." She lit another cigarette and held it poised over her drink. "You know, I never met a detective before. Homicide must be fascinating."

"Not really. It's like mortuary work—you never run out of customers."

As the outside door opened, Ragnon glanced around and saw Marshal Duff peering into the dimness. Spotting them, he called to the detective. "Sergeant—can I see you outside for a minute? Sorry to disturb you, but it's important."

Excusing himself, Ragnon followed the marshal out to his car. "What's up?"

"I thought you probably wouldn't want anyone else to hear this—you got a call from that Indian deputy, Antone, with a message from that Cruz fella down in San Ignacio."

"So what's the message?"

"Cruz wants another meeting right away. And he says to bring the money, because he's got a name for Two-Shoes—Hidalgo Valdez."

PART II
The Chase

FOURTEEN

Waiting nervously in the storeroom of a candle factory on the outskirts of Hermosillo, Sonora, Hidalgo Valdez ground out his third cigarette under his heel and moved again to the grimy, cobwebbed window that overlooked the dark factory yard outside.

"Puta madre," he swore softly, his hand trembling like a woman's as he wiped a wider clear space in the glass before fumbling a last cigarette from his pack of Delicados. The Señor Galindez was long overdue. He struck a match, cupped it to the smoke, then blew the match out viciously and inhaled deeply.

His first syndicate assignment had been a disaster, but he was sure there would be others. Perfection was not expected of a man the first time out, right? And he had brought back some guns; he had proved himself. It had not been his fault the plane had crashed. So why was he nervous? Why— He saw a car pulling up to the factory gate outside, a long dark limousine.

Peering intently out the window again, Hidalgo Valdez began to sweat. The yard itself was bounded by a high chain-link fence topped with coils of razor-edged wire. A lot went on here besides the manufacture of candles. He watched a guard come out of the lighted shack and open the gate—the same guard who had admitted him—then he turned from the window and left the storeroom, walking hurriedly down a short dark hallway to the office.

He was sitting in a straight-back chair by the desk, under the caged light bulb in the ceiling, waiting with exaggerated ease as the Señor Galindez came in through the main doors and followed a path lighted by a row of more caged bulbs spaced along the ceiling. The *jefe* had two of his henchmen with him, and he looked neither left nor right into the darkened areas of the factory, but came straight on to the office, which was also wired with heavy screen, like a cage. It was where the *jefe* had said to meet, and Hidalgo Valdez was here. Only suddenly he felt like an animal, trapped, but it was too late to run. Besides, he told himself, stifling his fears for the encounter to come, Hidalgo Valdez did not run.

Instead he stood up as the Señor Galindez entered, followed by his henchmen. The syndicate chief was not smiling. He simply stared for a long tense moment at Hidalgo, his eyes full of contempt, saying nothing.

"The failure was not my fault, *Jefe,*" Hidalgo finally said hesitantly, defensively, desperately trying to keep his voice from breaking. And still Galindez did not speak. "The fucking plane crashed. What could I do?" He was trying to keep the pleading tone from his voice—he was a man, no?

"Of course the crash was not your fault," the *jefe* said at last, softly. "It was what you and your compadres did after the crash that is your fault." His voice had almost imperceptibly hardened. "Your job was simple, burro. Take three men across the border, steal a couple of closed vehicles to meet the plane at the abandoned airfield, and haul the load to Phoenix. So the plane crashes; you abandon the stolen vehicles and return for another assignment, easy, no? We have planeloads going north all the time. Instead, you pull this stupid burglary and murder—for nothing!"

"I brought six guns, *Jefe*. I have them hidden. I can—"

"You brought back trouble, Valdez. Your weapons are nothing compared to the trouble. I had high hopes for you, and you disappointed me with trouble."

"Trouble, *Jefe?* What kind of—"

"Did you think to get away with killing a whole family, stupido?"

"It was nothing, *Jefe*—they were gringos! Besides, I like to kill. I enjoy it."

"See how you enjoy being hunted then, *pendejo!* Already there have been inquiries about you in San Ignacio."

"San Ignacio—how? No one even knows me there!"

"Someone knows *about* you," Raul Galindez said. "A gringo policeman who is coming after you." He turned to one of his henchmen who Hidalgo recognized as Lt. Chato Gomez of the Hermosillo police, who also happened to work for Galindez. "This one, Chato," he said derisively, "twenty-six years old last year when I bought his way out of the state penitentiary. Thirty years he was serving, the maximum, for killing a girl in Navojoa. But for this *pendejo,* killing her wasn't enough. He might never have been caught, but to prove himself he went back later in the day and had sex with the corpse."

Chato Gomez laughed, and Galindez smiled cruelly. "When I heard this, I had to see such a man; a man with style, with flair and imagination. I bought him out; I even bought his prison record and destroyed it. But he has two flaws, Chato—he cannot rise above himself, and he enjoys killing too much. I have wasted time and money on this clown with two-color shoes. He is not for me. Chato, Enrique." He looked at each of his henchmen, who were already slipping on dark leather gloves. "Teach him a lesson."

Pain was not new to Hidalgo Valdez. It engulfed him now as his swollen eyes focused unsteadily on the caged bulb in the ceiling, and he realized he was still in the office of the candle factory, alone.

It hurt to move, to breath, but he got to his feet, pulling himself up by a filing cabinet and cursing. Taking two uncertain steps outside the office, he fell, and then crawled slowly, painfully down the long lighted path under the caged bulbs that led to the front door. It stood wide open, and he could see the lighted guard shack and the gate beyond. The gate, too, stood open, as if beckoning, and he forced himself to his feet again and walked staggering, held upright only by his fierce raw outrage and his stubborn pride.

The guard watched in silence as he stepped carefully through the gate, and then closed it behind him. "You are lucky this time, *pinche cabrón,*" the guard growled through the steel mesh. "Lucky they didn't kill you."

Hidalgo Valdez didn't consider himself lucky. It only meant he would have to start over again. Life for him had always been a constant struggle to survive, to improve his advantage. And he had always found it necessary to step on the backs of others to find his own place in the sun. It had been that way ever since his childhood in the impoverished *vecindades* of Mexico City, when he had skipped school and obtained money by extorting it from younger children in Chapultepec Park.

Graduating to larger crimes, he had never been able to get the right breaks. He had led his own gang in the *vecindad,* and in between their petty crimes, he had held a variety of temporary jobs, usually working only for an employer he could steal

easily from. Killing anyone who got in his way had come natural to him, and the killing of the girl in Navojoa had not been
his first; it had simply been the one for which he was caught.

Then his big break had come with the syndicate contact in
the state penitentiary, and he had met the Señor Galindez.
"Ay," he cursed, and spat out a wad of blood and parts of a
broken tooth, pausing a moment against a building to let a flood
of nausea pass. That pig of a Galindez, he thought savagely. I
deserved another chance. But the Galindezes of the world do
not give second chances to the likes of me.

It took him the better part of an hour to make it the eight
blocks to a dingy ramshackle dwelling and push open the door.
"Madre Santísima!" Consuelo shrieked at the sight of him.
"What have they done to you, *querido?"* She guided him to the
bed, muttering *"Pobrecito, pobrecito,"* and began to look for
something to bind up his wounds.

"Let me get you to a doctor, Hidalgo," she whispered as she
brought salve and bandages and his hand stroked her swollen
belly beneath the thin dress. It was a child he had put there, his
third by this woman. He knew the others must be asleep in the
next room.

"No doctor," he told her, wincing. "They knew their business, Enrique and that Chato bastard. They can inflict much
pain and blood without serious injury. I will heal. Did you hide
the money like I told you, the silver dollars?"

"Yes, and the gold ring—under the bed, the floorboards."

"And the guns?" He let her ease him back on the bed, his
head on the pillow. "Where are the guns?"

"The others took the guns. Xavier said he knew where to
hide them safely and that you would approve."

"Yes, good, Xavier knows. At least we still have the guns."

"Ay, mi querido, mi vida—" She began crying as she worked
over him again. The bare electric bulb dangling from a cord in
the ceiling was harsh, and he covered his eyes with his arm. She
was a good woman, Consuelo; the best he had had. She wor-
shiped him. He would have to quit beating her so much, especially now that she was pregnant again. He groaned involun-
tarily as she touched a particularly tender spot. "Why didn't
they wait?" he asked her. "My compadres?"

"They did not think you would be back tonight. They will
return tomorrow. What did the *jefe* say, Hidalgo?"

"You see me, woman—you see what he said."

"Ay, but he will forgive you, no?"

"No. It is finished, this thing with the syndicate. I do not need them now anyway. I will be my own boss. I have Xavier and Miguel and Arturo, and we have the guns."

"But what did you do to anger him so, the Señor Galindez? The crashing of the plane? How could he blame you for that?"

"It was afterwards; what we did after the crash."

"What did you do?"

"Nothing serious, woman. We stole a few things, that's all." And he remembered then what Galindez had said. "But a policeman is after me, asking about me in San Ignacio." He spoke with a kind of amazed wonder. "A gringo policeman."

"A gringo?" Consuelo straightened, staring down at him. "A gringo policeman followed you across the border?"

"Yes." Thinking about it now, it seemed incredible. "That is why Galindez is so angry, that is why he wants no more to do with me." And suddenly, impulsively, he had a focus for his own fury. "But the fucking gringo will pay, Consuelo," he added slowly. "You will see. Whoever he is, he is a dead man. I am going to kill him."

FIFTEEN

Friday, March 12, 10 A.M.

"You brought the money?" Jacinto Cruz asked.

Tom Ragnon touched the old briefcase tucked under his arm as he climbed the steps of the police station in San Ignacio and joined the Mexican detective. "Fifteen hundred."

"Cash?" They stepped through the open double doors side by side and walked down the long, drafty, echoing hallway.

"Crisp new U.S. currency," Ragnon said, "guaranteed to please." They had reached the office at the end of the hall, where Cruz knocked once and then entered.

Comandante Maximiliano Hernández was standing at one of the high narrow windows, his back to them as he stared outside. Friday morning had dawned clear, the day bright with sunshine, and he was smiling broadly at the American as he turned around with a cigar poised in one hand. "Ah, Sergeant Ragnon, I saw your car turn the corner. We have been of some service, then?" He returned to his desk and sat down as Cruz went to the old iron-bellied stove and poured two mugs of coffee.

"It's a beginning," Ragnon said cautiously, "and we've come to an understanding." He nodded at Cruz, who was handing him one of the mugs after adding a splash of milk from a pitcher.

"Sorry there's no sugar," Cruz said over the rim of his own mug. "We, too, have a tight budget." His dark eyes were laughing.

The comandante had his own coffee already at his desk, and he invited Ragnon to sit and talk. But the detective saw no reason not to plunge right in. Setting his own mug down on the edge of the desk, he opened the briefcase, took out a roll of rubber-banded twenties, and laid it in front of Hernández. "Three hundred dollars, Comandante. Sergeant Cruz and I will be working the case together, unofficially. I'm here on vacation, but I need a guide."

"Of course." The comandante was still smiling as he swept the roll across his desk and into an open drawer. In almost the same motion he took from another drawer a stack of freshly printed posters, picked off the top one, and placed it in front of Ragnon. The four composite faces stared up at him, with a name added beneath one of them—Hidalgo Valdez. "These will be distributed throughout Sonora and Chihuahua," Hernández said. "Copies will also be sent farther south as well, but if they have fled there, I'm afraid it's out of our hands. In the meantime you have the services of Sargento Cruz."

"We are going to Hermosillo now, Comandante," Cruz said, "to see my cousin and determine if the fugitives are known there."

"And how much is *he* getting?" Hernández sneered. "This cousin?"

"Two hundred, Comandante."

"And you?"

"Five hundred." Cruz glanced at Ragnon. "We are dividing it."

"That's right," Ragnon lied quickly with a straight face. "Fifty-fifty."

"Of course." Comandante Hernández seemed skeptical, and Ragnon wondered for a tense moment if he was going to ask for the briefcase. But he only added, "I assume there will be more for all of us later?" It was more a statement than a question.

"We'll see how the investigation goes, Comandante," Ragnon answered carefully. "Catching this one"—he tapped the face with the headband and scar on the poster—"is important. Hidalgo Valdez is probably the leader, the one I especially want."

"Then I wish you luck, Señor. Here—take some of these for your own distribution." He pushed a dozen of the posters across his desk. "But be careful," he added, and his oily smile was condescending, "these are evidently extremely dangerous men."

In the car outside, Jacinto Cruz threw a battered suitcase into the back seat of the old Ford Falcon beside Ragnon's Navy seabag, then directed the American to the San Ignacio Banco Nacional.

"I thought for a minute you'd got our tails in a crack back there, Sargento," Ragnon told him as they pulled away from the curb. "I might not have been able to explain the extra five hundred if he'd wanted to take a look."

Jacinto Cruz smiled. "I have confidence you'd have thought of something. But it's best not to divulge the full amount we are working with. Comandantes can be greedy."

Pulling up in front of the bank, Ragnon opened the briefcase and handed his new partner another banded roll of bills.

"And the two hundred for my cousin, the lieutenant?" Cruz asked, putting the cash in a brown paper bag.

"I'll keep that till we get to Hermosillo and see your cousin." Ragnon smiled to ease the pain of his distrust.

"But we're not going to Hermosillo, Sergeant. Not right now. We're going to the coast."

"But you told—"

"It's also best not to tell comandantes the full truth," Cruz answered congenially. "You understand, no?"

"You're full of surprises, my friend. I thought you already went to the coast to check out the lead on that blue van?"

"No, the new lead came up here." Cruz was standing outside the car now, the brown bag in his right hand and his left extended through the car window, palm up. "Now the other two hundred, por favor? I'll get it all in the bank, change some into pesos for our expense money, and we'll send my cousin a money order."

By now Ragnon had taken out his pouch of Redman, and he tucked a pinch in his cheek, still hesitant.

"Trust, Sergeant." Cruz was still smiling ingenuously. "Remember?"

Tom Ragnon shook his head resignedly, then spat out the window and handed over the last of the fifteen hundred. But as he waited outside the bank for his new partner to return, he wondered why he felt as nervous as a getaway driver in a holdup. It was all turning out to be one big strain on his gut instincts and a cop's natural cynicism.

When Cruz finally returned, Ragnon had his own question. "This new lead you got—the name for Two-Shoes—where in hell did you come up with it?"

Now the Mexican police agent was hesitant.

"Trust, Sargento, remember?" Ragnon taunted him.

Cruz climbed in the car and directed him to the telegraph office. "We'll stop at that crossroads bar where the blue van was last seen and show the poster," he said, lighting up one of his cigarillos. "My cousin says nothing like it has turned up in Hermosillo, but his eyes will not be very sharp until he sees some money. My bet is still that they went to the coast."

"And this Hidalgo Valdez," Ragnon persisted, "who turned his name? Who the shit is he?"

"I don't know who he is, Sergeant. And my informant didn't know." He sighed. "She's a girl here in town—Angelina Zamora. She recognized his face from the poster. She met him about a week ago at a dance. He told her only that he was from the south, and he told her his name. She also saw one of the others on the poster with him, but never learned his name. She never even saw the other two."

"Maybe she doesn't know Hidalgo's name either," Ragnon said. "Maybe he used a phony; men do that, in the states and here too—give women a phony name."

"She thinks not. He was too full of pride, this one. Boastful. Pure machismo."

"About killing?" Ragnon asked.

"No, he didn't mention any killings. Just boastful in general, proud of himself, his manhood. After the dance he wanted to take her to a hotel, and when she refused, he became angry and threatening. Her brother was with her and she was afraid a fight would be provoked, so when this Hidalgo simply asked to park his blue van behind her house for a few days and pick it up later, she agreed to that. She does not know when he picked it up, only that she came home from work and it was gone. That was four or five nights ago."

"Where does she work?"

"In a local sewing factory. They make ladies underwear—bras, panties, things like that."

"And what made her come forward with this story about Hidalgo Valdez and his blue van?"

"She didn't. She saw the poster and mentioned it to a girlfriend at the factory. It got back to me, and I went to see her. She was afraid to talk—at first."

Ragnon stared at him as they rounded a corner. "Jesus, man, you mean you beat it out of her?"

"No, Sergeant." Jacinto Cruz looked bruised himself that the American would think this of him. "I just talked calmly to her. But being talked to by a Mexican cop can be very intimidating, no? Among ordinary people, everyone hates and fears the police. It—how do you say—goes with the ground."

"The territory," Ragnon corrected him.

"*Por seguro,* and the police are not always loved in the states either, am I right?"

"Not always, no," Ragnon admitted.

"But I would not seriously hurt someone, Sergeant, unless greatly provoked. You should know this. Some do, of course, but it is not my style." He studied Ragnon's face to be sure he understood. "You wish to talk to her yourself?"

"No," Ragnon answered, pulling up in front of the telegraph office. "Not unless you think she's got more information. Let's just get your money order mailed and get on over to the coast."

In the combination bar and store that squatted at the junction where the main highway south joined the road west to the gulf, they stopped to gas up and have a couple of beers while a jukebox blasted out a ranchero ballad. But no one had heard anything new about the men in the blue van, so they left the posters and Ragnon headed his old Falcon toward the coast, still a three-hour drive away over a paved but narrow road.

In the next town green and white streamers were being

strung around the plaza, and Ragnon asked what they were celebrating. "The president-elect is expected to pass through here on his way to Nogales," Cruz explained. "It is a great honor for them—and it is also hoped he will notice the potholes in the streets and maybe provide some money to fix them."

Cruz had to stop at a pharmacy and buy a national lottery ticket, and then they passed through three small villages where the Mexican detective talked to several people and left a few of the posters. But no one had seen or heard of anything, and Ragnon was beginning to wonder if they were chasing ghosts.

He finally let Cruz drive awhile, and got the first whiff of salt-sea air miles before they turned off on a sandy road and the scrub desert growth gave way to undulating dunes. Suddenly a dilapidated, abandoned motel appeared beside the road ahead, its sign dangling and its front windows boarded up. "I hope you're not taking me there for our honeymoon, Sargento," Ragnon cracked.

Jacinto Cruz laughed. "No, Sergeant, that place died a couple of years ago when they couldn't draw any turistas down from Puerto La Perla. But the fishing village is just over the next dune, down on the beach." And as they topped the rise, the Gulf of California loomed before them.

The village consisted of half a dozen wooden shacks built well above high tide, a concrete communal bathhouse, and several ramadas draped with drying fish nets. And a couple of long, narrow boats were drawn up on the sand where the tide was just beginning to turn. Ragnon glanced at his watch as Cruz pulled the car under one of the ramadas and turned off the engine. It was half past three in the afternoon.

"This is it?" the American detective asked. The only other vehicles in sight were a homemade sand buggy with a Volkswagen engine and two flat tires, and an old flatbed truck.

"It's the only fishing village for forty kilometers in either direction," Cruz said.

"I think we should have tried La Perla instead."

Cruz shrugged. "It's only forty kilometers north, a poor but passable road up the coast. But since we are here, shall we at least look around?"

"You look around, Sargento," Ragnon said, disgusted. "By the time I catch a few deep breaths of this cool sea air, you ought to be finished. I sure as hell don't see anything resembling a blue van."

While the Mexican lawman took one of the posters and knocked at the door of the nearest shack, Ragnon tucked a fresh pinch of Redman in his cheek and walked out past the bathhouse onto the beach. Stooping, he picked up a small clam-shell and sent it sailing out into the frothing tide. Chasing down killers in Mexico wasn't turning out to be quite what he had expected. He was even beginning to wonder if he'd completely misjudged Jacinto Cruz, and was maybe even being played for a fool, and the Pantana town council along with him.

"Oye, Sergeant!" Cruz called suddenly from another of the shacks behind him, and waved him over.

As Ragnon approached, the Mexican detective was shaking his head in frustration and disappointment. "Nothing, Sergeant, a false trail. No such men have been here, and no such van."

"Terrific. What do you mean by a false trail?"

"I meant my informant must have been misled, or mis-informed. He was a witness to the fight at the crossroads bar, but not previously known to me, so I had only his word. He thought the blue van came in this direction, but he was not sure. I took a chance and was wrong."

"Wonderful." Ragnon spat and looked again at his watch. It was almost four o'clock. "Well, what now? It's a long drive back to San Ignacio, or even to La Perla if it's a bad road."

"But why go back tonight, Sergeant?" Cruz was lighting one of his slim cigarillos as Ragnon sent another healthy stream of tobacco juice out onto the sand. "We have no more leads at the moment. We can stay here tonight and start again tomorrow."

"Stay here?" The detective looked up and down the empty beach and then at the shacks where a few brown faces—all women and children—stared curiously out at them. "I don't see any Hilton's, or even a Holiday Inn, Sargento, except that ram-shackle ruin back there beyond the dunes. And besides, in an-other hour I'm gonna be hungry as a bear in springtime."

Jacinto Cruz smiled, drawing deeply on his cigarillo. Even his eyes were laughing again. "Trust me, Sergeant. Tonight you will sleep like a child in its mother's arms. As for food, have faith that the sea will provide. And as for me, I'm going for a swim before the water gets too cold." And stripping down to his undershorts there on the beach, he ran out to meet the incoming tide.

Tom Ragnon shook his head wonderingly. It was a hell of a way to conduct a murder investigation, but when in Mexico . . . Leaving his clothes in a pile beside Cruz's, he followed him into the quick-chilling bite of the surf.

Later, with the lowering sun still faintly warm on their backs, they sprawled shivering on the sand above high tide and Ragnon laid it out for his new partner. "All right, Jacinto, we've got a name, maybe even his real name. But who is he? Where does he come from? A guy like this ought to have a record somewhere already. Where do we find it? What about a fingerprint check, can you do that? Something to match against what we've got."

"My cousin, the lieutenant, is checking this in Hermosillo. If Hidalgo's been in jail or the State Pen, there would be a fingerprint record and a write-up sheet on his background, of course. But even so, you understand it is a slow process and maybe not so accurate as yours. Our system is not as sophisticated, or as complete—we admit this. Besides, he could have bought his records and destroyed them."

Ragnon stared at him. "He could do that?"

"You can buy anything in Mexico, Sergeant."

"Yeah," Ragnon mused. "And the girl, Angelina Zamora, said he came from the south. But what if it's south of Hermosillo? Somewhere way south, like Mazatlán or Guadalajara, or even Mexico City?"

Jacinto Cruz could only shrug helplessly.

By the time they were dry, the sun was resting on the opposite side of the gulf, nesting among red-orange clouds that lay all across the horizon, and an offshore wind was rising, raising goosebumps through the salty residue on their skins. Cruz led the way to the bathhouse where a small boy brought them clean white towels and soap. The water from the spigots set in barrels mounted high inside the roofless concrete walls was cold but fresh. When they stepped outside again, with towels wrapped around their waists, Ragnon looked far out to sea, where the sputtering sound of outboard motors marked the progress of several long-prowed fishing boats heading for the beach on the tide.

"Here comes the day's catch, Sergeant," Cruz called to him, "and our dinner—with luck, huachinango! Tomorrow we can worry about chasing your killers. Tonight we relax, no? And everything is on me!"

Twenty minutes later they had changed into clean clothes at the car and Cruz had brought a bundle of driftwood from one of the shacks and built a roaring blaze in the gathering dusk on the beach. Then, as the fishermen unloaded their catch, he went over and bought a big Red Snapper.

By the time the fire was reduced to glowing coals, the Mexican lawman had brought a grill and aluminum foil and a bowl of sliced lemons and spices from one of the shacks. Ragnon had helped him carry them, along with two cartons of beer and two thick wool blankets, and then sat cross-legged by the fire and watched him fillet the fish expertly with a long knife.

"Christ, the beer's even cold!" Ragnon marveled, snapping a cap from one of the beaded bottles.

"One of the shacks is an ice house for the fish," Cruz told him, "and for the beer. The trucks come tomorrow; and yes, I asked the fishermen about the men in the blue van—nada. Salud." He waved his own bottle and drank in long swallows.

Tom Ragnon couldn't decide what he was enjoying most, the fish fresh from the coals and smoking, the cold beer, or the faint splash of reflected color still emblazoned across the clouds hanging far out on the dark gulf that had once been known as the Sea of Cortez.

"You know, Jacinto," he told Cruz, "I don't think there ever was a blue van. I think you brought me all the way over here for this damn fish dinner, and I have to admit it was worth every mile of it."

"Good, eh?" Cruz smiled, picking another smoking piece from the foil with his fingers.

"Beats the shit out of a Holiday Inn," Tom Ragnon answered.

When the beer was gone and the darkness had deepened and there was only the faint flickering whitecaps and the sounds of the surf, Cruz went back to one of the shacks and returned with a jar of cloudy liquid. "Pulque," he said. "Drink—it's fermented cactus juice. Only a man with balls drinks pulque."

Huddled in their blankets against the chill night wind gusting along the beach, they passed the jar back and forth in the darkness beside the still glowing embers of the fire, until Ragnon got a little dizzy. "All this is great stuff," he muttered finally. "But still no Hidalgo Valdez."

"Not yet," Cruz said. "But soon. Have faith, Sergeant. Have faith in Cruz and our destiny together."

Tom Ragnon knew his smile was a little crooked now, and he was already getting a buzz on. "All right." He raised the jar aloft. "To our destiny together, Sargento—salud."

"And to the success of our cooperative efforts." Cruz, too, was getting drunk. He was staring intently at the American detective as the wind sent a flair of sparks from the fire rushing skyward. "Are you married, Sergeant?" he asked.

"Separated. It's a long, long, ugly story." Angie, he thought, staring up at the seemingly sudden array of stars. Angie and her alley rat.

"I, too, have a wife," Cruz said, "by legal civil marriage, not by the Church. And a mistress. Both in San Ignacio. And because of me my mistress can't go to mass now. But she chooses me over God—that's very flattering, no?"

"Flattering . . . yes," Ragnon murmured, thinking of God with sudden warm memories of his grandfather, a Methodist minister, and how far he himself had wandered from that path.

"We are not the strong religious country you Americans sometimes think, Sergeant Ragnon." Cruz was deep in his cups now. "We are a nation of pageantry and emotions, but we overthrew the Church as corrupt and replaced it with corrupt government. I think we are more superstitious than religious—remember our saying about life being a matter of luck? Not Fate. Not Divine Guidance—just luck, good and bad. I tell you, Tomás Ragnon, Sergeant, with all our saints and artifacts and idols, we've got more gods than the Aztecs ever had. So drink up—there's plenty more pulque where this came from."

"Where?" Ragnon looked around expectantly.

"Over there." Cruz pointed vaguely in the direction of the shacks, all of which were almost invisible in the darkness. Except one, where a dim glow of lantern light showed through the gunnysack covering its doorway. "There," Cruz repeated drunkenly, laughing. "It's the best little whorehouse for forty kilometers in any direction. You want to give it a try?"

As he followed the Mexican detective in an uncertain weaving pattern up the beach toward the dimly lighted shack, something else occurred to Tom Ragnon, and he called out, "Hey, Jacinto—seems like we're depending a hell of a lot on this cousin of yours in Hermosillo, but you never told me his name. I should know his name, right?"

Jacinto Cruz looked back over his shoulder and shouted, "Gomez! His name is Gomez, Sergeant! Teniente Chato Gomez!"

SIXTEEN

Saturday, March 13, 6:15 A.M.

Tom Ragnon awakened alone; to a bleak dawn on a cold, empty beach, his body cocooned in his thick wool blanket and his head supporting a dull, heavy throb. Gradually he became aware of the hard sand under him, and from his prone position he could see the fog bank rolling in from the sea, while overhead the screeching gulls wheeled low over the exposed rocks and swirling eddies and shiny wet tidal flats.

By focusing intently he could make out a sailboat pulling to shore far down the coast. Then he rolled over stiffly and sat up, groaning and managing to catch his head in his hands before it fell off his shoulders. With a violent, involuntary shiver he looked over at the blackened remains of their fire and the bare bones of the Red Snapper still in the crinkled foil. Cruz's blanket lay where he had slept, but the Mexican himself was gone.

With a start he stared up and down the deserted beach, and then over at the row of silent shacks. The gunnysack curtaining the door of one of them stirred slightly in the chill morning air as slow realization and an eerie, senseless fear gripped him. "Ah, shit," he moaned, still staring around him and feeling foolishly deserted, lost. "Goddammit to hell." No Cruz, no fifteen hundred bucks—and no Hidalgo Valdez.

If there ever had been a Hidalgo Valdez, he thought bitterly. That was probably part of the scam too. "Shit," he repeated miserably, staggering to his feet and pulling the blanket roughly up around his shoulders. At least the sonofabitch had left him his car. He could see the back of it still sticking out of the ramada.

Then someone yanked aside the sacking covering the door of "the best little whorehouse in forty kilometers" and the face of Jacinto Cruz looked out on the dawning day. "Hola! Tomás!" he called, and waved him over. *"Vente pa cá!"*

As Ragnon staggered toward the shack, guilt and forgiveness and relief washed over him in a single wave. He thought his heart actually skipped a beat, like a girl's who's been asked to the prom at the last possible moment, or a drowning man pulled out of a well. His head still throbbed painfully, but the sea air helped even that as he pulled aside the sacking and ducked into the dim interior.

A smoking lantern still burned on a makeshift countertop, and he straddled a barrel at a corner table across from Cruz, who was smiling and eating hungrily. A short plump girl who looked vaguely familiar from the night before brought a chipped mug of hot black coffee and set it in front of him, and then a bowl filled with a pale porous-looking mass that made his stomach roil.

"Menudo," Cruz explained, still smiling at Ragnon's obvious distress and nodding at his own half-empty bowl. "Cow guts— the Mexican cure for a hangover. Eat, Tomás—it will make you a man again."

Ragnon's queasy stomach turned again, but he tightened his jaws, pulled up his bootstraps, and picked up the spoon. Strangely enough, it helped; that, and the sea air and the hot, black coffee. And finally, another fresh water shower.

His head was only throbbing faintly as he stepped out of the shower and toweled himself vigorously. He had indeed begun to feel like a man again, or at least human, when he looked up and found a little girl maybe three or four years old and as naked as he was, standing there and looking up at him expectantly with large limpid eyes while holding out a grubby little hand.

Pulling on his pants, he dug a peso note from his pocket and gave it to her. Jesus, he pondered angrily as she walked out the doorway and he finished dressing, what a fabulous, beautiful, lousy country.

Outside he found Cruz squatting alongside one of the rear tires on his Falcon, which was emitting a hissing sound. "What now—a flat?"

"No." Cruz moved around to the other rear tire. "Just getting back to business; letting some air out of the rear tires for the trip back."

"To San Ignacio? The road's paved, most of it."

"To Hermosillo."

"But we can't get to Hermosillo from here, not according to the map. Not without going back through San Ignacio. And why Hermosillo?"

"There's a road of sorts," Cruz answered, standing, "not on the map. It comes out at the railroad which leads to the highway into the city. And why not Hermosillo? We can save some of the time we lost yesterday by seeing my cousin, Chato. See what he has found out. Besides, there's a couple of small villages on the way that we can check out, just in case, and leave some posters."

Minutes later Cruz was easing the car off the paved road that would have taken them east back to San Ignacio and onto a narrow sandy trace that led vaguely off to the southeast. Ragnon reached for his pouch of Redman, and Jacinto Cruz laughed. "You do feel better, don't you, Tomás? I think we lost ourselves a little last night, but that is good, no?"

"You mean all work and no play. . . ?"

"I think that's what I mean, yes—hold the wheel." He let go and lit one of his thin brown cigarillos while Ragnon steadied the car on its uncertain course as the road seemed to grow sandier again.

Half an hour later they pulled into the first village, where Cruz asked around and left a poster. No one had seen such a van, or knew anything about such men. The two policemen got in their car and drove on. "How long have you been a cop?" Ragnon asked his new partner.

"Twelve years. Nine a municipal cop and the last three a special agent. But police work isn't a career in Mexico, Tomás. I'm afraid we're not very professional. It's mostly a means to an end, to survive. I learned carpentry and baking as trades, and I had my own small business for a while, but went broke through several unfortunate circumstances that were mostly my own doing.

"I had an uncle with political influence who owed me a personal favor and got me on the force. I only intended to stay a year or so, get some money ahead and go back into business.

But I found I really liked police work, and I stayed." He looked at Ragnon and smiled. "It pays just about enough to support my two families."

"With a little extra here and there," Ragnon pointed out sarcastically.

"*Por seguro.* The salary of a working man in Mexico, including policemen, is never enough to cover even minimal expenses, unless he works very long hours or at two or three jobs. I know it sounds like heresy or sedition," Cruz added soberly, "but I sometimes wish we had a government more like the United States."

"We've got our sore spots too," Ragnon said. "Every government has."

"I know. Every country has a political gang that runs it, no? But your gangs at least change every four years. Here the PRI has run everything for fifty years. Our democracy is a farce, but anyone who seriously opposes their hand-picked candidate can soon be fitted for his own coffin. And now we have more problems with runaway inflation and more devaluations, and a president-elect full of new promises no better than the old. So we live as best we can, Tomás, any way we can, to survive."

In the second village it was the same: another poster and more blank stares and shrugs from miserably poor people scratching out a living from their miserably poor farms. "Scared," Cruz explained their reticence. "They're all scared. Not of Hidalgo Valdez and his murdering friends, but of us, me, anyone who smells of the government, and rightly so."

Ragnon was staring thoughtfully at one of the posters, and the four composites stared back. "You know, partner," he said, "if this really looks like the guys we're after, they ought to be scared of *them,* and maybe we should too. None of 'em looks like anybody you'd want to dance cheek to cheek with."

Twenty minutes out of the village the road grew even sandier. Cruz kept the car in second gear and his foot on the accelerator, but the engine was soon lugging anyway as he shifted to first and tried to gun it through a drift of especially deep sand.

With the back wheels spinning and the momentum stopped, Ragnon told him to cut the engine; they were just heating up and digging themselves in deeper.

They got out, and while Ragnon opened the trunk and got out a folded entrenching tool and began to dig, Cruz gathered clumps of creosote brush from the surrounding desert and began stuffing them under the rear wheels.

Lurching forward, they drove a few miles and bogged down again; repeating the process of excavating themselves with the entrenching tool and creosote bushes, and letting even more air out of the rear tires. They battled most of the afternoon the same way, just to reach the railroad line where they could drive along the right-of-way beside the telephone poles until they reached the main highway and a taco stand and a carton of cold beer, which they finished while driving the last few kilometers into Hermosillo.

It was almost sundown as Cruz drove to a city park where he left Ragnon on a bench beneath a big iron statue of Benito Juarez while he went to find his cousin. Waiting, Ragnon got his boots shined twice by one of the myriad shoeshine boys with boxes, and bought enough chicklet gum from even younger children to stick his own taco stand together. A street vendor came by, selling candied fruits and sweetbreads, and Ragnon bought a half-dozen rolls. He was munching one hungrily as dusk fell over the city, and doubts once again began to needle the back of his mind. Where in hell was Jacinto Cruz? And what the shit was he doing here on a park bench in Hermosillo, Sonora, anyway?

Then his old Falcon came down the street and swung into the curb, and two men got out and came toward him. One was the Mexican detective, but Ragnon's eyes were on the other one, a slickly dressed, brutish-looking bastard who could probably have your guts for breakfast and never even get indigestion.

Cruz introduced him. "Sargento Ragnon—my cousin, Teniente Chato Gomez." Ragnon held out his hand, but Gomez ignored it.

"I have already given my report to Jacinto," Chato said in accented English, "but I wanted to meet you and tell you in person." He was not smiling, and his eyes were like cold hard marbles. "I have no liking for gringos."

"That's okay," Ragnon answered easily, "I don't plan on falling in love with you either." He threw Cruz a look: What's with this guy? "But I'd appreciate any help you can give us in catching these killers, as one professional to another."

"Chato says one of his informants saw four men in such a van gassing up at a station and heading south out of the city,"

Cruz said, "two days ago. They are by now in Mazatlán, or perhaps even turned east through the mountains to Durango. They were identified as the four men on the poster."

"So you have no reason to continue this pursuit, Sargento Ragnon," Gomez added, "unless you wish to involve the Federal Security Police in this too."

"I'll involve anybody I have to to get these guys, Lieutenant, and—"

"Mil gracias, Chato," Cruz intervened, "I think your car has arrived." He pointed to the long black Chrysler which had pulled to the curb behind Ragnon's Falcon and contained several men.

"Good-bye, Sargento," Gomez said with a definite ring of finality in his voice. "Your trip was for nothing. Your fugitives are gone."

As they watched the Chrysler pull out into the evening traffic and disappear, Cruz sat down on the bench and fired up one of his cigarillos. "You would like to kill me, no?" he asked, smiling.

"It crossed my mind, partner. What the fuck was that little scene all about? What in hell are we doing? You're dragging me all over Sonora for nothing. Let's just go back and start this thing over again in San Ignacio. Start with that girl—Angelina Zamora—and her brother. Did you interview her brother?"

"No."

"Why not? He may know something the girl didn't—or she may have left something out."

"But, Tomás, you heard my cousin, the teniente. They were seen getting fuel for their van. They were heading south. Mazatlán? Guadalajara? Is it not over? You're going to involve the Federales?"

"Would it do any good?"

"No. They are the same, even worse." He smiled. "Your only chance is with me, Tomás. Even if they have gone south."

"So you say. But your cousin, that Chato bastard, was feeding us a line of crap. I don't mean to insult you, partner, but he was lying. I could see it in his eyes. Christ, I could smell it, he was that obvious! And why would he lie? Just because he hates gringos?"

Jacinto Cruz took a last deep drag off his cigarillo and flicked it away. "He thinks you are all rich, Tomás, richer than he is.

And he is envious. That is why he hates gringos. I don't know why he was lying. Maybe somebody paid him more than we did. But you are right, he *was* lying."

"How do *you* know he was lying?"

"Because I didn't trust him, and described the missing van as being yellow."

"Jesus—" Ragnon, who had tucked a pinch of Redman in his cheek, spat off to the side into some bushes. "But you gave him the two hundred bucks."

Jacinto Cruz shrugged and lit up another of his cigarillos, shaking out the match and flicking it across the sidewalk. "Sometimes," he said, "in our business you have to pay to find out who *not* to listen to, right Tomás?"

SEVENTEEN

Sunday, March 14, 6:30 A.M.

The old walled hacienda, long abandoned, was ideal for their purpose. Nestled in the foothills with the great mother mountains of Mexico shouldering up into the blue sky behind it, the ranch buildings had fallen into disrepair. The rutted weed-grown dirt road was barely passable now, and led through an arched gateway in the adobe wall to the main ranch house, where the red roof tiles were broken and missing and the windows boarded over.

Entire roofs were caved in on two of the outbuildings, and the corrals were empty of stock. The nearby well was filled with the accumulated debris of years, and a faded red Dodge pickup was parked beside it. A second vehicle—a battered blue Ford van—was pulled up close to the front door of the main house, under a ramada that ran the full length of the building.

Smoke trailed from the big stone chimney, since at this altitude there was still frost on the ground until the sun got over the mountains. Inside, a mesquite log blazed on the grate of the massive fireplace which nearly filled one end of the main room. When a small side door opened and a girl came in with an armload of wood, the draft sent a shower of sparks rushing up the stone chimney, and Hidalgo Valdez cursed her whore of a mother and swore to give her the beating she deserved.

He was presiding at the head of a rough-hewn wooden table and benches, with Arturo Acosta and Xavier Castillo on one side and Miguel Tapia on the other. Drinking tequila with salt and limes, they all laughed at the barefoot girl who hurriedly deposited her load in the woodbox, but seemed more irritated than afraid. Dressed in a flowered blouse and full skirt, she began to clear away the remnants of their morning meal.

"Borrachones," she mumbled a little too loudly. They had been drinking all night, and she'd thought surely by dawn they would be satiated and ready for sleep, but instead they had simply ordered more food and more tequila. Now, as she bent across the table, Hidalgo reached up under her skirt and fondled her roughly.

Earlier, using a cracked mirror in an upstairs room, he had viewed his still-blackened eyes and swollen jaw. What was left of a broken tooth would have to be pulled, but for now the tequila deadened the pain. He glanced momentarily at the guns from the McNeal killings which were stacked in one corner, and in spite of this new addition to his small arsenal, his anger and resentment smoldered as he glared around the table at the others.

There was a small disagreement as to the importance of his taking vengeance on the gringo detective who hunted them, the gringo he held responsible for Galindez kicking them out of the syndicate. The gringo had, of course, given them this opportunity, too, something he had been not quite ready to attempt on his own. Now adversity had forced it on him and he was ready to act. But he still thought the gringo should pay.

Xavier, the oldest at twenty-nine, disagreed. He was a little drunker than the others and more inclined to speak forcefully. *"Ay, chingado cabrón, hombre,"* he was complaining, licking the salt and sucking a lime as he downed another shot of tequila, "we have much to do. Our contact must be firmed up in La Perla; we will need more ammunition for the guns; and the *mordida* must be placed in the hands of the right officials if we are to claim the northern border for our own small enterprise. Why waste time chasing a fucking gringo, hombre?"

"The gringo is chasing *us,"* Hidalgo insisted, his gaze moving around the table to include the other two, even Arturo, who was so drunk now his head was bobbing and his eyes were bleary. "How can we do business safely until he is stopped, eh?" He watched the girl disappear into the kitchen with an armload of dishes, and picked up on it. "We have Elena to serve us here. She carries water from the spring in the hill out back; she cooks, she cleans, she fucks. Here we can hide the guns, and from here we can burglarize the border towns all across Sonora, even into Chihuahua."

His look took in Miguel, who also appeared to be having trouble paying attention. "You say you can get the trucks to haul the loot, and Xavier has his contact in La Perla with a boat to haul everything down to Guaymas. So let Galindez run his empire of dope and machinery and whores. The burglary business on the northern frontier will be ours, something we can handle ourselves with only maybe one or two more. And not just rings and watches, hombres, but TVs and microwave ovens and stereos."

"All the more reason we should simply move ahead with our business," Xavier still insisted. "Just avoid the damn gringo, stay out of his way."

Hidalgo glared fiercely at him. "No. He has insulted us, is that not plain enough? He has come after us in our own country, and a Mexican cop is helping him—the fucking *agringado!*"

"For money," Xavier pointed out, shaking his head. "When the money runs out, the help will stop."

"Ay, no, you are wrong, hombre—you forget I, too, have worked in the United States. I have served time in their jails. For gringos, when they want something, the money never runs out. Jesucristo, I tell you my great grandfather was harassed by them. He had land across the border, land coveted by his gringo neighbors. They took his land and drove him back to Mexico."

"How could they do this?" Miguel asked drunkenly, fascinated.

"The fucking Arizona Rangers—in 1905 or six—I forget, they planted the hides of stolen cows in his barn and he had to flee before they caught and hanged him. But he got even." Hidalgo's smile was vicious. "Ten years later he was with Pancho Villa when he raided Columbus, New Mexico."

"But he never got his land back," Xavier said pointedly.

"No, hombre, but he got even! He got justice! He got revenge! He was able to hold up his head again as a man! Look!" He pulled a wrinkled poster from his pocket and spread the four composite drawings on the table before them. "We, too, are wanted men!"

Xavier shook his head. It was as if Hidalgo, too, dreamed of becoming a legend, like Villa. And maybe he could, but Xavier was still skeptical.

Arturo was squinting at the poster, and he grunted. "It does not look much like us, except you, Hidalgo, with your scar."

"Maybe I'd better grow a beard," Miguel suggested, rubbing his smooth jaw.

"And I'll shave mine off," Arturo answered. He looked up at Hidalgo. "Where did you get this?"

"Híjola, sons of whores," Hidalgo growled at no one in particular, and crumpling the poster, he threw it into a corner. "From my own contact in the north," he said. "They are distributing them all over. But it does not matter. The posters will stop when the gringo is stopped. Elena!" he shouted for the girl. "Where is that bitch?" And when she opened the kitchen door, "More frijoles, woman, more tortillas! We are hungry men!"

"And more tequila!" Arturo added, grinning through his beard and waving his empty bottle at the closing door.

When she came back, laden with a tray and two full bottles, Hidalgo slipped a hand beneath her skirt again. "Ay, you young she-goat, it's your hot flesh I'm hungry for."

"Okay, papacita," she taunted him, setting down the tray with an indulgent sigh. "One more time show me how much man you are, any way you want it."

Hidalgo rose up drunkenly, lurching heavily against the table and upsetting one of the bottles as he grabbed her, threw her over his shoulder, and carried her upstairs while she kicked and screamed in mock terror.

Xavier had saved the overturned bottle, and he passed it to Arturo, laughing. "Ay, compadres, that Hidalgo is a man with balls. He doesn't back down from anybody—not man nor woman nor gringo detectives!"

"Then we will go with him?" Miguel asked. "After the gringo?"

"Why not?" Xavier nodded, accepting the bottle back from Arturo and tilting it to his own lips. Wiping his mouth with the back of his hand, he added, "Our destiny lies before us, compadres. It lies with that rutting son of a whore up there."

Minutes later Hidalgo came back down the stairs alone, tucking his shirt tail into his pants. Lighting a cigar, he puffed to get it going, then picked up the shotgun from the arms stacked in the corner and brought it to his shoulder. Aiming it at the bright Mexican blanket hanging on one wall, he squeezed the trigger and blew a hole squarely in its center.

Pumping more shells into the weapon, he turned the gun on the boarded windows, shattering each in turn while the room filled with the shock of the blasts and the reek of cordite; and the girl, who had returned to the top of the stairs herself, cringed in real terror now as she stared in horrified fascination.

Setting the shotgun aside, Hidalgo grabbed a bottle off the table and held it aloft. "A toast!" he shouted. "We will not be shamed by a gringo dog! To the Villistas and my great grandfather, Candelario Valdez—all killers of gringos!"

"Ayee—ay-yi-yi-yiee!" the others yipped in approval as they, too, lifted their bottles to the killers of gringos.

Later, outside under the ramada, Hidalgo had reloaded the shotgun, and with his men gathered around him, raised the rubber-cushioned butt to his shoulder again and blasted two of the tires on the blue van. "We cannot use this one again, compadres. It must be known to the gringo." He looked at Xavier and nodded toward the red Dodge truck parked beside the well. "We'll use your brother-in-law's truck to go gringo hunting, eh? Or maybe steal one." And his next shot took out the van's windshield.

Oblivious to the cool light rain that was falling on Hermosillo, police agent Chato Gomez followed the bodyguard through the lush gardens surrounding the palacial white house set into a hillside on the outskirts of the city.

Inside he removed his raincoat, and was offered a drink by the maid while he waited. He declined, and minutes later was admitted to the Señor Galindez's large glass-enclosed veranda which looked out on the cloudy day and the rain-dampened garden. Galindez stood at the window, where he remained, his back turned to the lieutenant, while Chato made his oral report.

"The last load from the states was landed safely—mostly Sony Trinitrons and computer parts. The diesel engines and Uzi machine guns came in last night; no trouble. But the costs in bribes to the Federales is going up, and another peso devaluation will start hurting business."

"I'll take care of the Federales," Raul Galindez said, turning now from the window to face him. "And our people are already in Mexico City to make arrangements for a special exchange rate." He paused to light a thick Havana with a gold lighter. "What about the new route for the coke going north?"

"That's still being worked out."

"And the current price?"

"Sixty-two cents a milogram."

"I want that all handled, Chato—this week. Now what was the trouble you mentioned with one of our business enterprises?"

"It might be serious, *Jefe*. U.S. intelligence agents are investigating a shipment of reenforcing rods from our foundry in Cananea. Something about nuclear contamination."

"Where were they shipped?"

"Mostly around Sonora, but one load went north to a construction site in the states. That's the one they are concerned about."

"It's probably nothing." Galindez shrugged, and drew deeply on his cigar. "You know the gringos—they shit their pants everytime a bird falls out of a tree. What else?"

"There's this thing with Hidalgo Valdez, *Jefe*."

"Yes, you told me on the phone. The gringo detective and your cousin." He blew a couple of perfect smoke rings, then pierced them with his cigar. "That's interesting, Chato—the persistence of this gringo cop. That surprises me. I would have thought he'd have given up."

"You want them all eliminated?" Chato suggested. "My cousin too?"

"No—at least not yet. Not the gringo detective anyway. We don't need that kind of trouble. But not your cousin either—this Jacinto Cruz? He could prove useful in the north since Naco was killed. Can you recruit him?"

"I've already tried, several times. He can't be bought. A little *mordida* here and there, of course—he's taking money from the American. But it's for honest police work. *Por seguro, Jefe*, he is diligently hunting Hidalgo and the others." Chato smiled contemptuously. "He really goes after criminals. He works at it."

"And how much money is involved? How much is the reward?"

"Five or ten thousand dollars at most. This Ragnon is feeding it out as *mordida* through Cruz. And they *are* persistent. I told them they went south, but they didn't believe me. If we do nothing, I think they will catch him, eventually."

"It is something to watch," Galindez said almost to himself, "a couple of honest cops at work."

"Are you sure you don't want it stopped? Hidalgo is setting up on his own—some kind of burglary ring. Small scale but it could be trouble, like the contamination thing."

"Or it could be a useful diversion," Galindez said.

"Why don't we just put Hidalgo in a sack and dump him over the border—the other three too. They would be found there, identified, and it would be over."

"No. I want to watch them work, this Cruz and the gringo. Keep me advised as to how it progresses. As long as they don't get too close to any of our operations. Especially that clown, Hidalgo Valdez. If they do, any of them, including the gringo . . ." He drew a finger across his throat so the message was clear.

Teniente Chato Gomez nodded understandingly, but he still didn't like it. The contamination thing needed their full concentration, at least until they knew exactly what it was all about. But Galindez was the *jefe,* and Chato watched him take a thick envelope he knew was full of cash from a desk drawer.

Raul Galindez smiled benevolently. "You do good work, Chato," he said, handing the envelope to the police agent. "You serve us well."

EIGHTEEN

Monday, March 15, 2:45 P.M.

The sun was warm, the sky hazy.

"We haven't got much time," Jacinto Cruz said. "I got them both to agree to meet here at her house between work shifts." He directed Ragnon down a dusty side street in San Ignacio to a small blue and white house where a honeysuckle vine trailed heavily over a trellised porch roof.

Ragnon braked the car in front and saw someone peek briefly through the curtained bay window. "Angelina Zamora went on the evening shift at the garment factory," Cruz said, "and leaves for work at three thirty. Her brother Hector is a foreman over thirty women at the *maquiladora* plant, makes electronic gadgets. Works the morning shift and got off at two thirty. He has no English, but hers is good, so you can take her while I talk to him, *'sta 'ueno?*"

"She lives here alone?" Ragnon asked as they stepped across a couple of boards that bridged a drainage ditch.

Cruz opened the little wooden gate in the neatly fenced yard. "No, with her sister and brother-in-law. No kids. Sister's pregnant. Brother-in-law drives a produce truck between Agua Prieta and Hermosillo, and he's away a lot—including the week of the murders."

Cruz knocked on the door. The girl who opened it was in her early twenties, and far too skinny for Ragnon's taste. But she had delicate bones and finely honed features. Her brown cheeks were lightly rouged and framed by lustrous long black hair worn in a single braid that hung over her shoulder. But most of all her dark, troubled eyes gave her an elusive quality that was strangely alluring.

Without saying anything she motioned them into the small living room, which was clean and sparsely furnished with odds and ends. Ragnon noticed a crucifix hung on one wall, a scenic tapestry on another. A small black and white TV in one corner was tuned to a Nogales station, but the sound was turned too low to hear.

A woman in her thirties with a swollen belly sat at a softly whirring sewing machine by the bay window. "Angelina brings home extra work from the factory and her sister helps her with it," Cruz was explaining as a man in his late twenties emerged from a curtained doorway in the rear.

Hector Zamora glanced hesitantly at Cruz, but shook hands firmly with Ragnon as they were introduced. *"A sus órdenes, Señor,"* he said respectfully. His eyes were those of a man highly uncertain of whom he could trust.

"I'll talk to Hector out in the kitchen," Cruz said, guiding the young man by the elbow back through the curtained doorway.

Tom Ragnon looked again at Angelina Zamora and apologized for intruding on her time. Unfolding his copy of the wanted poster, he showed it to her. "Did Sergeant Cruz tell you we need more information about these men?"

She nodded, glancing up from the poster, a touch of fear in her own eyes now. "I don't know any more I can tell you, Sargento," she said softly, her voice as alluring as her eyes.

Nervously, Ragnon raised his hand to pat his pockets for his Redman, forgetting he was inside, and saw her flinch. "Hey—" He showed his palms in a peaceful gesture, and smiled. "What day is this?"

"What day? Monday."

"Then you're lucky, Angelina. I never hit pretty girls on Mondays."

Her confusion seemed genuine. He had missed with his shot of American police humor, but he knew her shy smile was real. "Let's just talk, okay? Just any little detail you might remember; sometimes they're important. And my compliments on your English—you must have spent some time in the states."

"No, I studied in school and then worked for two years at the tourist bureau in Hermosillo. I had to quit and come here when my mother got sick." The ice was broken between them, and the words spilled out freely while the sewing machine whirred steadily by the window, but the woman there seemed to pay no attention, or didn't understand. "When my mother died," Angelina was saying, "my old job had been taken, and Hector got me on here at the garment factory. But I am striving to better myself."

"You told Sergeant Cruz about meeting Hidalgo Valdez and this other man—this one here." He pointed to the one with the beard. "You're sure that was the only time you ever saw them?"

"Yes . . ." She hesitated. "Well, not really saw them, I guess, but something . . . the night they returned for the van."

"But didn't you tell Sergeant Cruz the van was gone when you got home from work?"

"I . . . was afraid. I wanted his questions to stop. And I didn't really see them . . . not their faces."

"What did you see, Angelina?"

"I got home from a movie just after midnight and had just

turned out the light to go to bed, when I saw four dark figures go into the backyard, get into the van, and leave."

"And this was when, exactly?"

"A week ago—last Sunday night."

"How do you know it was Sunday and not Saturday or Monday?"

"Because Sunday is my only day off, and no one was home but me. My brother-in-law had taken my sister to see his parents in Agua Prieta, and they didn't return until Monday morning, late."

"Okay, but you didn't recognize them as being definitely these four men on the poster?"

"No. It was dark, and they were too far away. But the moon was bright enough to see what they were carrying."

Ragnon almost held his breath. "What were they carrying, Angelina?"

She glanced around uncertainly, as if reflecting the same fear she must have felt that night. "I was afraid they might have seen my light and would try to get in the house, but they went directly to the van and put the guns in the back."

"Guns? They were carrying guns?"

"Rifles," she whispered tremulously. "They were carrying rifles."

The rest of his questions produced nothing else new or startling, and when Cruz came out of the back alone, he simply nodded at Ragnon and asked, "Ready?"

"Ready if you are." He offered his hand to Angelina Zamora. "Mil gracias, Señorita. You've been very helpful. We'll try not to bother you again."

She shook his hand shyly but firmly, her dark eyes not nearly so troubled now.

As they left the house, Cruz asked, "Get anything new?"

"A little—how about you?"

Cruz was lighting up one of his cigarillos. "Maybe a lot." He flicked away the match and closed the little gate behind them.

Back in the car they sat awhile and compared notes. Ragnon tucked a pinch of Redman comfortably in his cheek, then told Cruz about the four shadowy figures seen getting into the van with weapons.

Cruz was frowning. "So she lied about coming back after the van was gone."

"Maybe she just 'disremembered', Jacinto. She didn't really *see* them after all—not their faces. But she's a corroborating witness who can place them here in San Ignacio both before and after the fact. She's sure it was them, and the time is right. It's not as good as actually seeing their faces, but it fits in with everything else. What about Hector?"

"He saw the van too." Cruz took a long drag on his cigarillo and let the smoke stream out in force from his nostrils. "He says when he came by earlier that same night, it was parked in back, and he was angry that Angelina had let them park it there. He was also curious." Cruz smiled at the American. "He looked inside."

"And. . . ?" Ragnon turned his head and spat out the car window.

"Nothing much. It was empty. But he looked in the dash compartment and found the registration. The name on it was Hidalgo Valdez Contreras, the address some rural route and a name—Rancho Poste Quemado: Burnt Post Ranch."

"Jesus, where in hell is that?"

Cruz shrugged. "Hector didn't know. I don't either. I'll have to check around. But Hector's cooperative. He says he wants to help, says he thinks Hidalgo has someone covering for him now right here in San Ignacio, but he doesn't know who."

"So what have we got?" Ragnon asked, thumbing through the pages of his notebook and summarizing his thoughts out loud. "Hidalgo Valdez Contreras and his three buddies arrive here in their blue van four days before the McNeal killings. They meet the girl and after the dance leave their van behind her house, then cross the border on foot and undetected. They steal two campers the next day, but their drug rendezvous near Pantana goes sour with the plane crash so they abandon the campers and try to salvage something with the burglary at the McNeals' two days after that, with murder and rape as a sideline. Back across the border with stolen guns, they pick up the van just after midnight Sunday night, relax a little at the whorehouse, then get into a small snafu at the crossroads bar in the wee hours of Monday morning and disappear." He looked over at Cruz. "Where?"

"Not west to the coast, and evidently not to Hermosillo or farther south. What about Poste Quemado ranch?"

"Wherever the hell that is." Ragnon spat. "Who would know —the post office?"

"Perhaps. I'll try there. And I've got a son at the agricultural college over in Janos. They might know of it, or at least have a list of the area ranches."

"You have a son in college?" Ragnon asked.

"Ramón—eighteen." Cruz smiled nostalgically. "He is from an alliance of my reckless youth. His mother died, but he is a smart boy. I help him all I can."

"You *are* full of surprises." Ragnon closed his notebook and glanced back at the small blue and white house. "I think both the girl and her brother are still afraid," he said. "Not of us, but of Hidalgo and his friends—that they might come back. You realize they're evidently the only ones who know they were here —the only ones who can identify two of them? Or who will?"

"Except for whoever is covering for them here," Cruz added, starting the car. "Anyway, Tomás, for Hidalgo the contact with Angelina and her brother was almost negligible. He left his van, he came and got it. Why should he even remember them?"

"I suppose so," Ragnon said, spitting out the window as Cruz pulled the car out onto the road. Though he knew that for him, at least, Angelina Zamora would be hard to forget. "Okay, partner," he added, "let's go find me the nearest public phone— I want to call John Antone and find out if he's got anything new to report on the other side of the border."

Cruz had to stop first at a pharmacy to check the list of winning lottery tickets. He came out smiling. He had won back the price of his ticket, and immediately bought another.

When they reached the hotel, where there was a switchboard, the Mexican police agent waited in the car outside. Minutes later, Ragnon was the one who returned to the car grinning. "Our luck is holding, partner," he said, spitting.

"What does the Indio have?" Cruz asked as Ragnon got back in the car.

"Another name. They ID'd the body found in the plane crash —a gringo with a rap sheet for drug trafficking, kidnapping, and assault, but no connection to our fugitives."

"So what about the name, Tomás? You look like *you* won the lottery."

"I'm getting to that. John ran Hidalgo Valdez and his description through a computer. Seems our guy did seven months in California on a burglary rap two years ago. Printed and mugged and formerly deported after his release; they're sending a picture. But there was something else in the file." Ragnon was peeling back a page in his notebook. "A guy was picked up with him on the same charge—another Mexican national—but released for lack of evidence and turned over to the Border Patrol, who gave him a voluntary return to Mexico—"

"The name, Tomás—Jesucristo, the name!"

Ragnon had pulled out a copy of the poster and was printing a name under the one with the drooping mustache, goatee, and acne scars. "Xavier Castillo Estrada," he announced triumphantly, "Our second name."

"Híjola, hombre," Cruz muttered.

"And it gets even better, partner. No mug shot, but the description fits, and they fingerprinted him." He smiled exultantly at Cruz.

"And there is more," the Mexican said. "I can see it in your face!"

Tom Ragnon nodded smugly. "The bastard's left thumb print matches the one in blood on the McNeals' freezer."

"Madre Santísima—" the Mexican detective moaned softly.

NINETEEN

Monday, March 15, 7:45 P.M.

"More coffee?"

"Sure, bring the pot," John Antone said, taking his dirty dishes over to the sink and rinsing them. Tom Ragnon had broiled steaks and served them with ranch-style beans and a tossed salad, and he'd baked a frozen apple pie for dessert. "You're a damn good cook, Sergeant," the Indian deputy added, "for a white man."

"Gee, thanks—you think it would create too much of a scandal at the office if we got married?"

"You're not *that* good," Antone answered, smiling and watching the detective refill their mugs and place the pot on the warmer as they sat down again. "Besides, we're already married, remember?"

"That's right—how *are* Juana and the kids?"

"Growing an inch every day, including Juana." He laughed, and then grew serious. "How about you and Angie—any progress there?"

For just an instant Ragnon thought he meant Angelina Zamora, but he recovered. "I'm working on it. I haven't even called her yet," he said wearily, glancing at the wall clock. It was nearly eight P.M. He'd come back across the border about five, called Antone to meet him at his trailer in Pantana, then picked up a few groceries and some beer and put together a meal.

"You're not getting much sleep, are you?" Antone said, sipping his coffee and then nodding at the notebook and legal pad lying beside the briefcase on the coffee table. "And paper work even on vacation?"

"Just roughing out a homicide report for later, while it's fresh."

"Nobody ever thought you'd get this far, Sergeant."

"With your help, good buddy. How's Old Ironballs taking it?"

"You know him, he thinks you're crazy. But he's impressed. By the way, he tried to get hold of you yesterday. Another homicide and two men off with the flue, but it turned out to be just inside the city limits, so not our jurisdiction."

"You ever tell him I was back on this side, I'll kill you."

John Antone smiled. "How's this Mexican guy to work with?"

"You'd like him. He's got more guts than you could hang on a fence, and he's a good cop. I'm practically tagging along for the ride. He's the one really putting out."

"For the money—the *mordida.*"

Ragnon picked up the pot again and offered to pour, but Antone covered his mug. *"Mordida* is tradition in Mexico," the detective said. "It's the system. It's how things get done down there." He filled his own mug for the third time and promised himself it was the last. "And maybe for most of 'em that's the whole nine yards, but Jacinto Cruz is different. He's got a cop's natural instincts. I really think he'd help me on this now without the money. He wants them as bad as we do."

"But you're still taking him more money," Antone pushed.

"Yeah, another two thousand should do it. We're making progress, and like I said, he's not greedy. I'm going to talk to the councilman, Colonel Roberts, about it, and then go back to Mexico tomorrow."

"Maybe you should let Cruz handle that side himself now," the deputy suggested cautiously, "if you trust him. They must know by now you're after them, and they can't be that thrilled about a gringo cop."

"No." He thought about it a moment. "It's awkward at times, John. It's like we're almost on our own down there, Jacinto and me. There's no real organization. No one knows who to trust. But we do trust each other." He stared at Antone over his coffee mug, wondering if he understood. "We make a good team, Cruz and me. He's as wild a hair as I am, and it's working, for both of us. And now that you've got us a second name, it's really cooking."

John Antone nodded, then glanced at his watch. "I've got to go. I'm on duty tonight. Thanks for the chow, and I'll keep rooting around from this end. But take care down there, man, you and Jacinto Cruz both."

When the deputy had left, Ragnon sighed heavily and stared around him at the tiny confines of his trailer. It needed a good cleaning, but that could wait. The damned progress report could wait too. Everything could wait. It seemed like it was all on hold while the case wound tighter and tighter, like an old clock spring. Now, if it just didn't snap and go flying off in all directions . . .

He got up and paced restlessly, still thinking, knowing it was never any use hurrying a case. Each one seemed to set its own pace, and as long as it was progressing, unfolding, moving as if inevitably toward an affirmative close, it would work out in due time—if the assholes just didn't cut and run. He squeezed his temples as his head tried to ache. It was so quiet in the trailer, he could hear the hum of the electric wall clock. He took a couple of aspirin before consulting his notebook and calling Colonel Roberts.

A woman answered—the daughter—and he tried to think of her name while she called her father to the phone. The colonel was glad to hear from the detective, and yes, he could meet with him tonight, at his home, say in an hour.

Ragnon hung up—Wanda, Wanda Henderson—and he pictured the daughter that night in the hallway after the council meeting, and later at the steakhouse; what was it—three or four days ago—it seemed like a month. Then he dialed his wife's number. It rang and rang. He was about to hang up when she answered.

"Hi, Angie."

"Tom, you're back!"

"Temporarily. You took a long time to answer."

"I was in the shower. . . . Tom?"

"I'm here. I was just picturing you in the shower. How's everything? Kids okay?"

"Fine. Your chief called, said he wants you to contact him if I heard from you."

"You didn't."

"Maybe he's promoting you." Ragnon didn't feel like commenting on that one. He remained silent until she asked, "So, how did it go in Mexico?"

"Fine, no problems."

"You mean you caught them?"

"Not yet. Can I talk to the kids?"

"They're asleep, Tom. Come by tomorrow."

"I'm going back to Mexico tomorrow."

"Can't you let that Mexican cop handle it now?"

"Somebody already asked that. No, Cruz needs me." There was suddenly a long silence on her end of the line.

"I need you, too, Tom," she almost whispered.

"You've got your alley rat." A cheap shot, but he felt tired, angry.

"Don't call him that. I'm all mixed up, Tom. I'd like you to meet him. He's a lot like you."

"Then why did you dump me?" Another long silence hung in his ear. This conversation was going nowhere.

"Tom—call me again when you get back. And be careful down there." The receiver buzzed suddenly with impartial finality, and he was alone again.

"Bye, Angie," he said into the dead mechanism.

Angie's hand rested on the phone receiver for several seconds after she hung up. "I need you, too, Tom," she whispered again. But did she? She really did have mixed emotions about their relationship. Dammit, she loved him. She knew she loved the guy. Could it be their real problem was basic incompatibility, and they just weren't facing it?

She thought about Roy, her "alley rat." Was he really a lot like Tom? Roy was fun, outgoing, a socializer where Tom was a loner. But was that really where her heart was? And Tom certainly had his good points. He had filled a void in her life after the shock of grief of her first husband's death; a haven from the storm. And he was a better father than most men. So what was lacking? He was a good cop, she mused, and God knows, somebody had to do it. But why did he have to stay in field work? Why such resistance to promotion, to getting ahead? Maybe it was like his socializing, or lack of it—an essential part of his makeup. Whatever it was, she decided bleakly, it was killing their relationship.

After a long hot shower and shave Tom Ragnon felt better, but not much. At least he wasn't as tired, as he drove over to the councilman's ranch house outside Pantana.

"And he wants more cash?" Colonel Roberts asked after Ragnon had layed out for him what they had accomplished so far.

"Two thousand more should do it." Ragnon accepted the cold beer the councilman's daughter brought into the living room. Both she and the colonel were having margaritas, Wanda perched elegantly on the arm of her father's chair in her tight gold lamé pants suit, flirting shamelessly.

Colonel Roberts was studying the copy of the wanted poster Ragnon had spread out on the coffee table between them, the one with names penned in under two of the faces now.

"You're doing well, Sergeant," he said, looking up, "you and this Sergeant Cruz. Frankly, you've moved a lot faster than I expected, especially at this stage in the investigation. But do you think you can find this Burnt Post Ranch you mentioned, and that they'll still be there when you do?"

"No way of knowing that one, Colonel. But it's why I want to get back to San Ignacio tomorrow—by early afternoon if possible."

"All right, I'll relay what you've got to McNeal's brother first thing in the morning. I'll call around to the other council members, too, let them know how it's going. You should have another two thousand by noon."

"Thanks." Ragnon set his empty, foam-flecked glass on the table. "You know I'm going back anyway, Colonel—with or without the money—to do what I can. We're so damn close now I can taste it."

"I appreciate what you're doing, Sergeant. We all do." He rose and shook the detective's hand. "I'm sure there won't be any problem about the money, and good luck."

Wanda Henderson saw him to the door, her drink in one hand and a cigarette in the other. "You *will* come and see us again won't you, Sergeant?" she purred.

Tom Ragnon smiled. There seemed to be always one around —girls who liked to get next to homicide detectives, rubbing asses with all that death and danger and excitement shit. "Next time I'll try the margaritas," he said softly.

By the time he got back to the trailer, it was after eleven and a north wind was chilling the desert night—a persistent winter hanging on—and the radio was predicting frost. He was bone tired, but not sleepy, and turning on the TV, he got a beer out of the fridge and then tried to watch an old movie and relax.

Ten minutes later he had turned it off, even though it was *Gunga Din,* one of his favorites. He sat there in the silence, listening to the wind beating against the trailer walls and thinking about what exactly they had on this case, and what they didn't have.

That the bastards were still hanging around northern Sonora was what surprised him most. But he was sure they were, even though there were no facts to back it up—he could sense it. Yet surely they knew by now he was after them. Four guys, two of them with names now, and their blue van. Taking a pair of scissors from a night stand he snipped the poster into four separate faces and then studied each one in turn. Where are you now, slimeball? he thought. What are you doing right this minute? Drinking? Fucking? Sleeping peacefully? Or maybe killing again? He put the poster pieces aside and finished his beer. Where in hell was a Burnt Post Ranch in Sonora, anyway? he wondered. Antone hadn't heard of it, so that part was up to Cruz too; and then he wondered if the Mexican *would* work the case anymore without more money. He was tempted to try him.

The clock read 12:45, and he decided he'd call Angie in the

morning and at least talk to the kids. Then, for no particular reason, he thought of the dark-eyed Angelina Zamora in her blue and white house with the honeysuckle vine trellised over the porch.

He was still thinking about her, pleasurably, growing sleepier by the minute, when there was a light knock on the trailer door. Shaking his head to clear the lethargy, he got up and opened it cautiously. Wanda Henderson was standing on his doorstep, smiling. "Hi," she chirped, and held up a paper bag. "Thought you might be lonesome, Sergeant, or just want to relax, so I brought my margarita mix." He could feel the dumb, blank look he must have on his face as she added, a little miffed, "If you're busy I can leave of course. I don't want to intrude."

"No—no intrusion Mrs. Henderson." He stepped back, inviting her in; deciding there was time after all to let her rub asses with all that death and danger and excitement shit.

TWENTY

Tuesday, March 16, 9 A.M.

The battered red Dodge pickup that had jolted over the rutted dirt road out of the low foothills of the Sierra Madres in the early hours just after dawn, was like any dozen others in Sonora. Its paint was faded and scarred, its windshield pitted, its fenders dented and scratched. And the four men crowded into its broad front seat matched the truck.

The driver, who two days before had been fully bearded, had shaved. The man next to him, who had been without facial hair, now wore a scraggly mustache. Of the other two, one still wore his goatee and both had retained their thick mustaches. But the one on the outside, away from the driver, had also exchanged his mismatched sneakers for a pair of old boots.

"It's about four kilometers to the turnoff," Hidalgo Valdez told the driver. He had to raise his voice above the roaring engine because the muffler had a hole in it.

Arturo nodded, hunching over the wheel. "And we take the right fork to San Ignacio, eh?"

"If we were going to San Ignacio. Take the left—we're going over to the coast."

"To Puerto La Perla?" Arturo asked.

"To a fishing village forty kilometers south of there, for now. Xavier is going to contact his brother-in-law."

"But he is in La Perla," Xavier said, puzzled.

"So you will take the truck and go alone to see him. We will wait for you near the village. I want to be sure he has made the transport arrangements before we start stealing again."

"He already assured me it would be ready," Xavier said, as the truck bounced over a rock that thudded hard against the frame underneath. "And he is the owner of the boatyard, and even owns several boats."

"Then you should find everything in order," Hidalgo answered tightly, reaching across and lighting a cigarette off Arturo's.

"What about the gringo cop?" Miguel wanted to know.

"I have not forgotten that *chingado cabrón,*" Hidalgo said, forcing jets of smoke out through his nostrils. "Or his *pinche compadre.*"

Two hours later the scrub desert grew even sparser as the wind, rushing through the open windows of the cab, brought them the damp salt smell of the sea, and finally gave way to high, grass-tufted dunes. Topping a rise, they glimpsed the gulf and the fishing village in the distance, but Hidalgo pointed instead to some abandoned and bedraggled buildings squatting alongside the road a quarter kilometer ahead.

He directed Miguel to pull in under the sheltering concrete canopy and park beside the dry gas pumps of what had once been the office of a motel. "We're going to stay here?" Arturo asked.

"Get out," Hidalgo ordered, opening his door. "It's all right, I have used this place before. The roofs of the cabins are still sound. And do not despair—with the beach and village just over the next dune, there will be women and pulque and beer."

"Then why don't we just go on to the village?" Miguel suggested. "Why this place?"

"Because, burro, for the same reason I don't want all of us going to La Perla together. One man at a time is not so noticeable. Now take the blankets and lantern out of the back and carry them down to that end cabin. I'll drive into the village and get us some groceries and beer. When I get back, Xavier can take the truck to La Perla and contact his brother-in-law, while we wait for him here."

"We should have brought the guns," Arturo grumbled, helping the others haul the things out of the back.

"The guns are safely hidden," Hidalgo snapped, "and I have the one gun we need for the gringo cop—this one." Reaching behind the seat, he pulled on the butt of a sawed-off shotgun until it was half out of its hard leather scabbard, then shoved it back in. "Now take everything to the cabin and wait for me there."

The cabins were built in a horseshoe around a dry, cracked swimming pool. They set up temporary quarters in the kitchen of the last one and began playing cards. They played in silence, three ruthless, restless, uncertain men, with only the sharp snap of the cards on the table and an occasional vile oath, while the air in the room above their heads hung in smoky blue clouds from their cigarettes.

Thirty minutes later Hidalgo had not returned, and Xavier went outside to relieve himself. He didn't blame the other two for their impatience, but he knew Hidalgo was right to be cautious. It was regrettable but necessary to rid themselves of the police on their tail, so there would be no interference once they began the burglaries and the fencing of stolen goods.

For Xavier it was just as well the syndicate deal went bad. He had argued from the first that a small independent operation was best, and the idea to hit the ranch family after the plane crash had been as much his as Hidalgo's. But he regretted the killings as not really necessary. They should have known the gringos' reaction would be strong. A little rape maybe—women were to be used, no? But Hidalgo killed too easily. Still, he was the leader, and with his deep hunger for attention and recognition, he could remain so. Xavier had no greater ambitions for himself.

In and out of prison most of their lives, the crowded foul-smelling cells, the bad food, the beatings—all had become a way of life for the four of them. Xavier himself had seen his father grow old as a varnisher in a furniture factory until his lungs gave out, and swore it would never happen to him. Consequently he hadn't turned an honest day's work since he'd quit a job in a limestone quarry—breaking rock with a hammer at ten pesos a load—and turned to crime. Jailed the first time for killing a man in a street brawl, he had bought off the family, the witness, and the judge. He knew it had been generally the same with Arturo; only this last time Arturo had not been so fortunate, except that he had met Hidalgo in prison and been released two months ahead of him. Hidalgo had contacted him when he got out with the aid of Galindez, and offered him the chance to join them.

A construction worker and blaster in the mines, Arturo had worked illegally in the U.S., too, and had even been a policeman himself for a couple of years and a buyer of stolen goods on the side; until he had a falling out with his superiors over the percentage of the *mordida*.

Arturo had brought in Miguel, at twenty-two the youngest of the four. Half Indian and a farm worker from Sinaloa until he had joined the Army at sixteen for three years service, Miguel had got in a fight with a sergeant and deserted six months short of fulfilling his contract. Fearless, he complained a lot, but he followed Hidalgo blindly.

But it was Hidalgo himself who was the glue that bound them together, the planner and organizer who made them function as a unit, however uncertainly. Xavier had recognized the quality several years before when he had met him while working as a wetback in the states. Xavier had been sent home when they were caught after a burglary, but Hidalgo had spent time in a gringo jail. He, too, had turned to crime early. After working in a slaughterhouse for two years, washing and drying cow intestines, he had begun preying on turistas around Guaymas on the Gulf and decided it was a much better living than work.

Xavier returned to the card game and another twenty minutes passed before Hidalgo drove up with the groceries and beer. He was not happy. "They were here looking for us," he told the others as he watched Miguel light the old kerosene stove. "The gringo and his Mexican partner, three or four days ago. They were showing that damned poster, and had my name on it!"

"Ayee!" Arturo exclaimed. "Then you were recognized!"

Hidalgo shook his head. "I was alone and without the blue van, and it was dim in the shack. But you will all have to stay out of the village. The two cops took the old cutoff to Hermosillo, but they will not waste much time there." He turned to

Xavier. "So you better make it a quick trip to La Perla, compadre. Try to be back by dark."

Xavier was scowling thoughtfully. "And when I get back, what then?" Even Miguel paused at the stove, where the aroma of green chiles and onions frying in oil was beginning to fill the kitchen.

"Yes," Arturo added, "are we going to start robbing ricos along the border, or keep playing these games with a gringo cop?"

"*Cállate,* burro!" Hidalgo turned on them all. "It is now a matter of honor, hombres. Xavier will first assure us that the coastal contact is still good, then we can return to San Ignacio. The gringo will have given up looking for us in Hermosillo by then, maybe sooner, and we will find him."

"But should we go back to San Ignacio at all?" Arturo argued. "You and me were seen there, too, by that girl, Angelina. And there was her brother, too. We even parked the van behind her house!"

Hidalgo Valdez stabbed out his cigarette on the tabletop, grinding it hard into the worn wood. "You have a point, Arturo; so maybe we will just have to go back and make sure they don't talk."

TWENTY-ONE

Tuesday, March 16, 3 P.M.

"I kept out five hundred for Comandante Max," Jacinto Cruz said, patting his jacket pocket as he got back into Ragnon's car. He had just come out of the Banco Nacional, where he had deposited the Pantana council's latest reward payment just before closing time.

"I hope you kept out some expense money too," Tom Ragnon said, spitting out the car window into the street. "And what in hell are we paying Max for now?"

"We are still operating in his jurisdiction." Cruz cupped a match to one of his cigarillos. "He could make things difficult. This way it goes more smoothly, no? Besides"—he flicked the

match out the window as Ragnon pulled away from the curb—
"he has given us the use of his jeep."

"His jeep?" Ragnon glanced at his partner. "What do we
need a jeep for?"

"You think I was idle while you were back in Pantana, Tomás? I have located El Rancho Poste Quemado—an abandoned
hacienda in the foothills of the Sierra Madres, about a hundred
and fifty kilometers southeast of here."

Ragnon stared at him. "No shit? You found Burnt Post
Ranch? You never cease to amaze me, partner." He spat again.

"But for the last twenty kilometers the road is too rough for a
car, so Comandante Max has loaned us his jeep and says we can
swing around through the town of Ures and pick up some
soldiers. It has all been arranged with a Teniente Calderón."

"You're too much," Ragnon said. "I feel about as useful as
tits on a boar."

"But you have added a second name to our poster—this Xavier Castillo, no?"

"Antone did that. He hasn't been idle either."

"Anyway, we are making progress, *verdad?* And if you will
buy us a quick supper at Madrecita's, we can park your car
behind the police building, pick up the jeep, and be in Ures by
five thirty."

"You got a deal," Ragnon said, grinning and spitting out the
window again. "But you buy the gas for the jeep."

By six thirty in the evening a heavy cloud cover lay across the
entire northern range of the Sierra Madre Occidental, and the
temperature in the foothills above the desert hovered just under
fifty degrees.

A light rain was beginning to fall on Cruz and Ragnon and a
dozen Mexican soldiers under Teniente Calderón de Fuentes as
they parked their jeeps and trucks alongside the narrow rocky
road and fanned out on foot in a military approach to the
walled hacienda. In the gathering dusk Cruz and Ragnon
crouched behind a boulder and studied the main ranch house
beyond the wall.

"No smoke from the chimney," Cruz observed, his Colt .45
cocked and ready in his hand. It would have to cover them
both.

"Maybe they had a lookout on the road and saw us coming,"

Ragnon said. The rain, falling harder now, began dripping off his hat brim as he watched the Mexican lieutenant direct half his men around to the rear of the main building. For another five minutes they waited and watched in the wet, chilling silence.

But nothing moved around the rancho, and the only sound was the steady hiss of the falling rain, which gradually increased to a roar as the lieutenant signaled the rest of them forward and they all ran up to the wall. "I don't think they're here," Cruz said as he and Ragnon pressed against the adobe beside the open gate.

"But they've *been* here—look." Through the gateway Ragnon pointed to an old blue van parked under the ramada, its tires flattened, its right door missing.

Then the front door of the main house opened suddenly and they flinched back against the wall, but it was only a soldier who waved his rifle at the teniente as another soldier appeared at an upstairs window, shouting that the house was empty.

Following the lieutenant and the rest of his men across the front yard, where they all gathered under the long ramada, out of the rain, they paused to look closely at the van. Its tires and windshield had been shot out, its side blasted. A couple of empty shotgun shells lay against the wall. The engine was cold.

Ragnon peered in through the back window, confirming it was empty, then looked at Cruz. "Any chance of getting this dusted for prints, inside and out?"

Cruz nodded. "I will arrange it with the teniente." He had returned his automatic to its shoulder holster under his jacket. "They can tow it into Ures."

"I want to preserve anything we find inside too," he added as they went in through the front door, carrying flashlights.

More shotgun shells lay on the floor of the main room, and the wooden shutters had been blasted from the inside. "Somebody had quite a party," Cruz said, kneeling and brushing aside an empty tequila bottle as he stirred the ashes in the fireplace with a stick, then touched them with his hand. "Cold," he said. "They've been gone for hours, maybe days."

"Damn!" Ragnon swore. "To be so close!"

The stove in the kitchen was cold, too. A soldier was starting to empty some canned goods out of a cupboard when Cruz stopped him. When the Mexican lieutenant came in behind

Ragnon, Cruz asked him not to let his men disturb anything more until he and the gringo had been through the house themselves.

Teniente Calderón saluted quickly and went to gather his men in the living room, where they rekindled the fire while the two policemen continued through the house alone, and the rain drummed loudly on the tile roof overhead.

Upstairs they found a bare, stained mattress on the floor of one bedroom, and a few old clothes—men's pants and shirts and some dirty underwear. A second bedroom had a brass-posted bed and a wooden dresser, the bed stripped down to the mattress, and the dresser empty too.

"A woman's been here," Cruz noted as he emptied a trash basket out on the floor and poked through it with the stick he had used on the ashes downstairs. He shone his light on several tissues stained with lipstick.

Ragnon found further evidence in the closet where a red dress lay crumpled in a corner, and then Cruz pulled a pair of nylon panties out from under a bed. "If we could find the owner of these," he said, holding them dangling from the stick, "I'll bet she'd have a tale to tell."

"Maybe she'd know where they went," Ragnon suggested.

"Unless she was their prisoner."

"Or she might even be with them willingly." Ragnon stared around him. "Shit," he muttered as they moved to a third bedroom, which was bare. They found one of the wanted posters wadded and tossed in a corner. "They've probably scattered by now anyway," Ragnon said, feeling the disappointment keenly and stepping to a window, where he stared down at the front yard beyond the ramada roof. The rain had stopped as suddenly and quietly as it began, leaving the yard a muddy quagmire, effectively obliterating any tracks that might have suggested what kind of vehicle they left in. Except that it had to be a jeep or truck or another van, to negotiate the road. He wondered how long he and Cruz would have to wait now before the washes stopped running and they could get out themselves.

Turning, he was about to leave the room when Cruz, who was peering a little deeper into the dark recesses of the closet, pulled out a shoe and turned it over. *"Madre Santísima!"* he breathed, and dragged out the second half of a pair of mismatched sneakers. Both were black, but the right one had diagonal white stripes while the left had straight orange ones. He turned them over again to show Ragnon the soles—the same mismatched patterns of circles and diamonds that Antone had tracked from the McNeal ranch across the border to San Ignacio.

"Two-Shoes," Ragnon murmured almost reverently, and felt an odd and chilling sense of foreboding in his blood. "He *was* here, Jacinto." He looked around them. "Right in this room. He and the others, with their goddamned blue van parked outside!"

"But where are they now?" Cruz wondered aloud.

Downstairs again Ragnon had everything bagged and tagged for evidence by the soldiers, including the empty shotgun shells. He bagged the mismatched sneakers himself—he wasn't about to let them out of his sight.

They searched the house once more, but found nothing new. "No weapons," Cruz observed quietly. "The soldiers even looked in the well outside."

"Can we have this place searched more thoroughly?" Ragnon asked him. "I mean really torn apart and searched in daylight, and then a watch put on it for a few days—maybe a week, in case they come back."

"Por seguro, Tomás. I will speak to the teniente. It will not cost much. He will ask around about the missing woman too." They walked together back outside and stood beside the van, under the ramada.

Reaching in through the open doorway, Ragnon pushed the button on the dash compartment with his pencil eraser and the lid flipped open. He picked out the registration by one corner and looked at it. Angelina's brother had been right: Hidalgo Valdez Contreras, Route 8, Rancho Poste Quemado, Sonora, Mex. He was slipping it into a plastic baggie when a second piece of paper caught his eye. It was folded in the back of the glove box, and Ragnon fished it out with his pencil. Unfolding it carefully, he showed it to Cruz and held the light closer. It appeared to be some sort of receipt. "What do you make of that? It's from a Xavier's Boat Works in Puerto La Perla."

"Our Xavier?" Cruz wondered, holding the document by the corners. "It's for an outboard motor, used. It's not made out to Hidalgo; name on it looks like Arturo Acosta." He looked at the detective. "A third name for our poster?"

"Or a fake receipt and a fake name," Ragnon suggested skeptically, reaching for his Redman. "Has it got a date on it?"

"January twelfth, this year—a couple of months ago."

"Puerto La Perla," Ragnon mused. "That's north of that village we were at on the coast." He tucked a pinch of tobacco in his cheek, sensing the heat of the chase rising again. "But God, I hate to make that trip tonight."

"We can stay in Ures tonight, Tomás. I have relatives there."

Tom Ragnon nodded, feeling there was no use pushing it. But hopefully they were back on the track. "Seems like you've got relatives everywhere, partner," he said.

The streets were still wet from the rain in Hermosillo, and a bright quarter moon was rising, its silver rays glinting off the huge metal sculpture of Benito Juárez that dominated the city park. Two men sat on a bench beneath the statue and talked.

"The gringo and Jacinto Cruz got some soldiers from Ures and raided Hidalgo's hideout at Poste Quemado at sundown this evening," Chato Gomez reported.

"And found. . . ?" Raul Galindez asked, snipping the tip off an expensive cigar and holding it for the lieutenant to light.

"Hidalgo's van—abandoned. Lieutenant Calderón reports they took some clothes and shotgun shells they found and headed for the coast. They paid him to confiscate the van and check it for fingerprints, and to search the ranch for weapons in daylight tomorrow."

"And. . . ?"

"He checked with me and I've paid him more *not* to find anything."

"So they will still be there—Hidalgo's weapons?"

"Wrapped in heavy oilcloth and worked into the thatch of the ramada fronting the main house—a dozen assorted rifles and shotguns, and several pistols and revolvers. Ammo enough to start a small rebellion buried in back of the outhouse."

"And the woman who was there?"

"She evidently ran off—back to her village. You want her found?"

"No, she's not important." Galindez drew long and deep on his cigar. "What about Hidalgo and his compadres?"

"No one seems to know. Probably off establishing his burglary business along the border." Chato was lighting his own cigar. "Shall I find him and step on him now?"

"No, not yet. Not while the gringo is hunting them."

"There is more on the contamination thing, *Jefe.*" Chato shook out his match. "It *is* radioactive contamination."

Galindez scowled. "You mean radiation . . . like a bomb?"

Chato nodded. "We stole some old equipment stored in a warehouse and it went to our junkyard in San Ignacio and was later melted down at the foundry with some other scrap metal."

"But what exactly did we steal?"

"Some kind of cancer treatment machine with a dangerous core of cobalt pellets. Melted down, it wasn't destroyed; it simply contaminated the reinforcing rods that were made out of the melted metal. The shipment through El Paso into New Mexico was detected by a radiation alarm near the Los Alamos radiation laboratory. U.S. agents are keeping everything quiet, but if they continue the investigation of its source, it can bring unwanted attention to our operations in this area."

"Maybe you're right, Chato—this is serious after all. I'll have to think about it."

"And Hidalgo, *Jefe,* have you changed your mind about him?"

"I told you, Chato, after the gringo tires of hunting them, *then* we can step on Hidalgo and his friends, and Jacinto Cruz too." Galindez flicked his unfinished cigar across the sidewalk as the moon passed through a bank of cirrus clouds, fading the statue behind them to a thin, metallic gray. A tower clock two blocks away tolled the hour of eleven. "Then we can step on them all."

TWENTY-TWO

Tuesday, March 16, 11:45 P.M.

It was almost midnight in San Ignacio, too, and Angelina Zamora had finished the night shift at the garment factory. Most of the girls had already left the big, dimly lit, barnlike structure that was filled with rows of sewing machines set on tables and surrounded by boxes and bags of materials and scraps. But two of them, like her, had remained behind, selecting material to take home for extra piecework.

Angelina could sense the irritating presence of the foreman, who was hovering in the doorway behind them and waiting impatiently to turn out the lights. Hurriedly, she stuffed her pieces into a fiber bag, wanting to be sure she left with the others because the foreman—fortyish and fat, with thick greasy hair—had been getting more aggressive in his attempts to sleep with her.

She knew most of the girls already had, for favors, but she had stubbornly held out. It was always like that, wherever she worked—the men's brazen eyes and familiar hands, and crude, often open suggestions to have sex. She was not a virgin, but she was not promiscuous either. Having a watchful older brother helped. Usually he picked her up, but not tonight. Hector had a date himself tonight, and she wondered if he was the same way with the girls at the *machiladora* plant where he was foreman. She didn't like to think so, but she supposed he was like other men in that respect.

"Coming, Angelina?" one of the girls called, and she realized they were already at the door.

"Yes, wait for me." She gathered up her fiber bag.

"No need to hurry, Angelina," the foreman whispered behind her as she looked around at him inadvertently. "I'll be glad to take you home tonight." His frankly lecherous leer almost turned her stomach.

The other two girls were still waiting at the front door, and Angelina was about to join them when she stopped and stared. A man had appeared and was blocking the doorway behind them. Rough and dirty and mean looking, he was staring directly at her. And somewhere inside her head an alarm was ringing.

Then the other girls stepped aside as a second man moved in behind the first, and Angelina felt the shock of recognition as the foreman called to them from behind her, "What do you want, hombres?" He spoke firmly and with authority, though she thought with just a hint of fear and uncertainty too. And when she looked around to see what the foreman would do, a third man appeared at the back door, and she gasped and almost dropped her fiber bag. The third man was Hidalgo Valdez.

When she looked automatically for the fourth, she saw him lounging casually by the corner drinking fountain in the shadows, his drooping mustache and goatee barely visible. They had come back—all four of them! Her mind reeled with the improbability of it, and what they might want.

The foreman had seen the other two behind him now, too, and all the authority was suddenly gone from his voice as he whined, "Hey, hombres—what's going on? There is nothing to rob here, no money, nothing but—"

"Cállate, pendejo," the man closest to him hissed. "Close up and go home, and take those other two girls with you. Say nothing. Our business is with this one. Go on"—he smiled maliciously, his menace dominating the room without even displaying a weapon—"while you are still able to walk. We will turn out the lights when we are through."

Angelina, watching the two girls and the foreman disappear quickly out the front door, thought for a moment she was going to faint. Alone, with the four men approaching her, her legs turned weak and rubbery and her hands began to sweat as she clutched the fiber bag to her chest and tried desperately to think of some way out of her predicament.

Reaching out, Hidalgo took the bag gently from her hands, but there was something threatening about his very gentleness. The other three gathered around her, crowding her. "You remember us, no?" Hidalgo asked, setting the bag on the floor at their feet.

She shook her head, trying to ask what he wanted, but the words were caught by the fear in her throat and her mouth was dry.

"Yes—you remember." He took her arm, his grip painfully strong. "We came back at night for the van. You never did dance with me enough. And your brother—where is he?"

"I . . . don't know." The words came out in a squeak.

"But you know a gringo cop, don't you, Angelina? A gringo and a Mexican cop, asking questions about us—don't you?" His grip on her arm forced a small cry from her lips. "Here," he said. "Is this your machine? Sit down. We want to ask you about the gringo and his partner. What did you tell them—you and your brother? We want some answers."

She remembered the policemen: the tall gringo with the tough but somehow gentle face and eyes. He had been kind,

polite. He had put her fears to rest. She had been flattered to be
questioned by him. The Mexican officer, the *sargento*, was not
bad either, but she had sensed in him a ruthless determination,
a piercing ability to ferret out the truth by any means. She was
glad he had not questioned her again, though Hector had told
her afterward he had made no threats. She remembered, too,
what Hector had said he told him: about seeing Hidalgo's name
on the van registration, and the Poste Quemado ranch. Then
how had these men gotten away? What were they doing here?
And worse—what would they do to her?

Hidalgo's stinging slap across her face reminded her that he
was the one asking the questions. "Answer me, *puta*, what did
you tell the cops about us? You and your whoreson of a
brother!" She was sitting at the sewing machine now, and Hidalgo had moved around to stand behind her, his raw onion
breath just over her right ear. "What did you tell them?"

"Nothing . . . I . . . have not seen them."

His thick fingers knotted in the braid of her hair, yanking her
head back, the pain shooting down her neck and forcing a
shriek from her lips as she found herself staring up at the tangle
of light cords and dusty crossbeams and cobwebs that formed
the high ceiling. Hidalgo's voice again: "We know that's a lie,
you whoring bitch! You think we are fools? We have a source
here in San Ignacio. We know you talked to the gringo, you and
your brother!" Letting go of her hair, he reached around and
ripped open her blouse and bra, exposing her breasts. "What
did you tell the gringo?" he repeated. "Where is he now?"

Angelina stared in horror as one of the others leaned over
suddenly and held both her hands flat to the table while Hidalgo picked up a pair of pinking shears from beside the sewing
machine. Holding them in front of her face with one hand, he
used his other hand to pinch her left breast, forcing the nipple
to stand out straight and stiff. "Now," he whispered viciously,
"one of two things is going to happen in the next minute, you
puta bitch: either you are going to tell us what we want to know
about that fucking gringo cop, or you are going to get your
nipples snipped off with these shears, and your fingers stitched
together on this machine."

They left Ures in the last hour of darkness just before dawn,
getting up early and slipping out of the house before any of

Cruz's relatives were stirring. The early start had been Ragnon's idea; he didn't want to get bogged down with breakfast and long good-byes. He wanted to get over to the coast, to Puerto La Perla, and follow up their latest lead at the boatyard. Because his gut instincts told him that was where they might be headed, at least some of them if they had split up. And hopefully Hidalgo Valdez.

Jacinto Cruz was not so sure. He thought they at least ought to stop and check again in San Ignacio. Teniente Calderón and his troops had returned to Ures late at night behind them and reported finding nothing more at the ranch, though they had even torn out parts of the walls and ceilings. But they would return today for a daylight search, and then leave half a dozen soldiers on guard and encamped on a hill behind the ranch house in case the fugitives returned.

"What's that up ahead?" Ragnon asked, spitting out his side of the jeep into the chilly darkness as he studied the architectural mass that loomed against the star-strewn sky.

"An eighteenth-century Spanish church," Cruz said. "A ruin now."

The dark abandoned structure, its twin bell towers still standing stark and tall and silent, seemed somehow menacing as the road they were following made a long looping curve in front of it. Across the road a small village was surrounded by fields of beans and corn and already showed a pinpoint of light here and there from the kerosene lanterns of early risers.

As Cruz slowed the jeep going into the turn, its lights picked out an old red truck parked on the opposite side of the road and pointing back toward Ures. The truck's hood was up, the radiator was steaming, and two men were bent over the fender in the darkness. "Pull over," Ragnon said. "Let's see if they need some help."

"I thought we were in a hurry," Cruz said, braking.

"Humor me, I'm a Good Samaritan. I've been stranded myself."

Cruz pulled up on the shoulder across the road from the truck and in front of the church, but didn't shut off his engine. He talked above it, shouting to the two men still bent over their truck. When they answered, he turned back to Ragnon. "They say the radiator hose is leaking; they've lost their water. They're trying to make it to Ures."

"Shut this thing off and let's see what we can do," Ragnon said, swinging out of the jeep and feeling around behind the seat for the toolbox and a flashlight.

It didn't take long to find the leak. With a roll of black tape from the toolbox, Ragnon began binding the hole in the hose and told Cruz to see if the two men could find a container and bring some water from the village. "Then if they leave off the radiator cap, so there's no pressure, the tape should hold till they get to Ures."

As the two men returned, carrying three plastic jugs full of water, dawn was beginning to etch the eastern sky. When two more men suddenly materialized out of the shadows of the abandoned church and came across the road toward them, a tense uneasiness gripped Ragnon—four men?

One of them was still belting up his pants as Ragnon caught Cruz's look, which reflected his own. Canting his flashlight just a little so as to bring the face of the man who was filling the radiator into the glow, he heard the other one say, "Lift the damn jug higher, Arturo."

The one filling the radiator had shaved off his beard, but the face was the same, and Ragnon knew he could now pen Arturo Acosta beneath the third picture on their poster. The man helping him was younger—a long narrow face with a hook nose, and growing a scraggly beard—the only one of the four they still had no name for. Jesus, he thought. He didn't even have to guess who the other two were now as they came up behind the truck. His heartbeat nearly doubled as he moved closer to Cruz and whispered tightly, "Goddamn, man, it's them! All four of 'em! The other two must have been taking a crap behind the church or something. You got your pistola ready?"

"Ay, no, Tomás, it's in the jeep." Cruz's voice was husky and dry with his own tension. "I thought if I was going to work on the truck I didn't want the weight of the gun. I left it on the open lid of the dash compartment."

"Jesus H. Christ." But it was more of a prayer than a curse. "Then let's just ease on back across the road real careful like."

"I think it's too late," Cruz whispered as the daylight seemed to grow with alarming speed around them. "I think the one with the water jug suspects who we are—what do you think?"

"I think we're in deep shit, partner," Tom Ragnon said.

TWENTY-THREE

Wednesday, March 17, 6:10 A.M.

In the quiet village across the road from the church, a cock's crowing greeted the quickly spreading dawn. Tom Ragnon couldn't help wondering if it would be their last. Almost unconsciously he edged closer to Cruz and away from Arturo Acosta, who was emptying the last trickle of water from the third jug into the radiator. The younger one was still standing beside him, watching, and neither of them seemed overly suspicious to Ragnon. But the other two had moved up beside them now, and the detective's eyes met those of Hidalgo Valdez. The sonofabitch wasn't smiling.

"Don't you have an extra piece in your sock or someplace?" Ragnon whispered to his partner, regretting now that he hadn't chanced smuggling one into Mexico himself.

"No," Cruz whispered. "I never needed one."

Arturo slammed down the hood of the truck and tossed the plastic jug into the back as Ragnon whispered back, "You do now."

"I have a knife in my boot."

"Terrific—one down and what do we do with the other three, dance with them?"

But there was no time for further discussion as Hidalgo Valdez stepped to the open truck door on the far side, and Ragnon's blood froze as the fugitive pulled a sawed-off shotgun from behind the seat and braced it across the hood so that the barrel covered them both. He was smiling now, only not with his eyes.

Tom Ragnon had stared down a gun barrel at close range only a couple of times in his whole police career, and never a shotgun. It tended to melt his heart right down into his socks.

"Jesucristo," he heard Cruz whisper.

Hidalgo's smile was cruel, the smile of a man who would stuff a kid into a freezer and slam the lid. "You're cops," he told

Cruz in Spanish, shifting the barrel of the shotgun slightly, his finger curling a hair more tightly around the trigger.

"Cops—us?" Cruz feigned that even the thought was ridiculous. "You must be joking. What makes you think that?"

"What are you doing here with the gringo?" Hidalgo persisted suspiciously.

"Taking him to Puerto La Perla," Cruz improvised quickly with a partial truth, "for some fishing. He wants to rent a boat. Hey, what do you guys want, eh? We stop to help you and now you're going to rob us?"

It was full light now and here they were, Ragnon thought, all fucking four of them. He'd never dreamed of really catching them all still together. But instead of splitting up they had simply exchanged their blue van for a red truck, and one had shaved while another was growing a beard. ". . . your wallets and then your clothes," Hidalgo was saying in Spanish, and he was no longer smiling, even with his mouth. "Ju, too, gringo," he added in English. "Now!"

Cruz had eased out his wallet and tossed it onto the hood of the truck, and Ragnon did the same, knowing Cruz was thinking the same thing he was: as soon as they opened the wallets and found their police ID and shields . . .

But Arturo only grabbed the wallets and tossed them through the open window into the cab. "Now your clothes," Hidalgo ordered, "quickly, *cabrones,* take them off."

"Look, hombre, be reasonable—" Cruz started, but Hidalgo had moved around to the front of the truck, and his shotgun was leveled on the Mexican detective's belly. Cruz looked at Ragnon. "He means it—strip."

Ragnon shed his sheepskin vest and flannel shirt and saw Cruz covertly unfasten his empty shoulder holster and work it off unseen with his black leather jacket. His shirt and boots followed, and the fourth fugitive, who looked to be the youngest, began grabbing their clothes and tossing them into the back of the truck.

Ragnon didn't much like the thought that was rubbing against the back of his mind: that Hidalgo probably didn't want to get the clothes bloody when he triggered the shotgun. Then the bandit ordered Arturo and the younger one to cross the road and search the jeep.

Ragnon's eyes met Cruz's as the one they knew was Xavier

pitched their boots into the back of the truck, and they dropped their pants almost simultaneously. Fortunately the jeep had no markings, but its registration slip would be in the name of the San Ignacio Municipal Police, and the .45 was on the dash box lid, and a copy of the goddamned wanted poster was in it.

"I folded the poster between the seats," Cruz whispered as if reading his mind. He was bending low, as if entangled in his pants. "But they'll find the gun and registration."

"Callate!" Hidalgo ordered viciously. "No talking—and get out of your underwear too—everything!"

"Ayee!" Arturo shouted from across the road, where he was holding up the gun gleefully.

"So, you are armed." Hidalgo announced the discovery like a priest who had caught them in a mortal sin.

"Protection," Cruz mumbled lamely, tossing his green boxer shorts on the ground.

The fourth fugitive was rummaging in the back of the jeep and came up with a pair of binoculars. But even as he waved them, Hidalgo called to him, "Hurry up, burro, it's getting late, there will be people on the road. Bring the keys to the jeep!"

When Arturo and the other one had rejoined them, Arturo handed Hidalgo the keys. "Why not steal the jeep too?" he asked.

"Too risky," Hidalgo answered. He was tossing the keys in one hand and still holding the shotgun with the other. It would be so easy to kill these fools, he thought, but it was already daylight and the nearby village was stirring, so he decided against it. Instead, he suddenly hurled the keys behind him, sending them arching out into the greasewood desert. Then he looked with contempt at the two men standing naked and helpless before him, savoring the knowledge that their shivering was not simply from the cool dawn wind.

Stepping up to Ragnon, he jammed the shotgun barrel hard under his jaw, forcing his head back and lifting him up on his toes. "Beg, gringo," he growled in English. "Beg for jur life."

Tom Ragnon swallowed and held his breath, contempt in his own eyes but raw fear in his guts. In spite of the chill in the air around him, he felt the sweat starting to trickle down his sides and drip off his brows, burning into his eyes. But he clenched his jaw in stoic silence and decided he wasn't going to die like this, no way. He was about to make a final, desperate, and probably fatal move, when Hidalgo suddenly moved first, knee-ing him viciously in the groin.

Pain flooded over him, and as Hidalgo pulled the supporting shotgun barrel from beneath his jaw, he sank in childish weakness, moaning and doubling over on his knees in the road.

"You!" Hidalgo shifted his shotgun to Cruz now, shoving it against the lawman's hard, brown belly. "If you should happen to report this to the police, and you will, be sure to tell them a gringo cop in a black Ford Falcon is hunting me, too, and that I'm going to kill him—you understand, *cabrón?*"

Jacinto Cruz nodded, his eyes fixed on the eyes of the bandit, knowing now they were going to survive. He had known it when Hidalgo tossed away the keys so they could not follow him in the jeep. He was going to insult them, beat them, humiliate them; but the whoreson did not yet know they were cops, so he would let them survive, this time.

Their eyes still locked, Hidalgo asked him, "What is your name, *cabrón?*"

"Cruz. Jacinto Cruz."

"You have a look about you, Jacinto Cruz—I bet you were going to rob the gringo yourself, eh? But I beat you to it and robbed you too." His throaty laugh was not pleasant.

Watching the four of them climb in their truck and pull away, still laughing, Cruz memorized the license number, then muttered after them, "May your balls all roast in hell, and your transmission fall out." Then he bent over Ragnon, helping him to his feet. "Can you make it, Tomás?"

"Got to," the detective gasped, fighting the nausea and weakness that still swept over him in waves. "We've got to get that jeep started, and get out of here. When they open those wallets and see our police ID, they'll come back and spread us all over Sonora with that fucking shotgun."

"Then wait here, compadre—rest, while I hot-wire the jeep."

But as Ragnon struggled to straighten and gather himself, the sun topped the horizon and the long coppery rays stretching out across the desert glinted sharply off the jeep's ignition keys, which were dangling from a creosote bush not twenty yards away. Retrieving them, he crossed the road slowly to where Cruz was busy under the dash of the jeep. "Here," he said, pushing the cold metal against the Mexican's bare back, "try these."

Cruz raised up and stared at Ragnon, who was shivering again. *"Híjole,* hombre, you found the keys? Hey, Tomás, you're shaking—are you still cold?"

"Shit no, man, I'm still scared." He was grinning with relief. "I never had a sawed-off shotgun shoved in my face before."

But Cruz had pulled a folded blanket out of the back of the jeep, and holding a corner with his foot against the ground, he tore it in two. "Look," he said, handing half to Ragnon and pointing over toward the village where several campesinos had come out of their shacks to stare at them, two women and several children among them. "Let's put these around us before we shock somebody's grandmother, eh, and then we'll go."

Ragnon, draping the blanket scrap around his shoulders, eased himself into the jeep, letting Cruz get behind the wheel. He had just realized what a spectacle they must make: their lean-muscled bodies nakedly alike except for fleshtones. Cruz was brown all over, while Ragnon's bare hide was fish-belly white except for the contrasting tan of his face and neck and hands.

"I told you before," Cruz was saying, starting the engine and easing the jeep back on the road toward San Ignacio, "it's all a matter of luck. Bad luck this time that we lost them—but good luck, too, that we're still around to hunt again, no?"

Tom Ragnon, reaching behind the seat to assure himself that at least the bag containing the mismatched sneakers was still there, stared back down the road in the direction of Ures. But there was no sign of the bandits coming back. "Fucking bastards," he cursed them, "they got away with my last pouch of Redman."

TWENTY-FOUR

Wednesday, March 17, 8:20 A.M.

"How do huevos rancheros with tortillas and hot black coffee sound for breakfast?" Cruz asked as he parked Ragnon's car in the front yard of his modest adobe home.

"Like manna from heaven," the American detective answered. "I think my hands have finally stopped trembling, so maybe I could hold a cup." Arriving back in San Ignacio before eight o'clock, they had pulled the jeep in behind the police building, alongside Ragnon's car, dug fresh clothes out of the seabag and suitcase still stowed in the back, and changed there.

"My wife, she has no English," Cruz said, "but you will get along." As they stepped into the living room, the Mexican lawman was greeted joyously by four stair-step kids aged five to eleven. The older ones were girls, with their long black hair in pigtails, while the two boys were smaller copies of their father. All four were neatly dressed and courteous to a stranger, but their initial shyness wore off quickly, giving way to boisterous good humor as their mother came in and hurried them off to school.

Lupita Cruz was obviously proud of her children and her husband. "So you are the American detective," she said in Spanish. "Welcome to our home. Jacinto has spoken well of you."

"Mil gracias, Señora," Ragnon answered. "I can speak well of him too." She was pretty, long-legged, and wide-hipped, like he'd heard most Mexicans liked their women.

"Quickly, woman," Cruz interrupted them, "enough of your compliments. See if you can find us something to eat. We are hungry as wolves who have hunted all night."

"And did you catch anyone, *querido?*"

"No," Cruz glanced at Ragnon, "but we came close. Now hurry and fix us some breakfast."

They watched her disappear into the kitchen, and then Cruz asked Ragnon to sit down. The living room was sparsely furnished, but clean and bright, like the children. A colorful Mexican blanket was draped over the back of the couch, a votive candle burned beneath an icon in one corner, and a large print of *The Last Supper* was centered on the main wall. Ragnon had heard they sold a rat poison in Mexico City by the same name and he wondered if it was true. Sometime he'd have to ask Cruz, but right now he told him, "You've got quite a little family, my friend."

"And this is only half, remember." The Mexican was standing by a window, lighting one of his cigarillos. "I have a mistress and two more kids across town." He turned, sucking the smoke in deep and releasing it slowly. "But you know, compadre, for a couple of minutes back on that road, I didn't think I was ever going to see any of them again." He tossed the match in an ashtray. "Still, it was my own fault, *verdad?* I never should have separated myself from my gun."

"It was nobody's fault, or you could as well blame me for stopping to help them." He shook his head, still marveling at their narrow escape. "Jesus, Jacinto, it *was* close." He found himself staring at a picture hanging by the door, a picture he had known as a child in his grandmother's farmhouse in Missouri: an American Indian on a horse, his head and the horse's and the point of his spear all hanging down dejectedly. He thought it was called *The End of the Trail.* He hoped it wasn't some kind of omen.

"You know, Tomás," Cruz was saying, "I think we have underestimated this Hidalgo Valdez. He does the unexpected, he is unpredictable, the worse kind of fugitive. Why hasn't he run?"

"That's what I've been asking myself, partner. Why are they all sticking together? Just to chase us? Or are they planning something else? Because it sure as hell ain't brotherly love." He had turned and was staring at Cruz. "He's not afraid of us, Jacinto. Maybe it's as simple as that. Which reminds me, you're going to have to get yourself another gun. Any chance of getting me one too—unofficially?"

The Mexican studied him a moment. "Yes, Tomás, after what happened today, I think you are right. Wait here."

Disappearing into a back room, he returned in minutes with a worn leather gunbelt filled with greenish brass cartridges and supporting a holstered revolver. He handed it all to the American. "How's this? It's old, but it still shoots."

Tom Ragnon pulled the weapon from the holster, a heavy Colt .44 Peacemaker that must have been manufactured at least ninety years earlier. "Shit, man, it's beautiful." He sighted down the barrel at the Indian on the horse. "But will it shoot *straight?"*

"*Quien sabe?* It did for my grandfather in the Revolution." He smiled. "At least it will still make a big noise. I've got some gun oil you can clean it up with after we eat. Meanwhile I'll go call the comandante, then we'll have to return to his office and give him a full report."

In the comandante's office an hour later, Maximiliano Hernández was scowling up at the map of Sonora behind his desk as they walked in. His scowl deepened when he looked around at Cruz and the American. "So now your fugitives are wanted for a felony in Mexico," he said, clipping the tip from a cigar and striking a match on his desktop as he glanced at the notes he had made during Cruz's call. "You say, Sargento, that they took your gun and both your ID's, and a pair of binoculars from the jeep?"

"And our clothes, Comandante," Cruz added stiffly. "We were lucky they didn't take our lives."

"Huh," he grunted, shaking out the match and puffing to get a glow on the cigar. "Then we can arrest them for this now, *verdad?*" He looked at Ragnon. "When we find them."

"I'd prefer you didn't," Ragnon said carefully. "I don't want them taken on some half-baked gun charge and tried here in Mexico. I want them extradited for murder. Understand, Comandante?"

For an instant there was more than anger in Maximiliano's eyes; it was a look of hard, feral cruelty so obvious it was scary. "That might never happen, Sergeant Ragnon," he said softly, and then the eyes softened just a hair. "Better something . . ." He shrugged and sat down behind a cloud from his own cigar.

You blood-sucking leech, Ragnon thought, his own surge of anger whitening the knuckles of his clenched fists as he leaned forward on the desk. He was about to let it all out when Jacinto Cruz interrupted. "Let us do it our way, Comandante," he said just as softly, "por favor."

"It will cost more," Max said, avoiding either of their eyes now.

"We will get more—right, Tomás?"

Tom Ragnon shook his head disgustedly. "Christ, Jacinto, sometimes I wonder whose side you're on."

"You say they were headed for Ures?" The comandante was up and looking around at the map again, still drawing heavily on his cigar. "I have notified the police there, but once these fugitives find your ID's in your wallets, I doubt if they'll go back to that rancho."

"Teniente Calderón has left six soldiers posted in case they do, Comandante," Cruz said. "What about the license number on the red truck?"

"I have ordered it checked, but the truck was probably stolen, or at least the plates."

"The van was in Hidalgo's name," Cruz reminded him, "maybe the truck is too, or in one of the others."

Comandante Hernández shrugged, and reaching into a drawer, he pulled out a holstered Colt .45 and two extra clips, fully loaded. "You can sign for a new gun, Sargento Cruz," he said. "Your own department will have to issue a new ID, but I can make up an official letter that will do temporarily, and include Ragnon's name. And the binoculars will have to be charged against you too." He looked at the American and asked, "You *are* certain it was them—the men on your poster?"

"It was them, Comandante. I'm going back to Pantana and get warrants for the three we have names for, and one John Doe. Maybe you'd better notify the Hermosillo police again, in case they decide to head there now."

"They won't," Jacinto Cruz said. He had removed his Levi jacket and was strapping on the new shoulder holster. "They are out for blood now—ours." He walked over to a tall metal cabinet, opened it, and took out a lever-action Winchester rifle in a stiff leather scabbard. "We'll check this out too," he told the comandante. "It will better the odds against their sawed-off shotgun."

"There is the matter of more money," Hernández said casually, looking at Ragnon while Cruz signed receipts for the guns and a box of shells. "Five hundred more."

"Agreed," Ragnon answered, sighing heavily. "If we can still have the use of the jeep."

Outside, in back of the station again, Cruz was mounting the rifle in its scabbard on the driver's side of the jeep when he nodded toward Ragnon's Falcon, which was still parked alongside. "We've got company, Tomás."

Ragnon looked around to find Angelina Zamora standing hesitantly beside his car. She looked like a frightened deer about to bolt, her long hair unbraided and disheveled now; and she seemed shrunken somehow, and terrified, but determined. When he stepped around the car and moved toward her, he could see her face was swollen and purplish and both eyes were blackened. "Angelina, what happened?"

She took a step backward as he approached, as if he were a

threat too. "I shouldn't be here," she whispered, glancing fearfully around. "But they came back."

"Who, Hidalgo?"

She nodded. "All four of them. They knew you had talked to me. They said they had a source here in San Ignacio." Ragnon threw a look at Cruz as she continued. "They threatened terrible things if I didn't tell them what was said . . . so they know what my brother told Sergeant Cruz about seeing the Poste Quemado Ranch on the van registration. I didn't tell them that I saw them with their guns that night or they would have killed me. But you see why I cannot testify at any trial."

"When was this, yesterday?"

"Yes, last night, about midnight. My brother doesn't know I'm here, but I had to tell you—they plan to kill you both."

Ragnon reached out to take her hand, but she withdrew. "Let me take you home, Angelina," he said, sick with outrage.

She shook her head. "I can't be seen with you again, but I had to warn you. You were kind—" She turned away.

Just before she disappeared around the corner of the building, Ragnon called to her, "Angelina, please—"

Cruz caught his arm. "Let her go, Tomás."

Ragnon stared at his partner, helpless in his anger. "We've got to get those animals, Jacinto. She said they've got a source right here in San Ignacio—who, Comandante Max?"

"Probably. I told you I didn't trust him. Or maybe it's one of his policemen." Cruz took his arm again, gently this time. "By now they've found our ID's, Tomás. It's become a personal thing between them and us, especially you. I think it best if you go back to Pantana and stay there. I'll give the comandante his five hundred, just to appease him. It's all luck, Tomás, remember? And our luck has been running mostly bad on this one. I think it will get worse. Better let me handle it alone from here on in."

"Alone?" Ragnon turned on him. "You work it now alone? You must be nuts, man. I'm going back to Pantana all right, but only to get the warrants and start setting up extradition proceedings for when they're caught. You go get drunk if you want, but stay out of trouble till I get back. Then we'll take them— we'll take them together."

Jacinto Cruz looked closely at his partner, at this American detective who was more than a partner now; who had become a friend. "This one will not be caught, Tomás," he said slowly. "You understand? Believe me—he will be killed, but he will not be caught."

PART III
Death Raid

TWENTY-FIVE

Wednesday, March 17, 5 P.M.

In a small pulquería at the edge of the plaza in Ures, the four of them sat at a corner table drinking. Hidalgo Valdez was still fuming. The two cops had been using a jeep instead of the black Ford Falcon he had been told about by his informant in San Ignacio. That is what had thrown him off. He had paid good money and had not been told about them changing cars!

He was staring at the pictures on the two ID cards lying on the table in front of him. Taking another drink of pulque, he picked up the American's card and angled it to the light from the bar. That he had actually had the fucking gringo at the end of his shotgun and let him go! That they had tricked him, that he had their wallets and money and clothes, but not them.

"You are sure they recognized us?" Miguel asked, pinching the butt of his cigarette as he drew a last deep lungful of smoke.

"They knew it was us." Hidalgo slapped Ragnon's ID down beside the one that pictured the Mexican police agent. "Especially this Cruz—he knew." He picked up the American's badge, spat on it, and rubbed it on his sleeve until it shone.

As soon as they had opened the two wallets, and before they had even counted the money, they had found the ID cards and shields. Enraged, Hidalgo had turned the truck around and raced back to the abandoned church, but the jeep was gone. The two cops were gone. And his radiator was steaming again, so he knew he'd never catch them before they got back to San Ignacio. Limping back to Ures, they had spent the day finding a new radiator hose and fixing the clutch on the pickup, which had started to slip.

Across the table Xavier was chuckling over his pulque; something funny Hidalgo seemed to have missed. The others were laughing, too, but their humor only irritated him. "Why do you laugh, burros?" he hissed. "You think it is all one big joke?"

"A joke on the police, yes," Xavier answered. Behind them a jukebox was belting out a corrido, a folk ballad about a border bandit and his hopeless love. "Don't you see it, compadre?" Xavier had to raise his voice above the noise. "Naked—we left

two cops stripped bare on the road—it is *un gran chiste,* no?"
He elbowed Arturo beside him, who laughed even harder.

Even Hidalgo's stony features cracked a little then, and soon
all four were laughing boisterously, drowning out even the shrill
music of the corrido as Hidalgo allowed himself to ease just a
little the tension and hatred that had been building. Scooping
up a handful of the policemen's money, he held it aloft.
"Drinks!" he shouted. "Pulque for everybody! It's on the police!"

But his brief jovial demeanor soured quickly, and his moodi-
ness returned. "They had the *last* joke, compadres," he said
bitterly. "They lived. I had the gringo by the throat. I looked
into his fucking eyes and let him live!" He stared at the remaining bills they had taken from the wallets. All of it was gratify-
ing, but that the *chingados* had actually escaped him fired his
hatred anew and made his determination even stronger.

After finding the ID's in the wallets, they had gone through
all the clothes more thoroughly, finding the shoulder holster for
the .45, which Hidalgo now wore along with the gringo's sheepskin vest. There had been a knife, too, in one of the boots, with
a six-inch blade honed to keenness, and he stared at the ID of
the Mexican police agent again. He thought the knife was probably his—Jacinto Cruz, Sargento. He should have known the
pinche cabrón was a cop; he had that look in his eyes, the eyes
of a hunter.

And the gringo—Thomas R. Ragnon, Sergeant. He sat staring at the two ID's and barely restrained himself from crumpling them in his fists.

"So what do we do now?" Xavier wanted to know, recogniz-
ing the quick reversal of Hidalgo's mood. "That girl, Angelina,
told us they know about the ranch. And they were coming from
this direction. If they found the guns and turned them over to
the police here in Ures—"

"Maybe we should not be so free in spending the policemen's
money," Miguel suggested cautiously, glancing furtively around
as the corrido ended and another began about the *Rinches de
Tejas.*

But Hidalgo Valdez ignored him, scratching a match with his
thumbnail and cupping the flame to a fresh cigar. "We must go
back to the ranch and see if they found the weapons," he said,
shaking out the match and tossing it on the floor.

"If they have been there," Arturo offered, "it won't be safe to go back. The local cops might be watching it."

"We must know if they found the guns," Hidalgo insisted. "We must see for ourselves."

"We can always steal more guns," Xavier suggested quietly.

But Hidalgo Valdez was adamant. The new song playing on the jukebox was not very flattering to the Texas Rangers. He poured more pulque all around and then raised his glass decisively. "Drink up, compadres. We return to the rancho—now." Putting the ID's back in the wallets, he stuffed them along with the rest of the money into his vest pockets. "We did not gather a store of arms so some gringo cop can steal them from us. No, compadres." He rose and lifted his glass again. "A toast—to my great-grandfather who rode with the Villistas and who spat on the gringos as I spit on them now," and he spewed a great gob across the floor. "And who will ride again," he whispered almost inaudibly, "in me." And he drained his glass.

"What are you thinking of?" Arturo asked, a little awed by his performance.

"I am not sure." Hidalgo wiped his mouth on the back of his hand. "It is as yet but a spark at the back of my mind. But we will need more men, and we will need the guns. Because I am thinking of a town that would pay to send a gringo cop after us in our own land." He glared around at them all. "I will have to give it more thought, but it is bigger than a single gringo now, compadres. Him we will get, and more. For now it will be enough to get back the weapons, so drink up. If we leave immediately, we can be back at the rancho by dark."

It was dusk by the time they parked the red truck a mile down the rutted road from the rancho and walked the rest of the way to the old walled hacienda. Lying among the boulders and brush, they studied the main house through the binoculars they had taken from the jeep. No lights, and nothing moved. The place seemed deserted.

But as the darkness grew deeper, Xavier spotted a faint glow against the sky just at the top of the hill behind the house. "I think the place is being watched," he said.

"Perhaps." Hidalgo shifted his weight on the boulder, settling more comfortably. "Let's find out."

He sent Arturo around one side to scout the hill, and Miguel the other way to approach the house from the rear and see if it was really empty, and if the guns were still there. Twenty minutes later Arturo returned to report half a dozen soldiers camped around a fire among some trees on the hill. They were drinking heavily, and the one posted at the edge of the hill to watch the house was already dozing. Five minutes after that Miguel came scurrying back to the rocks at a crouch and told them the house was empty and the guns still concealed in the thatched roof of the ramada.

"So they are safe," Xavier said. "Leave them and let's go."

"No." Hidalgo stood up, staring at the house. "They must be moved. They could still be found in a more thorough search. We must slip them out and carry them back to the truck."

"And then what?" Xavier asked. "Where can we hide them?"

Hidalgo thought a moment. "On the coast. Your brother-in-law's. He's our contact, anyway, and we can hide them in the hold of one of his shrimp boats."

"Maybe, but then what?"

"Then we will take care of the two cops—we know their faces now. Everything else must wait until they are dead."

The next night in Hermosillo, Raul Galindez got a call from Teniente Chato Gomez. "Hidalgo Valdez returned to the ranch and got his weapons."

"I thought they left soldiers on guard."

"They got drunk or fell asleep or both. It happened last night. This morning they found the thatch torn away and the footprints of four men leading to tire tracks on the road a mile away."

There was silence on the line a moment, and then Galindez asked, "Where would he take them?"

"I don't know, *Jefe*. I'm trying to find out."

"Don't let this get out of hand, Chato. Perhaps I let it go too far—this fool could be trouble for everybody."

Chato knew better than to remind his boss he had wanted to eliminate them right from the first. Instead he said, "I think we should stop them now, *Jefe*. We've got enough on our plate. That shipment of radioactive rods is being traced back to our foundry. Soon the Federales will be sniffing around the junkyard, too, and maybe other places. Remember, there's the warehouse full of marijuana, and that hundred hectares of opium poppies under cultivation only twenty miles south of Cananea. One thing leads to another, and we can't pay everybody off, cover up everything."

But Galindez persisted. "What about the gringo cop?"

"He's gone back across the border."

"Giving up?"

"No, evidently bringing more reward money. I told you he is determined too. Why don't I arrange a simple accident on his return, and include Cruz too?"

"No." Galindez just wouldn't let it go. Chato could almost see the sly smile working across the face at the other end of the line. "I think I'd rather dump Hidalgo in their laps first. Then kill them all."

TWENTY-SIX

Friday, March 19, 8:05 A.M.

When Tom Ragnon and John Antone walked into Sidney Clayton Poole's inner sanctum, and the detective laid the clear plastic evidence bag containing a pair of mismatched sneakers on his desk, the chief of homicide looked up in obvious astonishment. "You found him? You found the gut-eating sonofabitch with two shoes?"

"Found all four of 'em, Chief," Ragnon said, spitting into the plastic lined wastebasket beside Poole's desk. "And lost 'em." Then he told Poole what had happened on the road from Ures.

The chief was incredulous, and for once, speechless. He rose, his jaw clamped tightly around a freshly lit and glowing cigar. When he finally spoke, his words were like nails. "The fucking greasers got your shield and ID, and Cruz's goddamned gun? They left you bare-assed naked on the fucking road like a couple of yay-hoos?"

"At least they didn't waste us, Chief," Ragnon said, glancing at Antone, whose expression gave away none of his amusement at the exchange. "Isn't that a point for our side?"

"Shit!" Poole fumed, very unwalruslike.

"You always did have a way with words, Chief." Ragnon

spat again into the wastebasket and settled himself comfortably on the black vinyl couch, motioning the Indian deputy to take a chair, since it looked like they were going to be here awhile and the chief wasn't known for his politeness.

He had returned to his trailer in Pantana late Wednesday night, after drinking heavily with Jacinto. But that had solved nothing. And exhausted with what he was facing in Mexico, he had awakened Thursday morning with a sour stomach and sore head, and simply crashed the rest of the day. By evening he still couldn't get it all together, but since there was no way around it short of suicide, he finally contacted Antone and had him arrange a meet for this morning with Old Ironballs. He was determined to get through it.

"We've got names now to go with the pictures of three of them," he continued, gritting his teeth. "We've got evidence linked with witnesses who can establish their proximity to the border at the time of the crime." He didn't mention the probability that neither Angelina nor her brother could really be expected to testify. "We've got their tracks and some matching prints and the shoes. We want warrants issued, including a John Doe for number four. And you might as well advise the powers-that-be to start untangling extradition procedures."

"But you haven't caught them, any of them," Poole pointed out unkindly. "You haven't even found any more of the stolen goods."

"We're working on it, Chief. And Antone got a description of the stolen weapons and their serial numbers from the insurance company."

"I'd like permission to go back to Sonora with the sergeant," Chief," Antone said. "With three of us—"

"No, goddammit—no way!" Poole had removed his cigar and was shaking his head vigorously. "I don't even want *you* going back, Rags. I'll get the warrants and see what the attorney general wants to do about extradition once they're in custody, so the case becomes official, but you've done enough jerking off down there. Let the pepper-bellies handle it from here. Let 'em earn their fucking reward money. How much have you given them?"

"Not enough. They want more. And Jacinto Cruz has earned his share. I've got to deliver it." He spat again, the tension mounting. He had never learned to live with rejection, and he could see it coming.

"The hell you've got to deliver it," Poole snapped. "You'll need my approval, Rags, and you haven't got it."

"I'm still on vacation, Chief."

"It's cancelled."

"I'll go over your head." Ragnon was reaching now, desperate.

"You sonofabitch!"

Ragnon grinned wickedly and spat. "Think how it'll look upstairs, political wise, with reward money provided at no cost to our budget and an ex-state senator's son's murderers almost caught, and my chief yanks me off the case when I'm working on my own time."

"Okay, smartass," Poole relented sourly, "but your vacation time runs out Sunday, so you've got till then to piss around in Mañanaland, then back to reality. Cases here are piling up too. And no, Antone—I sure as hell don't have to lose both of you!"

Ragnon looked at the deputy. "Sorry, John, but Jacinto and I can handle it down there. And I still need you to check out some things on this end."

"We're not really as close as I let on," Ragnon told the Indian deputy later over a brunch of beers and tacos. "We're only half sure of this third man's name, Arturo Acosta, or of his connection with the boatyard in La Perla. There may be none, but it's the only new lead we've found, and we're going to follow it over to the coast."

"You can be sure, Sergeant," Antone said, "at least of the name." And reaching for his notebook he thumbed through several pages. "Full name, Arturo Acosta Beltrán. He's been in the States before too. Worked as a powder monkey in a mine, and get this—on a construction crew two years ago, building a new electric power line north of Pantana." He looked up. "So they knew the area."

"Jesus, where'd you get all this?"

"His employment record. That FBI single-print computer check turned him from the index finger on the TV screen fragment in McNeal's truck. Seems when he worked for the construction crew he got in a fight and tried to open his foreman's head with a shovel. No charges, but they had him picked up by the Border Patrol, who fingerprinted him before tossing him back to Mexico."

Tom Ragnon laughed nervously, and Antone studied the detective's face. "That must have been hairy, man," he said, "when you had them altogether there on that road and a shotgun to your head."

"It was hairy as hell, John. I was scared shitless, even wondering what Angie would put on my tombstone."

"You better take a gun back with you this time. Better a broken Mexican law than your body shipped back C.O.D. And speaking of Angie, she called me a couple of days ago, said she wants to see you next time you're on this side." He was consulting his notebook again while he wiped his mouth with a napkin. "And a Wanda Henderson called—the councilman's daughter. She said to ask you: 'How about seconds?' " He looked up and smiled, "Whatever that means."

Ragnon thought a moment about the night in the trailer with Wanda, then shrugged. "I think I better go look up my wife. Maybe we'd better start facing our problems, or make this separation permanent."

"Sounds like a good idea, Sergeant. Now what were those things you told Old Ironballs you wanted me to check on?"

"Nothing. Just wanted to keep you handy on this side, because I really didn't want you sent over there with me either, John. No offense; we could use the help, but no use both of us getting our butts ground into hamburger if this whole pile of shit goes down the toilet."

Angie was working, but Ragnon picked up his kids at the house on Old Father Road and spent the afternoon with them at the park. Watching them on the slides and swings, and scrimmaging with a football, he wondered momentarily if it was all really worth it—his job, the tension, the hassle, the often stupid risks, and the almost endless frustrations.

But maybe this was what it was all about, these kids. McNeal's kid had played on a tire swing in the front yard. The swing was still there, the kid wasn't. Catching Hidalgo Valdez and his playmates wouldn't put Tad McNeal back in his swing, but it might help keep other kids from joining him. He whistled shrilly, calling to his two kids: then caught them one by one and held them tight.

Back at the house he left them inside with the sitter and sat down on the front steps to wait for his wife. Her car was in the carport, so he assumed she was taking the bus, until a sleek silver Continental pulled up to the curb behind his old Falcon.

As Angie got out, waved to him, and then bent over to talk to the driver, Ragnon knew with a lurch of his heart that this must be her alley rat. He watched the Continental pull away with a sharp squeal of tires as his wife turned and came up the walk toward him. "Hi—you're back," she called. She even looked glad to see him.

"Not for long." He got up. "I have to go back tomorrow."

Her face seemed to lose a little of its glow. "Come on in then, I'll finish up supper. Rosa should have it started. Have you seen the kids?"

"Took 'em to the park all afternoon—we stopped for burgers and shakes, so I'm afraid they won't be hungry."

"No harm done. I'll just pop a TV dinner in the oven for myself and have Rosa's supper as leftovers tomorrow." They were inside and she had turned to face him. "Are you all right, Tom? You look terrible. How did it go in Mexico?"

"We're close, Angie. We've got three names; we've even seen all four of them."

"You were *that* close?" The kids ran in, whooping and laughing and talking at the same time as Angie wrote out the weekly check for the sitter. Then, with the kids off in their room playing, the sitter gone, and a frozen dinner in the oven, she asked him again, "You were actually close enough to see them, but you didn't make an arrest?" She was sitting across the kitchen table from him, lighting a cigarette with the lighter he got her for Christmas.

"Things got complicated. We lost them. We'll find them again." He couldn't help comparing her to the councilman's daughter, and strangely, to Angelina Zamora, as she got up and poured them each a mug of fresh coffee. "I missed you, Angie," he said simply.

"I missed you too." Her eyes were full of the same message, but the guilt was there too—tit for tat, he wondered as he remembered the silver Continental, and couldn't help putting the barb in. "Was that your alley rat—bringing you home by the front door now?"

She made a face over her coffee mug. "I've found out a lot

about my alley rat. He's like you in many ways, but he's not you. Nobody is you, Tom Ragnon."

"Does that mean our separation isn't working out?"

"You haven't really given it a chance, have you, Tom?"

"I guess not. And you haven't really minded."

"Not enough to stop you. So, what shall we call it—a Mexican standoff?" She smiled.

"I know I missed the lieutenant's exam again, but I wouldn't have taken it anyway."

"I know that." She poured him some more coffee from the silex. "I found out I don't really care how many exams you miss. I just wish you didn't have to go back to Mexico. It's so scary down there. They're wonderful, the people, but the officials—for all their facade of civilization, they're still a primitive, developing country. Their police are brutal—their torture techniques something right out of the Inquisition. And their so-called democracy—they've had one-party rule for fifty years! Their elections are a joke, a sham—"

"Angie, they're poor and proud and overpopulated, and still struggling against the grain just to survive. But they *are* survivors. They've survived the Spanish and French and their own revolution. They'll survive themselves. Above all else they make do, they improvise; they envy us and hate us and need us. And we need them."

"But why do they need *you* personally? Why can't you and John Antone work it from this side now and let this Jacinto Cruz handle things over there?"

"That's what Old Ironballs wants too," Ragnon said.

"But you can't, can you? You won't. You've got to do it yourself, don't you?" Only her smile softened the accusing tone in her voice.

"Jacinto wants to handle it himself too," Ragnon said. "He says they won't be taken alive—they'll have to be killed."

"Then for God's sake, Tom—" she bit her lip.

"You know what my father wanted me to be, Angie? An architect. He was a construction worker all his life, and he always admired the architects with their rolls of blueprints and drawings. It broke his heart when I became a cop. He thought all wines taste sweet, all bankers have soft hands, and all cops are on the take. That's how bad I wanted this, Angie—enough to break my father's heart." He reached across the table and took both her hands in his own. "You understand why I have to go back? Why I have to help Jacinto finish this? You understand?"

"No." Angie shook her long black hair. "No, Tom, I don't understand. But why don't you stay here tonight, and maybe you can explain it to me. We can put the kids to bed early."

"You're sure you want to?" He smiled. "I don't own a Continental."

"Oh, God, Tom—you make jokes about everything. Just stay? Please?"

"Okay, Angie. I'd like that."

But later, as they climbed the stairs, he kept remembering the cold steel of the shotgun barrel tucked under his chin, and the eyes of Hidalgo Valdez above it; and the fear—the deep, primal, animal fear—and he wondered if maybe all his flip humor wasn't just his way of hiding his basic fears and insecurity.

Because he knew that for the past forty-eight hours he was really just trying to screw up the courage to return to Mexico.

TWENTY-SEVEN

Saturday, March 20, 3 P.M.

"Another name has come up," Jacinto Cruz said, raising his voice above the noise of the raucous little combo and shrill vocalist in the corner.

"What . . . a name?" Tom Ragnon scooted his chair around the table to be closer to the Mexican detective. They were meeting again in the Cantina Linda in San Ignacio and Cruz was drinking tequila with lime and salt while Ragnon sipped a Dos Equis beer, all beneath an overlaying smoky haze of marijuana. The small live band was blasting out *La Paloma* like it was a fandango instead of a love song, but though they had to talk above the noise, it also covered their conversation.

"What?" Ragnon cupped his ear to catch the name.

"Galindez—Raul Galindez!" Cruz said.

"Our fourth man?"

The Mexican shook his head. "A crime boss here in Sonora. An informant in Hermosillo gave me his name."

"What's the connection?"

"My cousin Chato works for him on the side—Chato Gomez, the lieutenant. Hidalgo Valdez also worked for him up until a couple of weeks ago, about the time of the murders. Galindez seems interested in our case. Tracks every move we make through Chato."

"Terrific." Ragnon drained the last of his beer, wiping foam from his lips and waving away the girl who had appeared with another bottle. Instead, he dug out his new pouch of Redman and tucked a pinch in his cheek. That's all they needed, he thought, as if things weren't hairy enough chasing this bunch of pricks all over Sonora without a Mexican crime boss sticking his oar in. And he was tempted again just to get out, leave the damn thing now to Cruz. But he knew he couldn't let it go, not when they were this close, and not when Cruz might get snuffed trying to handle it alone. At least with the two of them . . .

"You are nervous again, Tomás," the Mexican observed, smiling. "You always chew when you get nervous."

"I don't like it, Jacinto—our asses are hanging out in a cold wind."

Cruz shrugged. "You're just scared again, Tomás. You remember the shotgun, and I don't blame you. You didn't have to come back—I admire you for that, but I told you I could handle it."

"Quit bullshitting me. You and who could handle it? Comandante Max? We're practically working this thing alone."

"We *are* working it alone, Tomás." The Mexican's face grew somber again.

Ragnon worked his tobacco around to his other cheek. "What do you mean?"

"There is something else." Reaching into his pocket he laid a plastic baggie containing two large silver coins on the table between them. "U.S. Peace dollars," the Mexican said. "It's too dark in here to see the dates, but they are the same—1928." He pushed the evidence across the table to Ragnon.

They were tagged with the date and place they were found, but it was too dark to read that either. Only the coins themselves glittered brightly as the detective hefted their weight in his hand. "Jesus, man, you found their cache?"

"No. I didn't want to tell you until I was sure, but you remember Wednesday in the comandante's office when we checked out the guns? I saw them in his drawer and became suspicious. I went back later and picked the lock with my knife. He's got eighteen more like these—all 1928, uncirculated. I just deducted these two for evidence, so as not to excite him. I think we are caught in the middle of this, Tomás. Comandante Max is feeding information to Hidalgo Valdez, and to Raul Galindez, too, through Chato. He's being selective, keeping the chase going."

"Holy shit, Jacinto, isn't anybody on *our* side in this case but us?"

"Apparently not." Cruz smiled philosophically. "In fact our luck is running so bad that I'm not even sure about you, Tomás."

"You've been watching too much American TV, partner," Ragnon cracked back.

"But there is more." Cruz grew serious again.

"I kind of figured there would be." Ragnon spat into an empty tomato can he'd brought along for the purpose. "What else—is the governor of Sonora against us too?"

But Cruz was through joking. "Comandante Max also tried to hide the trace of the plates on the red truck, but I got it anyway."

"And I suppose *they* belong to El Presidente."

"They are registered to one Xavier Moreno of Puerto La Perla."

Ragnon frowned. "Moreno, not Castillo—so not *our* Xavier of Xavier's Boatworks, as in the receipt found in the van."

"Could be just a coincidence."

"But you think not. Maybe an alias?"

Jacinto Cruz lit one of his slim brown cigarillos and jetted the smoke through his nostrils. He was silent, thinking. "Maybe, but something else is in the wind, Tomás." He glanced around uncertainly. "Something not connected with our case, but important."

Ragnon raised his brows, spat into his tomato can, and waited.

"You mentioned El Presidente, and you know the president-elect is touring Sonora—we saw them putting up the colored streamers in Magdalena."

Ragnon nodded, wondering what he was getting at. "He went over to Baja California. He's due back in Nogales tomorrow. So what?"

"So this, Tomás—I bought another lottery ticket at the hotel today and there were at least half a dozen strangers registered as tractor salesmen. There haven't been that many tractor salesmen gathered in one place in Sonora in my whole lifetime, so I nosed around."

"And . . ."

"They are mostly Federales, but two of them are Spanish-speaking American agents."

Incredible, Ragnon thought. He's not smiling. "CIA?" he asked. "Drug Enforcement? American agents of one kind or another have been keeping a low profile in Mexico for years."

Cruz shrugged. "I overheard two of them talking. They've traced some kind of contamination across the border to a metal foundry in Cananea, and they're looking for the junkyard the contaminated metal came from and where else it was shipped."

"What kind of contamination?"

Cruz shook his head. "I don't know, it's all being kept hushed up. But the president-elect makes his speech in Nogales at nine o'clock tomorrow night, and it's customary for him to make a surprise, unscheduled visit to some insignificant village in the middle of the night to show his support and concern for the common people."

"And you think he might have picked San Ignacio this time? But how should any of this concern us and the four we're after?"

"It shouldn't, Tomás. It doesn't. So why do I have that uneasy gut feeling that bothers you sometimes?"

"Believe me, partner, most of the time it's just indigestion. Hadn't we better be getting over to La Perla? It's still our best lead."

"Of course." He glanced around the bar. "You want a girl before we leave? Another beer? Either one or both, it's on me."

"No, thanks," Ragnon said. "Let's just get on over to the coast. You got my hog leg handy?"

"All rolled up in the cartridge belt and tucked under the seat of the jeep. I even got you fresh bullets. And we'd better drop some more cash at the comandante's."

"No. After what you told me, I'm not wasting another peso on Max, or your cousin either."

"Would that be wise, Tomás? They will be suspicious. This way, as long as we know what they're doing—"

"No, goddammit." Ragnon spat hard into his can. "If we're on our own in this, then so be it. Fuck them. Let's get back to work."

"He will want his jeep back, Tomás."

Tom Ragnon smiled. "He'll have to catch us first."

"Okay, Tomás," Cruz grinned back wickedly, "fuck them. It's all a matter of luck anyway. Salud, compadre." And he finished off his tequila as the band broke into a wild rendition of *Cielito Lindo* and the female vocalist joined them.

"Sing, don't cry!" Cruz translated, raising his voice above both the band and the vocalist. "That's the story of Mexico, Tomás! Vamos!"

At Xavier's Boatworks on the coast the day was cloudy and cool. Gulls wheeled over the masts of a hundred shrimp boats moored gunnel to gunnel in the harbor and over the vast, stinking mud flats of the boat yard itself, where the black skeletal steel frames of new boats were braced starkly amid the brightly sparking torches of welders at work as the afternoon whistle blew.

A shack with a sign XAVIER'S was back-lighted against the lowering sunless sky, and inside, a fire burned low in an old wood stove where two men shared a bottle at a battered rolltop desk set against one wall. The open desk was cluttered with papers, and the small nervous man tilted back in a captain's chair was frowning. "I don't know, Hidalgo," he said, "like I told my brother-in-law, it is all arranged. A boat will be available on any day's notice for a clandestine cargo south to Guaymas. My contacts are solid. But this thing with the gringo policeman . . ." He shook his head, which was nearly bald, the few remaining strands of black hair plastered tightly across his shining scalp with brilliantine.

Hidalgo Valdez had moved to the window, where he rubbed a hole in the dusty pane and peered out. The town of La Perla was mostly shacks clinging to the rocky hillside above the harbor, with the more elegant beach homes of wealthy, mostly absentee owners scattered along the white-shell beach a mile to the north. "We have stored the arms temporarily in that third boat—the *Marielena,*" Valdez said, ignoring the man's complaints. "You said the shaft is bent and it won't be going out."

"I'm talking about—"

"I know what you talk about, hombre, but that is my end of the business. You tend to your end." He turned and ground out the butt of a cigarette in an ashtray that was already overflowing. "Getting rid of these two cops will discourage others in the future. I've already got something bigger in mind; the plan is still vague but it is forming. It is time a lesson was learned. And the name of Hidalgo Valdez will be a force to reckon with along the border."

The other man was still shaking his head skeptically. "If Xavier were not my brother-in-law—" The phone on the rolltop desk rang, interrupting them, and Xavier Moreno answered it, listening a moment and then handing it to Hidalgo. "Someone in San Ignacio."

"Yes. . . ?" Hidalgo Valdez listened, scowling. Then suddenly he smiled shrewdly. "Bueno, we will be ready." He hung up the phone and looked at Moreno. "That was my police contact. We are in luck. He says they are on their way here now— the gringo cop and his fucking *agringado,* Cruz."

TWENTY-EIGHT

Saturday, March 20, 5:45 P.M.

Under the cool and cloudy afternoon sky the rolling hills, covered with prickly desert growth, gave way suddenly to flat, rocky hardpan sprouting only greasewood bushes, until even the greasewood gave way to sand. They had taken the main paved road to Puerto La Perla, bypassing the turnoff to the fishing village farther south, and as they topped the final sandy dune, the gulf port lay before them.

The town itself was cupped into an elbow of the bay, clinging to the rocky hillsides, with the many boats of the shrimp fleet massed tightly along the stone quay. Several boat yards were scattered along the shore, and where the road forked—the right bearing away toward a long curve of white-sand beach and modern houses a mile away—they took the left, plunging down into the town itself, over rough potholed streets crowded with storefronts and cheap motels and bars, all bristling with gaudy signs and TV antennas.

"Over there," Tom Ragnon said, spitting, and pointing down a sandy street toward the various boat works. "I think I see a sign." The wind brought them the stench of the mud flats now, a smell that even the fresh sea air couldn't overcome.

The gate in the high chain-link fence was open, and Cruz drove the jeep on through to the office which consisted of a shack with a double carport attached and a faded sign: XAVIER'S. The carport was empty except for odds and ends of junk and litter, and an overturned rowboat set up on sawhorses; that, and a man who was standing in one corner, testing an outboard motor in a big steel drum of water. The motor was roaring and spitting and spewing noxious blue smoke that belched from the carport as Cruz pulled the jeep up alongside and got his attention with the horn. "Where can we find Xavier?" he shouted, pointing up at the sign.

The man, who had looked around at the sound of the horn, shut off the motor. "Xavier?" he asked. "I am Xavier."

"Xavier Castillo?" Ragnon asked, but his hair was too thin, his shaven face too full and clear of acne scars to be the Xavier on their poster, the Xavier he had seen on the road to Ures.

"No, my name is Moreno. Xavier Moreno." His eyes looked everywhere but at the officers.

Cruz got out of the jeep and showed him their temporary police ID and then the receipt they had found in Hidalgo's van. "Your boatworks?" he asked as Ragnon joined them.

Moreno studied their letter and the receipt a moment, then looked up suspiciously, glancing from Ragnon to Cruz as if uncertain of the authority here. He finally settled on the gringo. "Yes—I sold a motor. But I think you have me confused with my brother-in-law, the Xavier you mentioned before—Xavier Castillo."

Ragnon glanced at Cruz, then back at Moreno. "And he's here too—this Castillo?" he asked in Spanish.

Moreno shrugged, and his lips curled insolently with a sudden sneer of bravado. "I think you're out of your jurisdiction, gringo."

"But I'm not out of mine, Señor Moreno," Cruz reminded him softly. "So this Castillo, he's here in La Perla?"

"No." Moreno was scowling petulantly.

"But he's driving a red Dodge truck, Sonora plates, number UX-5244—your truck, Señor Moreno."

Moreno's scowl deepened. "My truck, yes—a red Dodge, I don't know the license number—he borrowed it. What is this all about?" His eyes darted to the gringo again, then back and forth between them, appearing to pretend confusion. "Why are you looking for him?"

Cruz pulled a copy of the wanted poster from his pocket, then carefully unfolded it on the fender of the jeep. Covering the names, he exposed only the faces. "Point out your brother-in-law, Señor Moreno, please."

"This one." Moreno put a greasy finger on the acne-scarred features with the drooping mustache and goatee.

"And the others? What are their names, and when did you see them last?"

Xavier Moreno shook his head, backing away. "I don't know them!" he protested. "I know nothing!" But tiny beads of perspiration had gathered on his smooth upper lip.

"Look over here," Ragnon said, kneeling and pointing out a footprint in the damp, packed sand near the water barrel. Barely legible was a Cat's Paw design in a right heel.

Jacinto Cruz turned his iron gaze back to Moreno. "Can we step inside your office a moment, Xavier," he asked gently. "We've got some more questions."

At the door they paused and looked down toward the harbor, where the sea of masts rose above the rows of shrimp boats. Myriad tire tracks led down to the dock, and two vehicles were parked at quayside, but neither was a red truck. "How does a boat parked on the inside ever get out?" Ragnon wondered aloud.

"Maybe the whole fleet goes out at the same time," Cruz said, pushing open the door and motioning Xavier Moreno inside. Then he looked at Ragnon. "Why don't you poke around out here, Tomás? See what else you can find."

Ragnon wondered uneasily if Cruz just didn't want him witnessing any third degree tactics, but he stepped under the shelter of the carport and began a methodical search for anything suspicious amid the usual clutter of accumulated debris, wondering how touchy they were about search warrants in Mexico.

The overturned boat was being caulked, and there were fresh tire tracks on the sandy floor. He knew they could check them against the two vehicles parked at quayside, but it didn't look like they were going to find anything more significant than the heel print. When he passed a trash can and glanced absently inside, he almost missed a familiar bit of green cloth barely hidden among the oily rags and bottles and cans. Reaching in, he fished out a pair of men's green boxer shorts.

Kicking over the can, he stirred the contents and found a once-white pair of men's briefs, size thirty-four Fruit of the Loom. "Jesus Christ," he murmured; the coincidence was too much. He raked through the trash with his hands, looking for other articles of clothing, or maybe even their discarded wallets, but the underwear seemed to be it.

"Looking for this?" a voice behind him asked, and he turned to find Cruz standing in the open doorway with Xavier Moreno beside him, his stringy hair disheveled and his nose bleeding. The Mexican detective was holding up a sheepskin vest remarkably smiliar to Ragnon's. "Found it hanging behind the door inside. Look in the pocket." He tossed the garment to Ragnon, who dug out a half-filled pouch of Redman.

Then the American held up the green boxer shorts. "And how about these—they look familiar?"

"Ay caray! Por seguro!" Cruz roared. "But what I want to know is who's got my boots and leather jacket?" He looked around at Moreno, who averted his eyes, then led him over to the water barrel. The man was still hanging tough and resentful, and Ragnon thought it was probably all they were going to get out of him, when Cruz suddenly caught him with a hard left hook to the belly.

Before Ragnon could speak or Moreno could catch his breath, Cruz had grabbed him by his thinning hair and dunked his head into the water barrel and held it. Cruz's other hand held Moreno by the seat of his pants, keeping him up on his toes and off balance while he burbled and gurgled and flailed helplessly at the steel sides of the drum. Cruz was staring at Ragnon and smiling grimly. "I think our bird will want to sing us a truthful song very soon, Tomás."

"I thought you told me you didn't work this way," Ragnon said tightly, his own fists clenched at his sides.

"Only when absolutely necessary—and we are close, Tomás, so very close!" He yanked Moreno's head from the barrel and let him hang on its side a moment, dripping and blubbering and gasping for air. Then he leaned down close to the man's ear and whispered gently, "Señor Moreno, suppose we go back over those questions about your brother-in-law and his friends again. And see if this time you can come up with some more reasonable answers."

Sprawled on a sandy hill above the town, Hidalgo Valdez adjusted the focus on the binoculars they had taken from the jeep and brought the scene below at Xavier's Boatworks jarringly close to view.

After the phone call from Comandante Hernández, he had borrowed Moreno's Volkswagen bus and gone to round up the other three, intent on setting up an ambush on the main road leading into town. But it hadn't worked out. He had found the red truck parked behind a whorehouse in the red zone and Xavier inside. But Arturo and Miguel had gone off to another bar, and it had taken half an hour to find them. By then he was afraid it would be too late, and he saw now he was right. Down below, the gringo had found the underwear they had thrown away, and the Mexican cop had tossed him the sheepskin vest Hidalgo had forgotten in his hurry to leave.

He glanced over at Xavier, who was sprawled beside him, wearing the Mexican cop's leather jacket and boots. "Let me see," Xavier was whispering, as if afraid of being overheard.

Grunting, Hidalgo handed him the glasses. "Looks like they're working him over."

"*Del ahogadito,*" Xavier said, focusing the lenses. "They're giving him the little drowning."

"You think your brother-in-law will talk?"

"No more than he has to," Xavier answered slowly. Behind them Arturo and Miguel waited in the Volkswagen on a sandy road at the foot of the hill. Xavier had parked his brother-in-law's red Dodge beside it. "They have a rifle now," he noted grimly, "in a scabbard on the jeep."

"And we have only the shotgun and their .45—the distance is too great. But we can still take them, compadre." He looked at

Xavier, who had lowered the glasses. "We'll leave the truck here and take the Volkswagen. When they come off the flats up into the town, there's an intersection with an abandoned gas station on one corner and a thick stand of salt cedars beside it. We can take them there."

Xavier's brows raised skeptically. "In open daylight—in the center of town?"

"It will be swift and sudden. Then we will ditch the Volkswagen here and head south in the truck."

Xavier handed back the binoculars. "What if they have my brother-in-law with them?"

"Then he will have to take his chances," Hidalgo snapped savagely. "These fucking shitheels will not get away again!"

TWENTY-NINE

Saturday, March 20, 6:15 P.M.

Xavier Moreno, his chest and nostrils still aflame from his ordeal, was breathing heavily as he watched the two policemen drive off in their jeep. Nervously, he started the outboard in the water barrel again; he had to do something to keep from shaking. But he had only lied a little. Mostly he had told the truth, or simply withheld information. He knew he could have evaded everything with just the gringo, but the Mexican cop was bad news.

Fortunately it had been dark when his brother-in-law and the others arrived in his red truck before dawn on Friday, and Moreno had not actually seen them unload anything. And even if the cops suspected, there was no way they could search all the boats. He'd had to admit only that they were the four in the poster. But he had insisted that he had no knowledge of any criminal activity, and wouldn't have ratted on his brother-in-law, anyway, who had just dropped by to borrow some money. It had a ring of truth. If that damned fool, Hidalgo, just hadn't forgotten the vest he'd hung behind the door, and had thrown their fucking underwear away in the desert somewhere instead of bringing it here!

He had finally admitted seeing them leave for town in the red truck about an hour ago. But he didn't mention that Hidalgo had stayed behind, received a phone call from San Ignacio, and then borrowed his Volkswagen.

Shutting off the boat motor, he spat blood into the damp sand at his feet and tested a couple of loosened teeth with his finger, wondering what that crazy Hidalgo would do now, and wishing his brother-in-law had never gotten involved with him. Or at least never involved him. A little fencing of stolen goods was one thing, but murdering gringos—he could lose his business, not to mention his life. He spat again, and fished nervously in his pockets for a cigarette.

Jacinto Cruz, shifting out of the granny gears, pulled the jeep onto the paved road and headed into the town. "If it's only been an hour since they left," Ragnon was saying, buckling on the old ̄.44 holster and cartridge belt, "with any kind of luck they should still be in town somewhere."

"With our kind of luck, Tomás, they'll be looking for us with a machine gun. So first I want to check in at the police station and see if we can get some help. Then we'll look for the red truck."

"At least Moreno let slip the fourth name for our poster," Ragnon said, printing Miguel Tapia under the long narrow face with the hook nose, then grabbing the door frame for a brace as the jeep dodged a pothole and wheeled around a corner into the first intersection. "But what's remarkable is that they're all still together. And I'm sure that much Moreno told us was the truth."

"I think if I could have kept him upside down in that water drum awhile longer, we could have got even more truth out of him." Cruz was just slowing down at the next intersection, where an abandoned gas station stood on one corner beside a grove of tall salt cedars, when a vehicle suddenly careened out of an alley across the street and slightly behind them, its tires squealing and horn blowing.

Cruz braked the jeep as the vehicle angled sharply in front of them and stopped, blocking their way. Ragnon already had the .44 out of its holster when he saw it was a Ford Bronco with a star emblazoned on the door and circled by the words *Puerto La Perla Policía.*

Two uniformed policemen, with Mauser rifles at the ready, were already out of the Bronco; while the youthful driver, in plainclothes and wearing a cowboy hat and mirrored sunglasses, sat staring at them over a .45 leveled in both hands.

"Well, at least we don't have to look for the police station," Ragnon observed shrewdly, easing his own weapon back in its holster. "I think it just found us."

"Just don't make any sudden funny moves," Cruz answered, "until I can explain."

As the two uniformed cops slowly approached them on either side of the jeep with their rifles leveled, Ragnon was vaguely conscious of another vehicle, a black Volkswagen bus, which pulled out from between the salt cedars and the old gas station and disappeared around a corner. Then the plainclothes driver of the Bronco walked over and stuck his cocked .45 in the American's face while he deftly pulled the old revolver from its holster.

One of the uniformed cops, his rifle held in one hand, jerked the Winchester from its scabbard as the kid in civvies, who was making Ragnon wonder if maybe Mexican cops were as dangerous as Mexican fugitives, pushed his sunglasses up on his forehead to expose his fierce glare and growled in Spanish, "Who the fuck are you, and what are you doing driving around town armed?"

"We're lawmen too," Cruz answered quickly. "I'm Sargento Jacinto Cruz with the State Judicial Police, and this is an American police sergeant from Mimbres County, Arizona. We're hunting four fugitives on murder warrants. We have credentials."

The young officer's expression changed slowly from dark suspicion to professional curiosity as he allowed them to show their temporary ID letter and the jeep's registration, along with the arrest warrants, while Cruz explained what they were doing in La Perla. Cruz also showed him the copy of the poster.

The youthful cop's dark face brightened; his white teeth flashed beneath his mustache. "I am Teniente Jorge Fierro," he said, handing them back their letter and registration and Ragnon his old revolver. "At your service." He was still looking curiously at the American, but he had holstered his .45. Then he motioned the uniformed officer on the other side of the jeep to return the rifle to its scabbard, and ordered both him and his companion to wait in the Bronco. "We received copies of your poster a week ago," he told Cruz, "but I see you have now added names."

"As I said, our information is that they are all four here in La Perla. One of them—Xavier Castillo—has a brother-in-law down at the boat yard with the same first name. They were all there about an hour ago, in a red Dodge pickup. They're armed and dangerous, and we were on our way to the police station to get some help."

"Then you have help," Lt. Fierro answered with the supreme confidence of youth. "We will try the zona roja first. I will lead."

"This Fierro," Ragnon said, spitting as they followed the Bronco around the corner, "he didn't even ask for money. You think he's on the level?"

Jacinto Cruz laughed. "I don't know him, but I've heard of him. Young he may be, but he owns one of those beautiful homes along White Beach, and his uncle has a controlling interest in half the port here. Maybe he has enough money."

"Nobody ever has enough money," Ragnon said as they turned sharply to follow the Bronco down a steep hill into an even raunchier district of bars and bordellos.

Twenty minutes later, with the sunset only a splash of pink that colored the clouds on the horizon, they had found nothing. But as Fierro led them on around the edge of the town and over a sandy hill that overlooked the bay, they found the red truck abandoned behind a dune. "There were two vehicles here," Cruz observed, pointing at the tracks. They had pulled their own machines up side by side and got out.

"Looks like two of them walked up this hill," Ragnon said, following two sets of footprints, their patterns indistinguishable in the soft sand. At the top of the hill he could see where the men had sprawled beside a creosote bush. "They were evidently watching the boat yard from here"—he glanced at Cruz—"and not so long ago," he added, pointing at two fresh cigarette butts thrust upright in the sand.

The others had come up behind them, and they all stood looking down at the shack with its empty carport.

"Was a black Volkswagen bus parked down there at Xavier's?" Fierro asked them, speaking now in heavily accented English.

"No." Ragnon glanced again at Cruz, realizing they had been so surprised at finding their clothes, they had forgotten to ask about a possible missing vehicle.

"It belonged to Xavier Moreno," Fierro said. "My thought would be they have now, how you say, changed—exchanged—the red truck for the Volkswagen bus."

"And split," Ragnon added, remembering now the black Volks that had pulled away from the abandoned gas station in town. Jesus, had they really come that close again?

Lt. Fierro was staring at him, not understanding. "Split?" he asked.

"Took off," Ragnon explained, "gone—*se fué.*"

"Ah, sí—split." Fierro looked at them both. "What will you do now?"

Tom Ragnon looked at Cruz. "I *saw* that damned black bus pull out of the trees back at that intersection! They were waiting for us!"

"So where could they go?" Cruz asked.

"There's no road north from here," Fierro said.

"And only a sandy track south to that fishing village," Ragnon added, chewing his Redman thoughtfully.

"Then my guess is back to San Ignacio," Cruz answered his own question, "or any point in between."

"Shit!" Ragnon sent a squirt of tobacco juice into the sand as they walked off the hill.

"I can call ahead," Fierro suggested. "Alert Caborca and Magdalena—Nogales and San Ignacio too."

"Yeah, thanks—do that." Ragnon stared at his haggard, distorted reflection in the young lieutenant's mirrored sunglasses, knowing how much good that would do. "And can you keep looking here, Lieutenant, just in case they've holed up someplace nearby?"

"Of course, Sargento."

"And can you put a watch on that brother-in-law's boat works?" Cruz asked.

"I can do better than that," Fierro said. "We've had suspicions of this Moreno for some time—some kind of smuggling with his boats. With your finding the stolen clothes at his office, and his admission about knowing the fugitives, I can place him under arrest."

"Just watching the place will be enough," Cruz said, "in case Hidalgo Valdez returns."

"It will all be taken care of," Fierro assured him, shaking hands firmly with them both. "You can depend on me."

But Tom Ragnon wondered cynically if they could depend on anyone now, except themselves.

On the way back to San Ignacio he was still deep in thought and said little.

"Why so serious, Tomás?" Cruz asked. "We will get them now. I can *feel* it."

"I was thinking about their almost getting us again, back at that intersection." And he was remembering the shotgun tucked coldly under his jaw, and the killer eyes of Hidalgo. "If Fierro and his men hadn't happened to stop us just at that moment, I bet the bastards were going to ambush us."

"Didn't I warn you, compadre?" Cruz was suddenly serious too. "This *hijo de puta* will not be taken. He will have to be killed."

THIRTY

Saturday, March 20, 6:55 P.M.

Forty kilometers south of Puerto La Perla the beach and the fishing village were shrouded in the gathering dusk and fog. The black Volkswagen bus had pulled under the shelter between two of the end cabins at the abandoned motel just over the dunes. Hidalgo and company had been in too big a hurry to bother ditching it for the red truck.

Instead of taking the paved road east to San Ignacio or somewhere in between, they had followed the narrow sandy coastal trace south, taking almost forty-five minutes to cover the forty kilometers. And with each kilometer, each jarring jolt and lurch of the bus on the sand-filled track, Hidalgo's anger and frustration and impatience had grown. Once again he had missed taking out the gringo. But somehow it didn't seem to matter anymore, because his final plan had taken form on that rough road too. And by now he had even convinced himself that missing them was a good omen for what was to come.

In the fishing village he had picked up the Medrano brothers, Juan and Fidel, who had been at sea when he was here before; and now there were six of them sitting around the table in the kitchen of the last cabin, drinking tequila from a common bottle and eating tortillas fried with cheese and green chiles. The kerosene lamp cast a grotesque play of shadows across their eager faces as Hidalgo unfolded the last details of his new plan.

"What about the gringo cop?" Arturo asked when he had finished. "You have not mentioned him since we got here."

"Fuck that whoreson! With luck we will get him, too, and that Cruz with him; but I told you before—this is bigger than one gringo now. With this plan we will show *all* the gringos." His enthusiasm was infectious as he gained the grins and nods of approval from the others. Even the overly cautious Xavier had succumbed to his charisma.

"Won't we still need more men?" Miguel suggested, looking at Hidalgo through the haze of cigarette smoke that coiled like a blue gauze veil around them all.

"That is where the Medranos come in." Hidalgo nodded at the two brothers.

"There's a man in Caborca who will join us," Fidel, the older brother said. "He just got out of jail. And another one in Magdalena—if he is assured an equal share of any loot."

"Equal shares for all who join us in this—I told you that," Hidalgo answered gruffly. "That will make eight of us, and plenty of loot for all."

"And the weapons?" Xavier asked pointedly. "They are still in La Perla, on the boat. My brother-in-law has probably been arrested. He may talk, and with certainty the boat yard will be watched."

Hidalgo frowned, still thinking everything through. "How long will he hold out?"

"Who knows? The man has balls, but they have their ways, *la chinga policía!*"

"But they can't search all the boats," Miguel interrupted. "They—"

Hidalgo silenced him with a look. "Moreno can tell them *which* boat, stupido. But even if we return now, the question is how to get at the arms ourselves if the boatworks is watched."

They all looked from one to the other, but it was the younger brother, Juan Medrano, who ground out his cigarette butt on the Formica tabletop and shrugged. "We have our fishing scow," he said, "Fidel and me. Suppose we go in tonight from seaward, cross over the decks of the other boats to the *Marielena,* and take them back out the same way?" He looked from Hidalgo to Xavier. "If we left now, we could be back here by midnight."

Xavier glanced at Hidalgo for approval. "It should work. They can take Miguel or Arturo with them to guide them to the right boat."

Hidalgo nodded agreeably, but he was still scowling. He had thought of something else. "What about our transportation when they get back? The cops will be looking for the Volkswagen by now."

"We also have a truck," Fidel Medrano said. "An enclosed ton and a half with dual rear wheels we use to haul ice for the fish."

"And it has a false center compartment where we sometimes haul wetbacks north," Juan added significantly.

"It's better than the Volkswagen for what we want." Fidel smiled at Hidalgo reassuringly. "It's big enough to hide the arms, and several of us too. With maybe three in the cab, we will just be heading somewhere for a load of ice."

"What about gas for your truck?" Xavier asked.

"We can siphon it out of the Volkswagen. Its tank is almost full." Hidalgo looked around at them all, his eyes gleaming now that it was decided. "But we will have to do it, hombres, before they break Moreno and find the arms themselves. Juan and Fidel will take their boat to La Perla. Arturo, you will go with them to find the *Marielena.* Then, with any luck, by midnight tonight we will have the guns back here, and we can leave before dawn."

"If your plan is to succeed, we should have an extra truck," Xavier said. "Another one with dual wheels, or a rear engine like the Volkswagen, if we're going to cut across the desert. And where do we find explosives?"

Hidalgo's smile was triumphant. "I know a place where we can steal both," he said, "near Magdalena. Now, hombres—are we ready?"

"Ayee!" Miguel whooped, *"Vámonos ahorita!"* The others

joined him as he stood and raised the nearly empty bottle aloft in salute to Hidalgo Valdez, who sat quite still, gloating and basking in his apparently growing power and strength.

Then he rose himself and grabbed the bottle. "To us! And to my great-grandfather and his Villistas—and to the killing of gringos!" Tilting it back, he drained it as the tiny cabin rang with shrill charro yips. Only Xavier still had any lingering doubts as to where it would all end.

There was no fog in Hermosillo. It was a clear, cool night as Chato Gomez reported to Raul Galindez at his palatial home on the outskirts of the city. "Hidalgo Valdez is out of control, *Jefe.*" He sipped at a rum and cola the servant had brought. "The brother-in-law of one of his men was arrested in La Perla. Somehow the gringo and Cruz traced them there and got the local police to help."

Galindez's face was grim. "Who is the police chief there?"

"Lieutenant Jorge Fierro."

"He's your informant?"

"No, he's another Jacinto Cruz—likes to earn his money doing police work. But one of his men is both greedy and reliable."

Galindez snipped the tip off a Havana cigar and flicked a gold Dunhill lighter. "Where is Hidalgo now?"

"No one knows. He was evidently in La Perla and got away. But something new is in the wind. He seems to be involving the Medrano brothers now, and whatever it is, he'll want the guns. My guess is they're hidden at the brother-in-law's boat yard."

"On one of the boats?" Galindez was squinting through a pungent cloud of cigar smoke.

"Yes."

"So the problem is which one. The harbor is full of boats now. You can't search them all."

"Only about a dozen belong to the brother-in-law," Chato said. "I'm having the names checked now, then they can be searched."

"I want it done quickly." Galindez had begun to pace the room nervously while Chato sat on the couch and watched. "The blame is mine—I let it all go on too long for my own amusement. Now I want the weapons and I want Hidalgo and his gang. He has played at being a crime boss long enough."

"And the gringo and Cruz?"

"Them too," Galindez said. "And what about this other thing—the contamination?"

"The Federales are in San Ignacio, *Jefe*. Coincidentally it's been chosen for the 'spontaneous' nocturnal visit by the president-elect. He will arrive about eleven tomorrow night via limousine for a midnight speech on the plaza, escorted by soldiers in jeeps and Federales in private cars. But with so many Federales already in town, it means they will be even quicker tracing the contamination to our junkyard. There may still be time to destroy our records, if we can do it now—before tomorrow night."

"You have the men available to do it?"

"Already in place, *Jefe.*"

Raul Galindez nodded thoughtfully, apparently satisfied. "Then take care of it, Chato. And when you have finished, take care of Hidalgo and his friends too."

"Bueno, *Jefe,* but we will have to find them first."

Galindez grunted. "You'll find them. Anyone with as big an ego as Hidalgo Valdez will not stay hidden long. Tomorrow is Sunday; maybe you'll find him in church, praying for his miserable little soul."

THIRTY-ONE

Sunday, March 21, 12:20 P.M.

Sunday in San Ignacio had not changed much in the past two hundred years. The old adobe church, erected originally as one of a string of Spanish missions across northern Sonora in the eighteenth century, had been burned twice by Apaches. Rebuilt, the ancient edifice still served the faithful, though after eleven o'clock mass there were more people congregated at Garcia's Bar two blocks away, where Tom Ragnon had agreed to meet Cruz.

The bar was full of men, and boys becoming men; most of them wearing clean blue jeans and white shirts, their Sunday best. And it was almost as quiet as the church. A murmur of voices, a quiet laugh, the click of balls scattering across the green cloth of three pool tables, and the clatter of cues; all while the warming sunlight streamed in through the open double doors.

But Jacinto Cruz was late. Ragnon, standing at one end of the bar and nursing a beer, caught himself glancing a third time at his watch and then at a side door where a man was wheeling in stacked cases of Tecate on a dolly. He guessed the chase was finally getting to him, and he sighed heavily.

They had looked for the black Volkswagen bus all the way back to San Ignacio without success. And there had been no reports of such a vehicle being seen in the several towns and villages between here and the coast. Which meant the fugitives had probably turned off on some back road and were in hiding, or had simply changed their transportation again somewhere along the way. Still, with all four identified now, he knew it was only a matter of time. So why this feeling of foreboding? This sense of impending dread? Like he was waiting in the eye of a hurricane.

A horn beeping insistently outside the open front doors broke his concentration. Then Cruz himself appeared in the doorway, his features ragged and drawn. "Trouble, Tomás," was all he said. "Vamos."

Leaving a dollar on the bar, Ragnon hurried outside and climbed into the jeep beside the Mexican. "What's wrong, man? You look like shit warmed over."

"You remember Hector Zamora, Angelina's brother?"

"Sure—the foreman at the *machiladora* plant."

"Not any more—he's dead."

"Dead? When? How?"

"The question to ask is 'who?' But not now." He swung the jeep down a side street, bouncing in and out of potholes and heading for the railroad tracks.

"Then how about this one: Where the fuck are we going in such a rush?"

"Madrecita's." He turned down the street along the tracks, pulled to the curb in front of the café, and signaled the old lady through the window.

Angelina Zamora was led out of the café by the old woman, who helped her into the back of the jeep. She looked worse than

Cruz and avoided the American's eyes as they drove off without any further conversation.

"Now where are we going?" Ragnon finally asked, turning slightly so he could see the girl. It was obvious she had already been told of her brother's death.

"We're taking her home, Tomás. Her brother-in-law is there this weekend. You're going to see that he takes her with him back to Hermosillo, and that they leave now."

"Who killed Hector—Hidalgo?"

Cruz glanced back at the girl, then lowered his voice. "Comandante Max."

"Max?"

"There are cells and an interrogation room in the basement of the police building. Max had him questioned there all night, but his men got a little overzealous with their electric prods and hot peppers in mineral water."

"Jesus Christ, Jacinto, why would they—"

"No more questions now," Cruz interrupted him as they pulled up in front of the small house with the honeysuckle vine trailing over the trellised entryway. "I'll explain later, Tomás. Right now she still trusts you, so get her on her way to Hermosillo before Max comes after her too. She was at the police building, looking for her brother, and now she knows too much for her own good."

As Ragnon helped her from the jeep, the girl came with him numbly, almost uncaringly; then he turned to Cruz. "But where in hell are *you* going?"

"I'll be back for you, Tomás," the Mexican answered curtly. "Just get her out of town—now!"

Standing beneath the flowery bower on the porch with his arm around her shoulder, Ragnon could feel her trembling beside him as they watched the jeep braking in a cloud of dust as it disappeared around the corner.

"What's happening?" she whispered in a voice so low he almost didn't hear it. "I don't want to go. What about Hector—his body? I can't just—"

Turning her, Ragnon held her shoulders so she faced him. "Angelina—listen to me." Her dark eyes were still glazed with the shock of her brother's death. Full acceptance would come later, but he had to get through to her now. "You're going back home—to Hermosillo. Your brother-in-law will take you, you understand?" She seemed so frail, so helpless, his heart went out to her. "Angelina, I'm sorry—about Hector, about all of this. But you've got to go; it's too dangerous to stay. Your sister will see to Hector now."

Her face, up close, still showed the fading purple bruises left from her experience with Hidalgo, but her dark sad eyes held understanding now. "You have been kind, Sargento," she whispered, and put a slender hand gently on his arm.

Only then did he realize how fiercely he was gripping her thin shoulders, and he relaxed his hands as the front door opened and the sister stood there with a man Ragnon assumed was the brother-in-law. "This is Carlos," Angelina introduced him. "He—"

"Take her home," Ragnon told him quickly in Spanish, "to Hermosillo—*ahora, hombre, ahorita; hay mucho peligroso aqui!*"

As the couple hurriedly led the girl inside, Ragnon started to follow, then turned at the sound of a vehicle braking in the street behind them. He thought for an instant that Cruz was back, but it was an old Chevy station wagon with two uniformed policemen in the front seat, and Ragnon felt a sudden familiar surge of adrenaline and dread. They had apparently driven too far before stopping and were now reversing the Chevy, both of them looking out their respective windows and studying the houses on either side of the street.

Stepping quickly inside the house, Ragnon ran through the rooms to the kitchen in back. The door was open and Carlos was taking Angelina out to his truck, which was pulled up in back. "*Andale, hombre!*" Ragnon called to him. "*Vayase—dése prisa! La policía estan aquí!*"

Turning, he ran back through the house and passed the startled sister, who was crossing herself and cringing in silent terror before a votive candle burning under a statue of the Madonna. Ragnon still wasn't sure what was happening himself, except that his every instinct told him Cruz was right—whatever had happened to Hector Zamora, for whatever reason, Angelina wasn't safe either. And he was the only one there to prevent them from taking her.

At the front door again he saw that the two uniformed cops had stopped the station wagon in front of the house and were getting out. Stall them, he thought, stepping out on the porch,

I've got to stall them—but where in hell was Cruz? *"Oígame!"* he called to them in a foolish greeting, "Qué pasó. . . ?"

They came unhurriedly through the little gate with their rifles still slung on their shoulders, one tall and thin, the other a squat brutish-looking hulk.

"Qué queres. . . ?" Ragnon called again, trying to keep their attention and at the same time deciding it would help the delaying tactics if he showed them some ID. But even as he walked up to meet them, the truck's engine came noisily to life out back and he saw by the quick expressions of concern on their faces that the fat was in the fire. And suddenly his own singular all consuming concern was simply that Angelina Zamora must get away.

The thin one was nearest, the other already starting to unsling his rifle and turn toward the rear of the house as Ragnon brought his knee up hard into the thin one's groin. As he doubled over, Ragnon chopped him a paralyzing blow on the back of the neck with the edge of his hand, thinking all the time— What am I doing fighting cops? And where the fuck is Cruz?—as the hulk turned back toward him in alarm and brought his rifle to waist level. But even as Ragnon stepped into him, grabbing the weapon by the barrel, jamming it hard against the startled man's belly and then jerking it from his hand, he knew he was in for a bad time. Because before he could use it himself as a club, the hulking Mexican was all over him.

Roaring like a maniac, the bull-strong bear of a man forced him backward, tripping him over a row of bricks that lined the sidewalk. Twisting himself as they fell together, Ragnon managed to keep the Mexican cop from falling directly on him; but even so, the landing on the hard ground stunned him momentarily, and he felt the man's weight roll over onto him and sinewy hands gather around his throat. Suddenly it wasn't just a fight, a delaying tactic—suddenly, with the breath being squeezed out of him and his ribs crushed, Ragnon knew he was fighting for his life.

Vaguely he heard the truck pulling out of the yard and another vehicle braking somewhere out front as he found his opponent's eyes with his thumbs; then he heard a thudding crunch and the weight was suddenly lifted. The hulk rolled away and

Jacinto Cruz was standing over him, the hulk's rifle reversed in his hands.

Ragnon, getting dizzily to his knees, felt his heart pounding and heard a shrill ringing in his ears. His whole body shuddered as he gasped for air. Then Cruz was reaching down and giving him a supporting hand. "Get up, Tomás. Come—get up!"

The detective struggled to his feet, his head clearing. Cruz had clubbed the hulk senseless and thrown the rifle down. The other cop was on his knees, one hand still holding his crotch and the other rubbing the back of his neck. He moaned softly as Cruz jerked the rifle from his shoulder and pitched it across the yard. "Let's go, Tomás," Cruz urged again.

"What's the goddamned panic, Jacinto? She's gone—she got away in Carlos's truck. Now will you tell me what the fuck is going on?"

"First, we've got to go get your car," he said as he guided Ragnon to the jeep and helped him in, "and then get you back across the border." Stopping at the station wagon, he reached in and pulled out the keys, then climbed back in the jeep, wheeled it around, and sped off toward the plaza.

"What I want to know, Jacinto," Ragnon said, easing his bruised ribs as they turned the corner, "is why we just had to dump on two of your local gendarmes. Because I know damn well that's a no-no, even in Mexico."

"Especially in Mexico, my friend. Now listen carefully while I tell you what has happened." There was something in the tone of his voice, this fearless hawk of a man, that was chilling. "Three things—one, about Hector Zamora. While we were in La Perla he found out through a mutual girlfriend that Max has been protecting Hidalgo, and he foolishly confronted him instead of waiting for us to get back. Max had him arrested and interrogated on the pretense that *he* knew something about Hidalgo and would not disclose it. It was only to frighten him— terrorize him into silence. But his men got a little too rough, or Hector had a weak heart—either way, the interrogation proved too much for him."

They had bounced through the potholes in the plaza and turned toward the fenced-in parking lot where Ragnon had left his car. A hundred yards beyond it the Mexican tri-color hung above the Customs building at the international gate.

"I had just gotten all this from a cop on duty," Cruz was

explaining, "when Angelina happened down there to try and get him freed, just as they were bringing his body out. The blanket slipped off the stretcher, and when she saw what they'd done to him, she got hysterical. I talked Max into letting me take her over to the café to calm her down, but I knew he'd be sending for her when he had time to think about it, since she'd seen too much."

"Holy shit, Jacinto—"

"Shut up, Tomás, and just listen." They had reached the parking lot and Cruz let the jeep engine idle beside the Falcon while Ragnon paid the attendant and he continued, "Point two —they just found Max dead in his office, a third eye drilled through his forehead and his brains splattered all over that wall map of Sonora behind him. They don't know if it's suicide or what, but it's going to get a little loco around here for a while." He waved his hand against Ragnon's attempted interruption. "And three—this concerns you, Tomás—I got a call from Chato Gomez in Hermosillo—"

"Chato?" Ragnon insisted on butting in now. "When did he come over to our side?"

"When it suits Galindez's purpose. He says the word is out that Hidalgo Valdez isn't just after you now; he's recruited more men and weapons and even explosives, and he's going to cross the border again, probably sometime tonight, and burn out that ranch in some kind of vengeance fit against all gringos."

"Burn out the McNeals' place? But it's vacant, there's—"

"It's your chance to get him, Tomás, without extradition, and the others with him. Now go—"

"Wait a minute, man, what about you? What about those two cops? Won't you be in trouble?"

"Jesucristo, compadre—go! This isn't the fucking United States—we do things differently here! Right now, while we talk, Max's brains and bone and blood are still dripping off that wall map—now go back and warn them about Hidalgo. I'll handle things over here. If we can stop him on this side, we will, but don't count on it now, there's too much confusion. You remember the contamination I spoke of, and the president-elect's little unscheduled visit to San Ignacio tonight?"

"Of course."

"Well, compadre, the junkyard is here in San Ignacio, and the contamination is nuclear radiation."

"Jesus, Jacinto, how could—"

Cruz waved him silent again. "Some kind of stolen cancer machine was melted down and made into 'hot' steel, which was then unknowingly shipped all over Sonora and into the States. The Federales and U.S. agents have tracked it back here to a junkyard, but they're not warning anyone. They don't want to alarm the public."

"What can we do?"

"We—nothing, Tomás. I must do something. I've got an uneasy hunch about this, but the comandante's death makes for serious complications, things you'd best not be involved in. Go, Tomás—you have your job now and I have mine."

They shook hands quickly as Ragnon studied the dark strong features of this man who had become a friend. "Jacinto, there's something else, isn't there? Something you haven't told me—"

"Good-bye, Tomás—go with God!" The Mexican agent withdrew his hand and shifted into gear, setting the jeep in motion.

"That's a strange thing for *you* to say!" Ragnon called after him.

Jacinto Cruz glanced back, laughing and waving. "Then good luck instead, Tomás—to both of us!"

THIRTY-TWO

Sunday, March 21, 7:10 P.M.

"Forget it, Rags," Lt. Poole said. "Nobody will buy a border raid without concrete evidence—something more than the fantasy of a two-bit spic detective—and you ain't got any. Who does this Hidalgo think he is, Pancho Villa for Christ's sake?"

They were alone in the detective squad room, standing beside Ragnon's desk. Getting the chief all sweaty on Sunday was bad enough, but it was ten minutes past seven by the wall clock above the Mimbres County map; Ragnon had been back in the city for over three hours and accomplished nothing. They simply didn't believe Cruz's story.

"Hidalgo whatsisname and his buddies can't really be that stupid, can they, Rags?" Poole was eyeing him over his half-lenses and chomping on the cold stub of a cigar that he didn't seem to realize was out. "Come over the border and raid an empty ranch? Shit, to come over the border at all would be a crazy risk, even for another burglary. But to hit the same place before anything's even been replaced? Don't you think they'd have the brains to scout it first?"

"I don't pretend to figure the guy, Chief; he's unpredictable. But it's reliable information or Cruz wouldn't have passed it on." Yet even Ragnon had to admit that part bothered him, too, the target being the McNeals' again. Even just for vengeance it would be too risky. Except that evidently there was to be no risk at all, since neither Poole nor anybody else believed it.

"Look, Rags, be reasonable," Poole said, "what could we take to the County Attorney, never mind the State Attorney General—an uncorroborated tip from a Mexican cop? What's he been smokin' for Christ's sake? We've checked with DPS and Customs and the Border Patrol; they haven't had so much as a sniff of anything like this. There was some kind of search conducted among the fishing boats moored in Puerto La Perla this morning, but they evidently didn't turn anything. Tell your greaser friend as soon as he gets something solid—"

"It's tonight, Chief, goddammit." Ragnon spat into the steel wastebasket, ringing it like a bell as Poole winced. "It's some kind of macho thing, a matter of pride, honor—an uptight emotional vengeance raid, not a reasoned response to a kiss on the cheek! And it's a chance to grab him—nail them all. Give me a tactical SWAT team—half a dozen men. I'm not asking you to turn out the National Guard for Christ's sake!"

"And make myself the jerk-off of the department? You think I'm really that stupid, don't you, Ragnon? You tell that Cruz to catch 'em down there and we'll extradite. That's what we've been dishing out reward money for, goddammit—you tell him to stop 'em down there!"

Ragnon was still bothered by Comandante Max's death, too, which he couldn't figure out and hadn't bothered to lay on the chief along with everything else. His fight with the two Mexican cops over Angelina had excited him enough. "If they do intercept them down there," he said to Poole, "the Mexican officials will probably want to try them themselves—on reduced charges. A short sentence and they'll walk."

"So what's so different about our justice system?" Poole fired up his bronze horse desk lighter and was cupping the light to the stub of his cigar. "I'm telling you we've alerted everybody but Santa Claus about a possible border crossing—that's all we can do."

"I'll go over your head, Chief," Ragnon threatened again.

But this time Poole only grinned sardonically. "Fuck off, Rags. That won't work this time. Captain's already said no too. I've got two more homicides I need you on now, and your vacation is over. I want your ass back here at eight in the morning ready to work, or I want your shield."

Tom Ragnon sighed resignedly. "Hidalgo Valdez already got my shield, Chief." He spat again. "And I'm gonna get him. See you around."

Full of anger and frustration, he drove the forty miles back to Pantana in less than forty minutes. He didn't even have a plan, didn't know what he was going to do or anything he could do. He only knew if Hidalgo Valdez was going to return to the McNeal ranch, he was going to be there too.

As he pulled into the driveway beside his trailer, he noticed a familiar motorcycle parked out front, and found John Antone in civilian clothes, sitting in the darkness on his doorstep.

"What in hell are you doing here?" Ragnon asked, unlocking his door, switching on the lights, and motioning the deputy inside.

"I heard about your dilemma," Antone said, "and I figured you'd strike out with Old Ironballs. But I'm still your other partner in this, right—unofficially? And I'm off duty tonight, so . . ." He shrugged. "How can I help?"

"Jesus . . ." Ragnon shook his head wearily, started to heat up the coffee in his silex, then realized there was no time. He opened two beers instead. "I'm not sure how anybody can help, John," he said, handing him one. "That's why I didn't call you myself. They tell you what Cruz told me about Hidalgo actually planning to hit the McNeal place again—tonight?"

"That's what I'm here for, illogical as it sounds. The bastard just might do it."

"Shit, John . . ." He smiled at the irony—Hidalgo was playing right into their hands, and they were helpless. Or maybe not quite helpless. "Did you bring your piece?"

"I brought my cannon." The Indian deputy raised his jacket to expose the holstered .44 Magnum on his belt.

"Well, I don't think even that's gonna be big enough for this, but we've got to try. Let's go find that Marshal Duff, see what kind of ordnance he's got." But as he reached for the trailer door, there was a knock, and when he opened it, he found Jacinto Cruz standing on his doorstep. On the street behind him a battered green Plymouth with Senora plates was pulled up behind Antone's cycle.

"I crossed just before the gate closed," Cruz said in answer to his questioning look. He nodded a greeting to Antone.

"But what are you doing here, man? What about the contamination and the visit from your president-elect?"

"The visit was cancelled. He flew back to Hermosillo from Nogales, and the Federales say the contamination is now under control."

Ragnon stared at him skeptically.

"Radioactive cobalt pellets, Tomás, the source of the contamination, were traced to a pickup truck parked in the junkyard. The stolen machine was hauled to the yard in the truck and taken from there to the foundry in a bigger truck, along with more scrap metal. I notified our health officials and they'll have to trace all the shipments, see who was exposed, and get everything cleaned up. But my uneasy hunch was right—Galindez was involved. It is his junkyard and his foundry. The Federales are rooting all over both places. So after advising the health officials, I came straight here."

"I sure appreciate your help, partner, but—"

"I came because there's also new information on Hidalgo's target. I called that Marshal Duff, but I don't think he believed me. It's not the ranch Hidalgo's going to hit, Tomás, it's the town—this town."

"This—Pantana? My God, Jacinto!" It was all coming too fast, but at least this made some kind of bizarre sense. "Are you sure, man? He's raiding the *town?*"

Cruz pulled a telegram from his pocket and handed it over. "From Lieutenant Fierro in La Perla. I also talked to him on the phone. He says Hidalgo's got eight or ten men now, and weapons he smuggled off one of the boats by sea. His information has it that Hidalgo plans a hit-and-run raid on Pantana itself to burn it down. And he's probably already across the border. A construction yard was broken into outside Magdalena early this morning and a dual-wheeled truck stolen. The tire prints of a second truck matched those of one known to belong to the Medrano brothers, two fishermen from that village south of La Perla who also dabble in alien smuggling. A fireworks factory was burgled a couple of hours later, and the tracks of both trucks used there matched the construction break-in."

Ragnon looked at Antone. "Fireworks means explosives."

"And Arturo Acosta has worked with explosives," Antone said grimly. "He knows how to use them."

"So when is your SWAT team due?" Cruz asked.

"I'm afraid *we're* the SWAT team at the moment, Jacinto," Ragnon said. "They didn't believe me either; but they will now." He held up the telegram. "We've finally got something solid. Let's get over to the marshal's office and his base radio."

But as they started out the door, Cruz caught Ragnon's arm. "Can I see you alone a minute, Tomás?"

"I'll wait in your car," Antone told Ragnon. "I about froze my nuts off driving down here tonight on my cycle."

"What is it, partner?" Ragnon asked, but he could already sense it was more bad news.

"About Comandante Max. He didn't commit suicide, Tomás. I killed him."

THIRTY-THREE

Sunday, March 21, 8:25 P.M.

"You *what?*" Ragnon was stunned. "*You* killed Max?"

"I used that old .44 revolver and then put it in his hand. It can't be traced. I killed the *pinche cabrón,* Tomás, and good riddance, no?"

"My God, Jacinto, we've been chasing murderers all over Sonora and then *you* kill the comandante? For God's sake, why?"

Jacinto Cruz shrugged expressively. "For what he did to Hector Zamora, for a dozen past betrayals and corruptions. For simple bad manners, what does it matter? I killed him."

"It's got to matter, man, or what's it all for?"

Cruz lit a slim cigarillo and stared at the American. "There were other Hectors, compadre. I witnessed other things, too many things over the years, but I could never prove anything. I speak from the heart, Tomás. We pay for what we do in life. It was time for him to pay."

Holy shit, Ragnon thought, feeling drained and helpless. "And you really think you got away with it?"

Cruz shrugged again. "I doubt it, Tomás. Our system is not as efficient as yours, but it functions. And he had friends in high places."

"At least you're over here; we can get you a lawyer. Now *they'll* have to extradite."

"No, Tomás, I just came to help you get Hidalgo. When that's over, I'll go back and face it."

"We'll talk about it. Right now we better get over to the marshal's office before we have to face Hidalgo's gang alone."

Antone and Ragnon drove over in the detective's car, with Cruz following in his old Plymouth. The Indian deputy wondered at his partner's strained silence, but he didn't intrude. They found the marshal watching TV with his wife in his trailer next to the office. Ragnon could see Archie Bunker's face on the big color screen in the living room behind him while he stood in the doorway and the detective showed him the telegram and explained the urgency of their visit. But Edwin Duff still wasn't convinced, and not unduly concerned. Mexican bandits were something he read about in Max Brand or Louis L'Amour, or saw in old TV reruns.

Reluctantly, he finally agreed to get his keys and turn on the base radio while Ragnon asked to use the phone to call his chief. "It's out in the kitchen, Sergeant," Duff said, and the detective heard him tell his wife there was nothing to worry about, "just a little police business."

But when Ragnon picked up the wall-phone receiver, the line was dead. Something was wrong, and his scalp prickled as his senses picked up on it, gathering swiftly on the edge of panic. "How long's your phone been out?" he asked Mrs. Duff.

"It was okay an hour ago, Sergeant. Try the one in the office."

Across the patio, in the marshal's office, Duff had switched on the light and was sitting at the radio as Ragnon moved to his desk and picked up the phone there. It was dead, too, and he looked at Duff. "Is this phone connected to the other—" The deep double boom of distant explosions were followed by the office light flickering and then going out.

"What in hell was that?" Antone asked.

Cruz had stepped quickly to the window. "The lights are out all over town."

Marshal Duff had flicked on his cigarette lighter and was holding it high as they all exchanged the same intense, knowing glances. "First dead phones and now the juice," Ragnon said softly. "I think Hidalgo has already arrived."

"God damn!" Duff breathed. "The power line's northeast of town—they must have blown up a transmission tower. We're blacked out!"

"Including your radio," Antone said. "And I brought my bike instead of the jeep."

"Where's *your* jeep?" Ragnon asked the marshal.

"In a garage in the city." Duff's face had gone pale under his tan. "Transmission went out yesterday."

"Edwin. . . ?" Duff's wife was calling across the patio. "What happened to the lights?"

"You've got no emergency generator?" Ragnon asked.

Duff shook his head. "Council voted it out since we've got no hospital." He turned and called across to his wife, "Millie, find that camp lantern! It's in the back of the hall closet—and bring it over!"

"How about a CB?" Antone asked. "Somebody in town must have one."

Duff scratched his head. "Colonel Roberts, he's got one in his truck!"

"Find him," Ragnon said, "and show him this telegram." He handed him the paper. "Tell him to call the Sheriff's Department for a helicopter SWAT team. Have 'em notify the Border Patrol and the state police too."

"What about the National Guard?"

"This will all be over in an hour—too late for them. We may not even be able to hold them off till a SWAT team arrives."

"We?" Duff's voice had grown a little faint. "You mean the four of us?"

Duff's wife came into the office then, holding up a lantern with brightly glowing mantles. "What's going on, Ed?"

"No, the three of us," Ragnon was saying. "You're going to

find Roberts and his CB." He reached out and took the lantern from the marshal's wife. "Thank you, Mrs. Duff. The town's about to have some unpleasant visitors—bandits. It would help if you could find a flashlight and then go round up the rest of the council members—start evacuating the town, just in case we can't intercept them before they get here."

As both the marshal and his wife turned to go, Ragnon set the lantern on the desk. "Wait a minute—where are the keys to that gun cabinet over there? We'll need some heavier weapons."

"Here." Duff tossed him a set of keys as he followed his wife out the door.

Ragnon looked over at Cruz while he unlocked the cabinet. "You sure you want in on this, compadre?"

Jacinto Cruz smiled wryly. "Do Mexicans eat tortillas?"

"I mean it, it's really not your fight, man."

Cruz looked hurt. "After all we've been through together in this, you can tell me it's not my fight?"

"Sorry, but you're not even armed, or are you?"

"What? And violate the laws of the United States? Not me. I'm in enough trouble, *verdad?*"

"Then you may as well take your pick." Ragnon had opened the thick wooden doors to expose several racked guns, and he pulled out a drawer filled with boxes of shells in assorted sizes.

Cruz chose a Browning semi-automatic rifle and a Colt .45 pistol. Antone lifted a .30-30 carbine from the rack, and Ragnon picked a .12-gauge automatic shotgun. They all scooped out boxes of appropriate shells and filled their pockets.

Then Ragnon tucked a fresh pinch of Redman in his cheek, picked up the lantern, and held it high to throw more light on the wall map of the county. "Now, John," he said, "you know this area best. Where's that transmission tower that just blew up?"

Antone pointed to a dotted line angling northeast of Pantana. "The transmission towers run along here, following this big wash."

"Madre Santísima," Cruz murmured, "that's only about four miles from town!"

"Except that they can't come straight across the desert from there," the deputy explained. "Too much erosion has left deep gullies and arroyos slashing all across here, and they all empty into that broad sandy wash."

"Then they'll have to swing clear back around the way they came," Ragnon said, "and with luck we'll have a SWAT team here by then."

"Not necessarily." Antone put his finger on the map again. "The wash curves here behind the power line and meanders southwesterly about ten miles to cross under the highway bridge a mile north of town. They can use it for a road."

"But the wash will have steep sides too," Cruz pointed out.

"Sure, but if they've got heavy trucks they *can* get down into it by just caving in the soft bank. Getting out would be the problem, and the only way out is here by the highway bridge—a cement ramp. They can't go farther down the wash under the bridge because it's too low. They'd have to come out here."

Ragnon spat into a nearby wastebasket. "Then I'm betting that's the route they'll take; it's quickest."

"*If* they knew about the ramp," Cruz pointed out.

"Oh, they know about it." Antone looked at Ragnon. "Remember that report on Arturo Acosta—he worked on the crew that built this power line."

"Then they probably planned to use the wash all along," Ragnon said, "because to even reach the power line across the desert they've got to have either dual-wheeled trucks or four-wheel drive, and either one will get them down that wash."

"So if they're coming down the wash right now, here's where we'll have to stop them." Antone pointed out the bridge again on the map. "Or at least delay them. But two trucks and eight or more men with arms and explosives?" He looked skeptically from Cruz to Ragnon. "How are we going to do that?"

"You don't have to go, John," Ragnon said. "Christ, it's your day off. You either, Jacinto, it's not your problem now. Both of you can stay here and help Duff evacuate the town. I can create some kind of diversion until the SWAT team arrives."

Antone looked at Cruz and smiled. "Shall we whip his Anglo ass now or later? He wants to play Cowboys and Indians all by himself."

Cruz turned to Ragnon. "You play poker, Tomás?"

"What's poker got—"

"Then you know it's the same in life—you play out the hand you are dealt, no? So quit trying to deal us out of this game, compadre, until it's over."

Tom Ragnon looked fondly at them both. "Okay, smartasses,

let's do it. I've got something in mind, but we'll need some extra gas—at least five gallons."

"I've got two jerry cans in my trunk," Cruz said.

"That should do it. Get one of them and let's go." Ragnon turned out the lamp and spat out the open door. "Our one chance of stopping them is at that ramp. We'll take my car; it's expendable."

THIRTY-FOUR

Sunday, March 21, 9 P.M.

The town was already astir as they drove through—a lantern light here and there, dark figures scurrying with flashlights, voices calling. Tom Ragnon just hoped Duff had found Roberts with his CB, because he had no real confidence that his little diversion could really work. There just wasn't any other choice.

Leaving it all behind them, they reached the highway bridge north of town in moments and Ragnon doused the lights as he pulled off and parked beside the wash, halfway between the bridge and the cement ramp. Shutting off the engine, he took a deep breath, and the sudden chill he felt had nothing to do with the cool night air.

With moonrise still a couple of hours away, and a cloudy night, the darkness was complete. He glanced at the luminous dial of his watch. "It's been twenty minutes since the explosion," he said, "so with maybe ten miles of sandy wash to cover, they should be getting close."

The others said nothing as they all got out, pausing to listen for long seconds while they stared into the shadows along the wide wash. The slight breeze stirred the branches of a lone mesquite tree growing on the bank nearby as they checked the loads in the shotgun and rifles.

Tom Ragnon, patting his pockets for a chew of tobacco, found his pouch of Redman empty and felt the remaining shreds of his confidence running out of rope too. He tried to reel it back in, but it seemed like everything was finally catching up with him: the strain of the past two weeks of almost unrelenting pursuit; the shock of Cruz's incredible confession; and at last a final impending confrontation. He felt depleted, enervated; and suddenly the unanswerable questions belabored a mind heavy with fatigue and uncertainty: What if it didn't work? What if he had guessed wrong and Hidalgo Valdez wasn't even coming down the wash at all? And what if—

"What's the plan, Sergeant?" John Antone prodded him gently, jarring him out of his intense anxiety. "Maybe you should clue us in before they get here."

"What? Oh, simple—I block the ramp by parking my car sideways across the top."

"But with trucks they'll push right through it," Cruz said.

"Not if it's burning—they've also got explosives."

"Unless they used them all on the transmission tower," Antone suggested unkindly.

"That's a chance—"

"Quiet, hombres!" Cruz hissed. "Listen—something's coming!"

From out of the darkness far down the wash came a low, distant rumbling accompanied by a grinding whine, like machines laboring in low gear. "Looks like we've got company, girls," Tom Ragnon said, feeling the anxiety drain away even as the adrenaline began to flow.

With his car parked sideways across the top of the cement ramp, Ragnon opened the front and rear doors on his side and Cruz handed him the jerry can of gas while the rumbling sound along the wash grew steadily louder, more insistent. Christ, he thought, as he poured gas over the front seat and then the back, could there be more than two trucks—more than eight or ten armed men?

Leaving the can on its side on the backseat, with the last of the gas gurgling out over the upholstery and floor, he ran back to where the others were waiting with the guns. "John, you take your rifle out on the bridge. When they get here and see the ramp blocked, they ought to stop while somebody gets out to investigate. That's when you'll yell 'police' in Spanish and order them all to freeze."

"They won't," Cruz said grimly.

"I know they won't, goddammit, but it'll give us a minute. You have one of your cigarillos lit and glowing, and I'll run it up and toss it in the car. John, you'll start firing when you have to, but run along the bridge rail, shooting over it and yelling like there was a dozen of you. By then I'll be covering the other flank with my shotgun. Jacinto, you lay out here with your Browning trained on anything that tries to come through the light around the burning car."

"They're here," Cruz said then, and there was no time left to discuss it. Turning his back, he shielded one of his cigarillos while he lit it, and Antone sprinted for the bridge as a truck without lights rolled out of the deeper, blacker shadows along the far edge of the wash, with another following close behind, their engines rumbling.

Both trucks eased to a stop at the foot of the ramp, engines idling noisily as one of the drivers called out to the other in Spanish, *"Hola—qué está?"*

Ragnon turned and reached for Cruz's glowing cigarillo, but the Mexican shook his head. "You spilled some gas on yourself, Tomás, I can smell it. I'll do it. You go ahead and cover the other flank." And he ran for the car.

"Alto!" Antone called suddenly from the blackness along the bridge. *"Páresen, hombres—somos policía! No se mueven!"* Meanwhile Ragnon, gripping the shotgun in both hands, ran to cover the opposing flank. He saw in his peripheral vision the glow of Cruz's little cigar as it arced through the open front door into his car. Then the Mexican detective hit the ground and rolled away from the whoosh and roar.

The interior of the car was an inferno, lighting the wash and several armed men who were standing motionless in front of the lead truck. Antone was still calling to them from the bridge, demanding their surrender; and Cruz, partially shielded by the blazing car, foolishly stood up and began shouting in Spanish, too, ordering them to throw down their arms or be shot; that they were surrounded.

Ragnon, on the other flank, knelt beneath the mesquite and fired one round from the shotgun into the air. "Hidalgo!" he yelled. "Hidalgo Valdez! Throw down your goddamn weapons —it's over!"

For that one instant it looked like it was going to work. Antone was in place behind the bridge rail with his rifle leveled. Cruz had his Browning ready, too, and none of the figures in the wash had moved.

Then the gas tank on the car exploded and it all fell apart. In the new and leaping brightness the still armed fugitives scattered around the trucks as one of them called out, "Is that you out there—Tomás Rag-non, Sargento? *Chinga tu madre, gringo!*" And they all began firing at once.

In the confusion the first truck backed into the second, evidently trying to keep any explosives left away from the searing heat, while Ragnon took out its front tires with two quick blasts and felt the butt plate jarring heavily against his shoulder. He heard the sharp crack of Antone's repeating rifle as he moved at a crouch along the bridge rail, but Cruz's Browning was strangely silent.

Ragnon got off two more rounds with the shotgun, taking out the second truck's windshield and the driver along with it. He was about to call to Cruz then, when he took a hit himself—a thin burning sensation at first, he couldn't believe it until his right leg gave way under him and he went down.

After that things got a little blurred. Pain washed over him in waves and there was a sticky wetness along his inner thigh, then a blessed numbness as he realized someone was crawling along the ground toward him. With the crawling figure backlighted by the fire, he couldn't tell who it was, and he scrambled for the fallen shotgun even as Cruz called to him in a voice obviously weakened and hoarse with pain, "Tomás—"

Jesus, thought Ragnon, he's hit too; as a distant whap-whap-whapping sound borne on the wind invaded his consciousness and he saw two distinct bright white lights in the distant sky. He could hear Antone's rifle, still firing from the bridge, while the return fire was sporadic now, and he realized Cruz was beside him, pulling off his belt. "I'm okay," Ragnon gasped, and the Mexican nodded. *"Por seguro,* Tomás—here, bind up your leg, tight. You'll live. I won't—I'm bleeding inside."

"Oh, shit." Ragnon got the belt cinched tightly around his thigh, and then helped Cruz until they were both braced against the trunk of the mesquite. Ragnon groped for the Mexican's wound, found it, and pressed against the soft wetness of his side.

"Something hit me when the car blew up, Tomás," Cruz whispered. "It's deep inside."

As the firing ceased Ragnon could hear the sound of the choppers approaching, and could feel the Mexican's grip weak-

ening. Panic seized him. "Jacinto—" The Mexican's blood and
pain seemed to be mingling with his own as they held onto each
other and the tree trunk. And Ragnon realized that even Antone had stopped firing as the whirring beat of the chopper
rotors grew to a vibrating roar, and he could see their landing
lights making bright widening pools by the bridge as they settled on either side of the highway and armed camouflaged figures spilled out of them.

"A final stroke of bad luck for me, eh, Tomás?" Cruz gasped.
"I told you, *toda la vida*—" But he couldn't finish. He tugged
instead at a pocket of his jacket and withdrew a paper. "My
lottery ticket—give it to my wife. I checked the list before I left
—a winner, enough for both my families. First time I ever won
big, Tomás. Crazy, no?" He tried to smile but the effect was
ghastly in the dying light of the burning car. "Luck, compadre," he whispered again. *"Toda*—I'm cold, Tomás. Why am I
so cold?"

"Hang on, Jacinto!" Ragnon tugged the jacket tighter around
him, willing him to live. "Goddammit, man, they're coming—
hang on!" He could see Antone and two camouflaged figures
running toward them, and the fugitives in the wash lying
spread-eagled on their bellies.

But Cruz's fist, knotted tightly in Ragnon's turtleneck
sweater, suddenly relaxed, and the dark head sagged heavily
against the American's chest. "Jesus, Jesus, Jesus," Ragnon
murmured, rocking his friend like a child. His words were more
of a prayer than a curse.

EPILOGUE

"This is a fine fucking mess you've gotten us into—you know that, don't you, Rags?"

Tom Ragnon was on crutches and eased himself down on the vinyl couch, the better to endure the tirade he knew was coming. How's the leg, Rags? Old Ironballs could have asked. Mending nicely, thanks, Chief. No bones broken. End of sympathy.

Instead Lt. Poole had thrown the crime report on his desk with his customary contempt. "You're hit in the leg with a slug from Antone's rifle that ricochets off one of the trucks; the Mexican cop is killed with a slice of jagged metal blown off your car; and Hidalgo Valdez steps into the line of fire from his own men! You know what all that looks like in a shooting report, Ragnon? It looks like shit!"

"Hidalgo's dead; the others are in custody or dead too," the detective answered wearily. "What can I say, Chief? Sometimes it all just doesn't work out by the book." His leg was beginning to throb again. He was physically tired and emotionally drained. He just wanted to get this bullshit over with.

"I'm just not happy about all this," Poole was saying, looking like an unhappy walrus. "As far as I'm concerned, it was a botched job right from the start, very unprofessional. You were just damned fucking lucky, you and Antone."

Chewing savagely, Ragnon spat hard into Poole's wastebasket, watching the old bastard wince. "Jacinto Cruz said that, too, Chief. He put it all down to luck, and for him it was as bad as it can get. He was where I should have been when that damn car blew. That should have been me that got my ticket punched."

"But it wasn't, so count your blessings. There sure as hell won't be any citations for this, but that Pantana town council has voted you an award."

"I'd rather see Jacinto light up one of his cigarillos. He was a good cop. Anything else?"

"Yeah, the council has also agreed to split the rest of the

reward money between Cruz's two families." He looked up, scowling, and stared a moment at the detective. "How long's the doctor giving you, Rags?"

"A couple of weeks."

"Okay, go home and get some rest."

Ragnon struggled up from the couch, wincing as he adjusted his crutches and hobbled toward the door.

"Wait a minute."

The detective turned and found Poole glancing back through the report. "What's this bullshit about the Mexican president-elect cutting short his visit in Sonora due to a threat of contamination from radioactive material traced to a junkyard in San Ignacio?"

"I don't even want to talk about that, Chief. Maybe that's all it was—bullshit. The Federales and CIA and everybody else was involved. Jacinto notified the Mexican health officials and I called the FBI. I also dropped a word in the ear of an investigative reporter, so maybe we'll read all about it in the papers. Can I go now? I'm going back down to San Ignacio this afternoon for Jacinto's funeral. He gave me a winning lottery ticket to split with his families too. He had it in his pocket."

"Jesus H. Christ, will wonders never cease?" Lt. Poole was shaking his head and scowling again over his cold cigar. "But you really think that's smart, Rags?" He was squinting over his half lenses. "I mean going back down there so soon—especially after tangling with those two spic cops?"

"I probably won't even see them, and if I do, I doubt they'll want to be reminded of it. Besides, Antone's going with me."

"Oh, sure, you'll make a great pair. But that reminds me—you may as well get used to him. His promotion to detective finally came through and he'll be your new partner. I'll let you give him the tidings of great joy."

Tom Ragnon smiled. "Finally some good news."

"Oh, and one more thing, Rags—the county turned down reimbursement for your car, since you were officially on vacation at the time."

"Terrific—now can I go?"

"Sure. I just want to say I think the best thing about this whole fucked up mess is you getting back with your wife. I was beginning to hate that goddamned answering machine of yours with a purple passion."

Outside in the hallway Antone was waiting on one of the benches. "You tell him about us going back to San Ignacio for the funeral?"

"I told him. He wasn't all that thrilled." He had decided to wait until they were settled somewhere over cold beers and burritos to tell him about his promotion. The deputy was already wearing civvies, and in his tweed sportcoat with leather elbow patches he even looked like a detective, so that was the first thing that would have to go.

"What I want to know is," Antone continued as they moved slowly down the hallway side by side, "are you going to tell the Mexican authorities what you told me about Jacinto confessing to killing the comandante?"

Tom Ragnon paused and stared quizzically at his new partner. "What confession? Shit, John, I'm not even sure now I heard him right. No . . ." Balanced on his crutches, he dug around for his pouch of Redman and tucked a fresh pinch neatly in his cheek. "No, John, I think I'm just gonna let the Mexicans sort that one out for themselves."